# ZERO DAY
# THREAT

## R.M. OLSON

ISBN-13: 978-1-7771778-1-2

To my children. Even though this isn't a kid's book, as they so helpfully suggested it be.

*ZERO DAY THREAT:*

*A threat that exploits a previously-unknown security vulnerability in a system.*

# 1

Jez was going to die in about two minutes and thirty-seven seconds.

That was how long it would take to get to where the stark hallway she was being prodded down crossed the maintenance tunnel.

In front of her, a set of doors hissed open, the orange artificial lights humming off the steel-coloured walls. She glanced up at the balding, heavyset guard in front of her. He glowered, and she gave him a toothy grin.

Or maybe …

She twisted her wrists against the heavy magnetic cuffs linking them together. There, in her closed fist, something sharp and smooth and hard.

The guards hadn't noticed her palm it when she left the cell.

Maybe, in two minutes and twenty-two seconds from now, she'd be a free woman.

Honestly, after three weeks in a prison cell on this plaguing prison ship, she wasn't entirely certain she cared which.

There was a guard in front of her, the heavyset one, and two behind. The sharp 'click' of their black boots echoed off the bare metal walls of the hallway.

Her heart pounded, her body tingling with a sort of tense anticipation.

She couldn't stop grinning.

Probably made her look suspicious, but what the hell.

The first day in her cell, she'd memorized exactly how many steps it took to get from one side to the other, along each wall and then diagonally. She'd counted each one of the prefab squares that made up the wall. She'd tried to convince the guards to tell her their names, and when they hadn't, she'd made up names for them and turned them into a dirty, but quite funny, poem and recited it aloud until someone had come and told her to shut up or they'd close off the window bars.

By day two, she was ready to lose her mind.

And now, three weeks later, she was finally doing something about it.

"Excuse me, is this prisoner Jez Solokov?"

She jerked her head up, and almost ran into the balding guard. He turned and glowered at her again, and she glanced in irritation at the person who had interrupted her countdown.

A woman in a worn pilot's coat stood in front of them, medium-brown skin, shoulder-length black hair, a pleasant smile and a slightly martial air, exactly like a million other people Jez had met. She was thoroughly average, and thoroughly forgettable, except ... except she wasn't. There was something about her, a charisma that pulled at you like gravity, and despite herself, Jez found she wanted to like this woman. She wanted to trust her. She wanted, somehow, to make her happy.

Which meant, of course, she didn't trust her as far as she could throw her, and with her hands locked behind her back, that wasn't very far.

"Yes." The balding guard was smiling now, as if he, too, wanted to make this woman's day just a little easier. "This is her. What do you need?"

"Some minor administrative business. Nothing important. But if it's possible, I'd like a private word."

"We're transferring her to another cell block. The guards in the previous one threatened to revolt if we didn't." He chuckled. "You sure you want to talk to her?"

The woman smiled again, an accommodating sort of smile. "Please. I do hate to put you out, but we could step into a room just now, if you and your guards would keep watch at the door."

"Well—" He hesitated, and the woman looked past him to Jez. She smiled, and for just a moment Jez glimpsed something under that bland, forgettable expression, something sharp and intelligent and dangerous.

"Jez," she said. "I have a … proposition that might interest you."

"Sorry," she said, in a tone of voice that made it very clear that she wasn't at all sorry. "Busy now." She lifted her handcuffed arms in a gesture of mock apology.

"Prisoner," the balding guard began, turning to scowl at her, but the woman held up a hand.

"No, I apologize for the bother. I'll come find her later. The last thing I want is to inconvenience anyone."

She smiled, giving Jez a knowing look, then turned on her heel and walked away, boots clicking on the smooth floor.

Jez stared after her for a moment, a slight pang of unease twisting in her gut.

The woman seemed to know her. But she could swear they'd never met.

The guard was still scowling at Jez. "Get a move on, then, if you're so eager to get to your cell."

One of the other guards prodded her from behind, and she stepped forward.

She shrugged internally. Crazy people everywhere.

And in about—forty-eight seconds ...

She caressed the smooth bit of material hidden between her fingers. She'd had it when she'd been picked up for smuggling—hard, like metal, but it wouldn't show on the scanners. She'd managed to secret it in places she didn't really like to think about when she was being searched, and for three weeks she'd been working on it. Filing it. Tinkering with it.

And in just under forty-eight seconds now, she'd figure out if it had been worth her time.

Ahead, the heavy, utilitarian maintenance door jutted a few centimetres out of the wall, marring the spartan smoothness of the hallway. She sucked in a breath, a familiar jolt of adrenalin flooding her brain and pumping through her muscles.

Three.

Her grin widened.

Two.

She'd missed this.

One.

Her foot hit the floor in front of the tunnel door and she made what she hoped was a convincing stumble, falling awkwardly to the ground. The balding guard turned in annoyance and bent to pull her to her feet. She closed her eyes for half a second, savouring the moment, then twisted up on her shoulder and slammed both booted feet into his face. The heel of her boot connected with his nose with a satisfying 'crunch,' and he stumbled backwards, clutching at his bloodied face.

The other two guards were already going for their pistols. She shoved the bit of metal into the connection between the cuffs and depressed the trigger.

The makeshift cuff-cutter twisted and bucked in her hands.

The cuffs stayed firmly shut.

Damn.

She rolled out of the way as a laser blast burned a black mark into the floor where she'd been lying only a moment before.

She was doing this with her hands behind her back, then.

She rolled over her shoulder and staggered to her feet, then bent sideways and kicked out as hard as she could. Her boot met the guard's crotch.

The guard stumbled backwards, but her only reaction was an annoyed grunt.

It was the female guard. Jez was zero for two at this point.

She spun and tried again with the other guard, the male one. This time she was rewarded with a strangled wheeze of pain, but the female guard had caught her balance and was bringing her weapon to bear. Jez turned and fell backwards into her, the razor-sharp edge of her makeshift weapon sticking out between her fingers. The guard reached out instinctively to catch her, and then gave a shout of agony as the knife cut through her palms.

At least the thing was some use.

She braced her shoulders against the shouting guard and shoved herself upright, then sprinted for the maintenance-tunnel door. Opening it required her to turn backwards and squat down awkwardly as she fumbled with the lever. The balding guard was still clutching his face, and the guard she'd knifed cradled her bleeding hand, but the male guard she'd kicked was fumbling on the ground for his gun. She tried not to catch their eyes as she worked. If there

7

was ever a socially awkward moment, this was it.

At least she wasn't reciting rude poems to them. That had to count for something, right?

The handle gave, and she pulled the door open with a jerk and stumbled inside, pulling it shut after her with the toe of her boot. Then she ran.

Her footsteps echoed off the hollow tunnel surrounding her, the flickering maintenance lights casting long shadows. It would only be moments before they'd be after her. Maybe a minute—they'd wait for backup, probably.

Her grin felt wider than her face. OK, so the cuffs thing hadn't worked, but the rest of it had been spectacular. This was definitely worth it.

She came to a juncture in the tunnel and paused for a split second, orienting herself. She'd gotten a good look at the outside of the prison ship when they'd flown her in, and she had a pretty decent guess where the escape pods would be.

Be a little harder to hotwire one with both hands cuffed behind her back, but she'd cross that bridge when she came to it.

Left. She had to go left, and then she had to go down. She'd planned on using the ladders, but with any luck there'd be a lift or something. Ladders were probably beyond her skill set at present.

She pounded down the new hallway. There were boots behind her now, and shouts. They didn't know where she was going yet, but it wouldn't take them long to guess.

She skidded to a stop in front of a small alcove. Here was the ladder, which she couldn't use, but maybe …

She slipped inside and jammed the toe of one boot against the heel of the other, wrestling with it until at last it gave.

The footsteps were getting closer.

She pulled her foot free of the boot and kicked it as hard as she could down the ladder shaft. It fell with a satisfying amount of clanging and crashing, and she slipped backwards and wedged herself into the corner in the deep shadows of the alcove.

A moment later, three guards piled into the tiny space and glanced up and down.

"The pods are down there," one of them growled.

"How'd she get out of her cuffs? She couldn't have gone down the ladder with her cuffs on."

"How'd she plaguing well incapacitate three guards and take off in the middle of the plaguing day?" the first guard shot back. "Down. Now."

With a fair amount of cursing and stumbling over each other, they started down the rickety metal rungs. When they were gone, Jez allowed herself a smile of relief.

One obstacle down. Now it was just a matter of—

"Bravo. That was very well executed."

Jez spun, her heart just about coming out of her mouth.

From the dim corner on the opposite side of the alcove, the woman in the pilot's jacket smiled, eyes sharp and amused.

Even now, Jez felt herself relaxing at the sight of this friendly woman, her mouth turning up into a smile.

Nope. Bad idea. She tightened her grip on her makeshift weapon and braced herself to run for it. The woman held up her hand and stepped forward, detaching seamlessly from the shadows.

"Don't worry. I won't alert the guards. I'd say you have … three minutes before they find you. So." She stopped in front of Jez. "Would you like to hear my proposal?"

"No," Jez growled. The woman stood between her and the exit now, but if she had enough momentum …

"It will take only a moment."

"A bit busy, thanks. Could you move?"

The woman gave her a regretful shrug. "I'm sorry we couldn't do business. I think it would be to our mutual benefit. But—"

Jez braced herself for the inevitable shout for help. Instead, the woman held out her hand, palm up. Jez stared at it, frowning.

Inside the woman's upturned palm was … a chip. A pod chip.

"To one of the transports," the woman said, offering it. "It's the least I can do. You've impressed me very much."

Jez glared at the woman and shook her cuffs. The woman gave a slight smile and stepped forward, slipping the chip between Jez's fingers. Then she stepped back.

"There's a lift just down the hall to the right. Go down three floors, turn left, take your first right, and you'll be at the pod station. The chip will let you into the station, into the pod, and start it. After that, it's up to you." She glanced around. "I'd hurry. If you're quick, you'll reach it before the guards on the ladder do, but there's more on the way."

Jez hesitated. This whole thing was a terrible idea. But … it wasn't like things could go much more sideways. She tightened her fingers around the chip, turned, and ran.

The stranger's directions were, to her surprise, accurate. She made it through the airlock doors to the transport pod station with no trouble, and stared at the pods arrayed in front of her.

Much better than escape pods. And, added bonus, no auto-tracking on them.

Boots approached from down the corridor. She darted to the closest pod, stepped inside, and, with some twisting, managed to maneuver the chip into the sensor. The control panel glowed green, and she grinned.

She was going to pull this off. She was actually going to pull this off.

Five guards tumbled over each other into the pod station. She jammed the door button with her knee, and the pod slid closed with a 'whoosh' as laser-blasts glanced off its rounded sides. She grinned and half-turned so she could make a rude gesture through the tiny porthole, then glanced quickly over the control panel. She'd have to turn backwards, squat, and peer awkwardly over her shoulder to reach the controls with her cuffed hands, but she was a pilot. She could have fired this thing up fast asleep, pass-out drunk, and high as a kite, and flown it like a dream. Handcuffs just made it interesting.

They figured out what she was doing a split second later, and even in her awkward position she was rewarded with the dawning look of panic on their faces as they ran for the airlock.

She paused for a moment to give them a chance, then, as the doors sealed shut, she pushed the launch button with her elbow. There was a familiar sucking sensation as the pod's pressurizer kicked in. Then the atmosphere in the pod station puffed out in an icy vapour as the bay doors slid open, revealing the clean black emptiness outside.

Her territory.

Tears pricked at the corners of her eyes.

It felt like forever. Three weeks in a cell, locked away from all of this, but it had felt like three lifetimes.

She breathed in, for what felt like the first time in ages. Then she nudged the steering column with her straining fingers, and the pod lifted delicately from its docking port and boosted out the opening. The last thing she saw of the prison ship was the port doors closing gently behind her, framing furious faces of the guards behind the protective plex of the airlock.

As soon as she was out, she set the pod to steady on course and turned to assess her prospects.

Enough fuel for an atmospheric entrance, a landing, and a tiny extra thrust to get her moving in the right direction. Enough oxygen for maybe four, five hours, plus the emergency store. Meant for nothing more strenuous than quick jaunt planet-side. Maintenance tools, nothing fancy, but enough to pop her out of her cuffs.

When she had the time to spare.

If she lived through this, she'd have all the damn time in the world. The thought was a little like a drug, and it sent a rush of warm satisfaction through her chest.

From the corner of her eye she could see other docking port doors opening, tiny dots in the hull of the rapidly shrinking prison ship. They'd be after her in a moment.

She gave a blissful smile, and nudged the steering thruster in the direction of deep space.


The ships were on her in under a minute. She had a head start, yes, but then again, she was in a transport pod.

There were two of them, small and sleek, designed for both space and atmosphere. They were crossed with the three black stripes that meant, everywhere in the system and to everyone on the outside edge of legality, trouble. Or police, which was generally synonymous.

Her heart thudded a quick pattern against her ribcage, her fingers tingling with anticipation.

Before, on the ship, she'd been playing on their terms. Now they were playing on hers.

Their first shot clipped her pod on its starboard side. Her shoulder slammed into the cockpit window as the pod veered sharply off course, accelerating in the wrong direction. She swore under her breath as she wrestled with the steering stick.

She didn't have any extra fuel to course correct—she needed everything she had for what was coming next.

A blinker flashed on the dashboard, and a voice boomed into the cramped cockpit.

"We're not here to hurt you. Give yourself up and we'll take you in easy. That pod isn't built to survive in deep space."

She mashed the com with her knee and gave an assortment of creative suggestions as to what they could do with their advice.

"You've been warned. Stand down or we'll shoot."

"Good luck with that," she called back.

They converged on her, one from above, one from below. They were clearly hesitant to shoot—she was no threat, and anyways, they probably assumed that if she wouldn't see reason, she'd at least eventually run out of fuel. Then they'd just pick her up.

She smiled.

This was the fun part. When they thought they had you.

This was always the fun part.

She leaned backwards and, with straining fingers, grasped the entrance-fuel button. She needed it for re-entry, yes, but if she came in at just the right angle, she wouldn't need nearly as much as they'd provided.

Almost close enough …

She jerked down on the lever, lifting her un-booted foot and yanking back on the steering column with her toes at the same time. The pod shot out a cloud of crystallized fuel, and there was loud cursing over the com as the ships swerved to avoid it. The pod spun on its axis in the roiling cloud of exhaust, almost knocking her off balance. Ahead, the dark bulk of the upper ship loomed in her pod's window. She kicked off the fuel switch, shoved the steering column forward, and, with sweating fingers, flipped the thruster. When the pod came, at last, to a gentle halt, it sat nestled in the blind spot behind the cockpit like a tick on a swamp-rat's ear. She shut off the power and leaned back, smiling to herself.

There were confused shouts and swearing from the com as the ships turned to locate her. But she'd gone dark. There was nothing to locate.

One of the pilots swore loudly. "Well, she'll be dead in a few hours anyways," he grumbled into the com. "That's all the oxygen those pods hold. Good riddance—I've never met such a damn crazy lunatic in my life."

Damn crazy lunatic. She liked the sound of that. Maybe she'd take that up as her next call sign. A little long, but it had a certain *je ne sais quoi.*

The ship she was hiding behind made a slow turn.

At just the right moment, she flipped the thruster on for half a second—not enough to attract attention, just enough to give the thing a tiny shove. Then she shut the pod down again, letting her momentum carry her.

She held her breath as the pod drifted away from the bigger ships, but no one seemed to have noticed—flying dark like this, she wouldn't show up on any sensors, so unless someone was tracking her with a visual, she didn't exist.

She waited one long moment.

Two.

Three.

The ships, their shapes receding in the distance, waited at the docking ports for the bay to depressurize and the doors to open.

She let out her breath. She was free. And ... she let go of the controls for long enough to glance over her shoulder at the planet that loomed green and white on the horizon. Yes. She'd calculated it just right. She'd come in at exactly the angle for an easy pass through the atmosphere—or as easy as it could get in a transport pod.

She turned and sat back in the control seat, tension draining from her shoulders. Her whole body was light, as if prison had been a rock sitting on her chest, crushing the life out of her.

And now she was free.

It was better than being drunk. It was better than anything in the world.

She'd be home in no time. Then, with any luck, she'd pick up another ship, another job … She stared out at the familiar, comfortable blackness of space surrounding her, letting her thoughts wander down pleasant tracks.

In the prison ship, far behind her, a woman in a worn pilot's coat stood at a window, hands clasped behind her back, watching the tiny pod drift towards the planet's surface.

Perfect angle. Impressive. And the pilot would have done the entire masterly maneuver with her hands cuffed behind her back.

The woman smiled to herself. It was even better than she'd hoped.

She turned away, her sight smile reflecting off the dark glass with the blackness of space and its endless stars behind it.

# 2

Jez's day was not going according to plan.

She scowled down at the com on her wrist, the spare one she left in the basement in case of emergencies. "Look Talliel, we had a deal. You said you had a job for me."

"I said I had a job for you three weeks ago, when you hadn't lost a ship and weren't on the run from the law," the voice in the com growled back.

"It wasn't my fault!" she snapped. "They messed with my controls. Some new EMP tech I couldn't shield against. Come on! You know I'm the best pilot you have."

She could almost hear him shrug. "Look, Jez. I like you. But you've been tagged. They'll be watching for you. I can't risk the law coming after me."

Damn him to hell.

"You're a plaguing smuggler, for all the seventeen demon's sakes!" she exploded. "I can't believe—"

The com went dead. She swore disgustedly, and kicked at the threadbare sitting cushion, the only thing in the bare basement that gave the faintest nod to comfort. Her toe caught it in an especially threadbare section, and it burst, vomiting cheap, manufab'ed stuffing across the floor.

She swore again, louder, but there was nothing left in the dilapidated apartment to kick. She kicked the dingy pre-fab walls instead, and then swore again and rubbed her toe.

She didn't even have two plaguing boots.

She'd brought the pod down the night before in the middle of a marsh, and had managed to bum a ride from a passing swamp-miner. The driver, a squat, surly man, had dropped her off just outside the city's force-shield, and she'd had to hoof it in from there. She'd worn three blisters into the sole of her bootless foot before she got back to the basement apartment she kept as a sort of safe-house.

Now, five hours and countless com-calls later, she was starting to wonder if it had all been worth it.

Grounded. That was almost as bad as being in a cell.

She paced across the small space for the fiftieth time that morning and ran her hands through her tangled hair.

Damn it to hell. Damn everything to hell.

For half a moment she thought back to the woman from the prison ship, the woman with the worn pilot's coat and the pleasant, competent, compelling air.

She'd had a proposition, she'd said.

Well, whatever it was, Jez was singularly uninterested in propositions that were presented on the decks of prison ships by people who looked like they worked for the government.

She sighed, and picked up her com again. She bit her lip, then, reluctantly, tapped a familiar pattern and waited as it buzzed on her wrist.

She wasn't sure she was ready for this. But it had to be better than a crazy woman, right?

"Jez?" came a male voice, low and slightly husky. She smiled. Pyotr may be an idiot, but she couldn't deny he had a sexy voice.

"Hey Petrush," she said. "Been a while."

"Yes. It has."

Not good. His voice had a definite touch of ice to it.

"Sorry I haven't called. Been on a long run. I just got in." She paused, and put on her most persuasive tone. "So, I hate to do this when we've just caught up, but I have a bit of a favour to ask you. You know that old ship of yours?"

There was a long pause. She tapped her fingers against her hip. Come on, Pyotr, you knucklehead. Be a good boy.

"I seem to remember last time I saw you, you said you were done runs for a while. You were going to spend some time with me. And then you never showed up."

Damn.

"Oh. Yeah." She tried to sound casual. "Something came up last-minute."

"So last-minute you couldn't call me on your com to let me know?"

"Listen, I—"

The com went dead.

Jez sighed heavily and dropped into the sagging cushion, which belched out another puddle of manufab.

It was fine. She'd be fine. She could steal a ship or something. Not like it would be her first time. Someone would want a pilot like her, even if the law was after her.

Her ship.

The jolt of the memory was like jarring a broken bone.

Her beautiful ship, the awful grinding, rending sound it made as it tore itself to pieces on that damn asteroid, the controls, usually so sensitive under her fingers, refusing to respond, the thrusters refusing to fire ...

The police never should have caught her. There was no way they should have caught her. She had blockers and everything, but they'd had some new EMP tech she'd never seen, and it had shut down her ship. Killed it. And her ship and her freedom and basically her whole life had broken itself to pieces on the rough space-rock.

She pulled up the com and swiped the holoscreen up with one finger.

She shouldn't do this. She knew better. But she swiped across it anyways, and an image appeared. A young man, no older than twenty, with a sullen face and dark, wavy hair that hung over his eyes. He was glaring straight in front of him.

"Tae Bezdomnikov," the caption read.

She stared at the picture for a long time.

She'd overheard them talking about him when they brought her in. An inventor. A techie. The man who'd created the EMP device the police had used to crash her ship.

She slapped her hand over the com, and the image disappeared.

He'd just better hope she never ran into him, that was all. Because she'd spent three excruciating weeks dreaming up ways to make him pay. What kind of psychopath invented tech like that, and then sold it to the government?

They called her a lunatic.

It would be fine, though. She'd gotten out of worse scrapes before, right?

She glanced around her at the bare, grungy apartment, the sad, spreading pile of manufab creeping across her bootless foot.

At the moment, though, she couldn't think of any.

* * *

The afternoon sun slumped dim and dingy over the skyline of Prasvishoni, light oozing reluctantly though the grey fog that always seemed to shroud the city. Jez paused on the rickety prefab stairs leading out of her basement, a familiar depression washing over her as the thin rays failed to penetrate the grimy air or bring even a modicum of warmth. The first thing she'd realized about this place, when she'd come here four years ago, was that no matter the weather and no matter the season, it was always slightly dank, and slightly clammy, and slightly too cold for comfort.

Didn't matter. She'd be back in space soon, in a cockpit, with stars and nebula stretching out around her in glowing patterns, a steering column that fit into her hand like it had grown there and controls her fingers knew as intimately as the body of a lover.

But for now, she was stuck on the ground. Would be, until she found another plaguing ship and someone to fly for. It wasn't like she was picky. She just needed a break. One break.

She sighed and turned away from the anemic sun, back to the guttering artificial lights of the dingy basement she called home.

She grabbed her mildewing jacket off the peg, where she'd left it a month and a half ago, pulled on two more-or-less fresh socks over her bare foot, and stalked up the grimy stairs and out into the grimy street.

"I need someone who's dependable," Yulio had said apologetically, before breaking off the call. "You're good, but I can't trust you. Can't always work alone, you know. Going to get you killed one of these days, and then I'll lose my investment."

Screw him. Screw everyone. She was a good pilot, for crying out loud. What did they want? Pretty common knowledge she wasn't a team player, and she'd always done fine.

Until now.

The streets were crowded at this time of day, plodding clusters of people slouching past, heads down, collars of their long, bedraggled jackets pulled up around their ears. Hurrying, in a listless, despondent way, to get somewhere to wait—the food rations line, or the clothing rations line, or the government aid application line, or the line for some form or other that they had to turn in, before midnight tonight or risk a penalty, which the government had forgotten to announce until the day before.

Waiting. An endless, hopeless, emotionless, purposeless sort waiting. That's what people did in this plaguing system. They waited.

But not her.

That wasn't what she was made for.

She was made to bloody fly.

The greyish-white, mildewed walls of buildings rose up around her, each apartment complex identical to the one before, each bare office building the image of the one on the street across from it. There was a dash of colour in a window here or there—a dyed rag drying on the sill, a bedraggled potted plant—but somehow, it made the whole scene even more depressing.

When she reached the rations store three blocks down, there was already a line of at least thirty people, waiting with a sort of sad hopefulness to buy their week's worth of slightly stale rations. They stood quietly, any ambition or impatience bled out of them ages ago by an endless lifetime of lines.

She rolled her eyes. She wasn't that hungry. Probably had some dried rations in her apartment somewhere that she could scrounge up. They kept forever.

The face of the woman from the ship floated, unbidden, to her mind. She shook her head determinedly.

Nope. The woman had definitely been bad news.

She turned, wrapping her arms around herself, and started towards home.

She was within a block of it when a voice called from an alley, "Hey! You!"

She should have run. Instead, she turned.

By the time she realized what a bad decision that had been, it was too late. Three beefy-looking individuals hemmed her in from all sides. The leader, a tall, muscular woman, gestured her into the alleyway.

She glanced around once, wildly.

No escape.

She sucked in a long breath, and did as she was told.

A man was waiting, leaning up against the wall of the alley. His face was thick and brutal, and his muscles had muscles.

She recognized him at once.

"Jez!" His fake-jovial tone sent a shiver down her back.

"Hey, Antoni." She tried to make her voice casual. Her heart pounded, adrenalin jittering in her brain.

"Boss lady's been looking for you for a while," he said. He cracked his knuckles against each other.

This wasn't going to end well.

She lowered her voice conspiratorially. "Doesn't surprise me. I think she has the hots for me, to be honest."

May as well go out in a blaze of glory.

Antoni dropped the jovial tone. "Doubt it. But that ship you stole from her a few years back—she was pretty fond of that, I understand."

Jez grinned. She couldn't stop grinning even though it was stupid, even if she wanted to. "Oh, that piece of junk? Let me guess, you're tracking me down because she wanted to pay me for taking it off her hands."

His fist caught her in the stomach before she had time to brace herself, and she doubled over, wheezing. Antoni laughed, the sound hard and cruel.

"Oh yes, Jez. She wanted to reward you. She was desperate to reward you. That's why she sent us." He leaned over until he was looking her straight in the eye. "And she wants her damn ship back."

His meaty fist slammed into her rib cage, and she staggered backwards against the wall, panic jolting through her brain. He stepped up close to her.

"Where is it, Jez?"

She tried to draw in a breath and choked on it, and he hit her again, his open hand connecting with the side of her face and sending her reeling.

She was going to die. The realization sent prickles of ice down her spine.

"Where is it?"

"It's gone," she choked out. "Hit a damn asteroid."

The words hurt almost as much as the blow.

He paused, and gave her an appraising look.

"Long story. Wasn't my fault. But tell Lena I can work it off. I'll fly for her for a while, give her a cut. How's that sound?"

He laughed again, and shook his head in genuine amusement. "Oh Jez. My dear, dear Jez. The only thing Lena wants more than her ship back is to never see your face again. I don't know if she could control herself if she did."

"I am pretty damn hot," Jez wheezed, trying for a smile.

He hit her again, and this time she went down, spots dancing before her eyes.

"Enough laughs," he growled. "That ship was her pride and joy.

You have three months to get her a new one, or the money to pay for one." He leaned closer. "And believe me, Jez, that ship wasn't cheap."

He tilted his head to one side, considering her. Then he drew back his foot and gave her one last kick to the ribs. She gritted her teeth again tears of agony, but she had to admit he'd been judicious. Could have hit her a lot harder.

It was hard to appreciate that, though, as pain danced like lighting before her eyes.

She managed to haul herself up on one elbow as he walked away.

"Tell Lena she's too old for me anyways!" she called after him, choking out the words through the metallic taste of blood. He paused, his shoulders tensing. Then he just shook his head and kept walking, the other three thugs following behind.

She lay there for a long time after they left, staring up at the dingy grey walls of the alley.

She'd made it four years. It was bound to catch up with her some-time.

If she'd had her ship, this would be a minor setback at worst. She'd disappear before the next morning, and it would take Lena another four years to find her again.

But she was land-bound now.

Damn that Tae Bezdomnikov.

She'd never forget the paralyzing feeling of watching her ship, out of her control, drifting towards the asteroid. The desperation, the helplessness, the wrongness of it—the one thing in her world that she could always control, ripped away from her. She'd woken from nightmares of it for weeks.

Losing the ship was bad. Crashing was bad. Where she was now, beat up in an alley—that was bad. But none of it came close to that paralyzing helplessness, watching, waiting, unable to act.

Slowly, she rolled to her side. Even more slowly, she struggled to her feet. She swayed for a moment, caught herself against the wall, and limped towards home.

On the bright side, Antoni hadn't killed her. He could have, pretty easily, but he hadn't. So that meant Lena wanted her ship, or her money, more than she wanted Jez dead. That was a definite plus.

Jez wasn't sure if she was relieved or insulted—to be honest, she'd thought Lena hated her more than that—but it was a plus.

But she'd damn well better get herself back on a job. Because she'd worked with Lena for long enough to know. She'd get one more warning. Maybe. And then the calculus would change, and she'd be more useful as an example than she was as an asset.

# 3

Jez stumbled painfully down the grimy steps to her apartment and pulled open the door. She limped inside, pushed the door shut with her foot, and leaned against it. It took her eyes a moment to adjust from the pale, weak sunlight to the orange, weaker flicker of the artificial lights.

Then she jumped back and swore.

Ensconced comfortably in Jez's much-abused cushion was a figure that was instantly, unsettlingly, familiar.

A long pilot's coat hung on the peg beside her.

The woman smiled up at Jez pleasantly, and Jez could hardly fight the urge to smile back and offer her a glass of sump.

Which was completely stupid, because first, the woman was an intruder. Second, she had no sump to offer and no money to buy any, and third, if she did, she could bloody well use a whole bottle herself at this point.

The woman studied her with a concerned frown. "Are you alright? You didn't crash, did you?"

Jez swore again and leaned against the wall, wincing at the pressure on her bruised ribs. "I'm fine. Thanks for the concern. What the hell are you doing in my house?"

The woman rose, brushed herself off, and gestured to the cushion. "Sit. You look like you need it more than I do."

Jez stared for a moment before her battered brain finally gave up trying to make sense of this stranger calmly offering her a seat in her own house. She found herself dropping ungracefully into the cushion, glaring at the woman the whole time. The stranger didn't seem to mind, or even to notice. She put her hands behind her back and paced slowly across the tiny, dirty space and back again, then stopped in front of Jez, hands clasped behind her back, legs apart, like a woman accustomed to keeping her balance on a shifting ship's deck.

"I must say, Jez, you made quite an impression on me. I'd heard of you, but I had no idea that you were quite so accomplished. You didn't want to talk about my offer on the ship, and to be fair, it wasn't a situation that offered opportunity for nuance. But I feel that here we'll be able to have a discussion."

Jez just stared. Finally, she blurted out the first coherent thought that made it into her head.

"Who the hell are you?"

The woman chuckled. "I'm sorry. I feel I know you so well that I'd forgotten you'd have no idea who I am. My name is Masha."

Jez stared at her blankly, and the stranger—Masha—gave a gentle smile.

"I don't expect you to recognize the name. I'm not important, certainly. But I've been searching for someone like you."

"Someone like me," Jez repeated sullenly. "You could probably pick up half a dozen girls with my dashing good looks."

Masha leaned forward, and once again Jez caught that disconcerting flash of intensity behind her gaze. "But how many of them could pilot a transport pod with their hands cuffed behind their back, and outwit two police ships? I need a pilot Jez. And I don't just need any pilot. I need the best pilot in the system."

Still, Jez stared.

She didn't trust this Masha woman. Didn't trust her as far as she could throw her, and even without hands cuffed behind her back, in her current condition that wasn't very far.

But …

"What's the pay?" she asked bluntly.

Masha smiled again, a flash of something like triumph behind her expression, and Jez cursed herself.

What's the pay. Anyone else would have asked, what's the job. But she was desperate, and she'd given herself away.

Not that it mattered. She was desperate. And right now, the pay was all that mattered.

The pay, and getting back in the sky. She could almost taste it, the intoxicating freedom that was better than all the sump in the world. She wanted it so badly her fingers hurt.

"The pay," said the woman, crouching so she was eye-level with Jez, "is more than you can possibly imagine."

"That's hard to believe."

"Believe it," Masha whispered.

For someone so remarkably unremarkable, her eyes were magnetic, compelling, electrifying.

"What do I have to do?"

"What you were born to do, Jez. Fly. I have a contract from the government, and I need a pilot. If you do this, you'll get a full pardon, and more money than you know what to do with."

"Oh, I know exactly what to do with money."

Masha smiled and straightened. "I'm certain you do. So." She raised an eyebrow. "Are you in?"

Everything in Jez's mind was screaming at her that this was a bad idea, while simultaneously suggesting she offer this nice woman her seat and sit down with her for a friendly chat.

But … she glanced around her dingy apartment, the mildewed walls and the guttering lights.

At this point, what did she have to lose?

"I'm in," she said in a low voice.

"Excellent! I was hoping you'd agree." Masha lifted her brown pilot's coat from the hook and brushed it off fastidiously before she shrugged it on. "Come. I'll take you back to meet the team."

Jez stopped abruptly. "Team? Hold on. I don't work in teams."

Masha considered her for a moment. Finally, she said, "Well, Jez, this is how I see it. You're on the run from the law. You need money, desperately. And you want to fly. I can see it in you, you need to fly like you need to breathe. So here's the deal—you get what you want. Everything you want. And you work in a team, because I tell you that that's the only way you're going to get it."

Jez glared at her sullenly, but Masha had already turned towards the door.

Damn her.

She was right.

Reluctantly, Jez pushed herself to her feet and followed.

It wasn't the walk she minded so much. It was awful, with every step revealing another bruise she'd overlooked, her blistered bare foot catching every loose rock, and every breath so painful on her bruised ribs that she briefly contemplated not breathing altogether. But that wasn't the worst thing.

She glared at the woman striding ahead of her.

The worst thing was that same panicked, gut-clenching feeling she'd had when the controls of her ship betrayed her, for the first time in her life.

She was flying blind, and she wasn't the one steering this ship. All she could do right now was follow and hope against hope they weren't headed for an asteroid.

She was still lagging sullenly behind, a long walk, a painful flight of stairs, and a short, dingy hallway later, when Masha pulled open a door and gestured Jez inside.

Reluctantly, Jez stepped past her into the room and glanced quickly around.

It wasn't empty.

Working in a team, Masha had said.

She took a deep breath to steady herself, swore out loud as her ribs protested, and glared at the people who had both turned at her entrance.

To her right sat a short, stocky woman, resting her pale, but impressively-muscled, forearms on her knees and watching Jez with an expressionless face. Despite herself, Jez felt an immediate flood of affection for this woman, whoever she was. Her light-brown hair was shaved short against her head, and she was wearing stained, tattered work clothes that made it immediately apparent that, first, she took whatever it was she did very seriously, and second, she didn't give a damn what anyone else thought.

It was kinda hot, actually.

She managed a grin at the woman, who in return gave her a stare that said very clearly, "piss off."

Also kinda hot.

On the other side of the room sat someone who looked like the universe proving it could make opposites. He was a young man, maybe a year or two older than Jez, with olive skin, cropped dark hair, and the overall air of a soft scholar-boy. His posture somehow managed to be both formal and comfortable at the same time, and he looked like he'd woken up with good intentions, got halfway through making himself presentable, and then forgotten what he was doing. His eyes, however, were unsettlingly sharp and astute, and he was watching her closely, a small frown creasing between his eyebrows, as if she were a puzzle that needed solving.

A slight unease sparked in her chest. She could probably knock him down with one punch, but that didn't seem to bother him in the slightest. He had the calm self-assurance of someone who didn't worry about a fight, because he would have found a way to win it before the other person had realized it had begun.

The door swung open again.

"Ah," said Masha. "And that's the last of us. I'm glad you made it back."

She turned to the person who'd just arrived as the door clicked shut behind him.

It hit her like a slap in the face. Dark, wavy hair, dark skin, a scowl that looked permanently drawn on his face …

Tae bloody Bezdomnikov.

"That's the bastard who crashed my ship," she growled, and lunged at him, ignoring the pain jolting through her ribcage.

"What the hell are you talking about?" he shouted, jumping back. Then two arms that felt like ships clamps closed around her, so tightly she couldn't breathe. She struggled ineffectually, twisting her head to see her attacker through the spots of pain dancing before her eyes.

It was the stocky woman. Her face, still mostly expressionless, managed somehow to look smug.

Jez relaxed, partly because she wasn't going to out-fight this woman, and partly because she was about to pass out.

"Jez, meet Ysbel," said Masha in a pleasant tone. Ysbel let go of her disdainfully, and Jez gasped in a breath, swaying on her feet. Masha caught her arm and smiled.

"Why don't you sit? It's been a long day."

Again, Jez found herself collapsing awkwardly into a proffered chair.

She drew in a few more painful breaths, until the black crowding the edge of her vision faded away, and then she grinned with an effort.

"Nice to meet you, Ysbel. Couldn't keep your hands off me, I see."

Ysbel looked at her with a flat expression. "Piss off."

She had a heavy outer-fringe accent that made the words sound something like "Pees oaf," but Jez picked up the general meaning.

Masha ignored the exchange.

"The man sitting across from her is Lev. Lev, Jez."

The scholarly-looking young man gave her a friendly nod, but he was still studying her intently.

"Pilot, are you?" he asked, his voice soft, but intense.

"Yeah." She glowered at him.

"Flew with Lena a few years back, I believe."

"Yeah. So what?"

He sat back, still studying her. "Nothing."

There was something in his eyes that belied his words.

"And over there we have Tae."

The dark-haired young man had stalked to the point in the room farthest from her and dropped into a sitting cushion. He was currently glowering at the entire room.

Jez scowled and grabbed the arms of her chair as if to push herself up. Ysbel gave her a warning look, and she subsided.

"Bastard," she muttered in the man's general direction.

He glared at her. She could almost feel his anger, distorting the air like a heat wave. Like *she* was the one who'd wrecked *his* ship, got him landed in jail, and been responsible for their current predicament.

Fine. That would just make this all the more satisfying. One of these days she'd meet him when Ysbel wasn't around …

But she needed this job. Thanks to that bastard sitting in the corner, she needed this job. So she contented herself with scowling.

# 4

*earlier*

Tae Bezdomnikov was running for his life.

He pounded down the narrow streets, head bent low, and turned a sharp corner.

There. Ahead. He dove into an alleyway and flattened himself against the mildewed wall, trying desperately not to breathe as his heart hammered its way almost out of his chest. The dark, cylindrical form of a police drone slipped past the alley entrance, and he counted slowly to three, then sank to the ground, gasping for air.

"Tae?" A tall, lanky boy of about seventeen materialized from the shadows, and a girl, a little younger and a little shorter, followed. Tae scrambled to his feet, a mixture of panic and relief flooding through him.

"Caz, Peti! Did the drone get visuals on you?"

The girl, Peti, shook her head, eyes sparking with mischief. "Come on, Tae. How long have we known each other?"

Tae sighed and grabbed them both in a bear-hug, some of the tension draining from his shoulders. "I wasn't sure you'd make it."

He let go of them reluctantly and stepped back to look at them.

After five months in prison, he hadn't realized how much like home seeing their faces would be.

"We missed you, Tae," said Caz softly. "We were all frantic after you'd got locked up. But I kept telling them you'd find a way to get back."

Peti leaned forward with a conspiratorial whisper. "So. How did you break out of jail?"

Tae hesitated. "I didn't," he said at last.

Something about the memory made him uneasy. If he was being honest, everything about the memory made him uneasy.

Masha made him uneasy. She had from the moment he'd seen her, sitting in his jail cell like she belonged there. But what she'd offered had been too good to pass up. And far, far too simple to con her out of.

Which made him even more uneasy.

Caz and Peti were watching him curiously. "So I'm just imagining you're standing here in front of me, then," said Caz. Tae shook his head, trying to push back the unease.

Sometimes you just caught a break. That was all. That was all this was. A piece of luck, for once in his life.

"No, I'm here. I'm out." He took a deep breath. This was the part he'd been dreading. "I—but I'm heading off-planet. I came to say goodbye."

They frowned, like what he'd said hadn't made any sense.

"What do you mean?" asked Peti at last. "I thought—I mean, you're out, right? The other kids are all waiting for you. We told them—"

He shook his head, trying to make his voice harsh. "If I come back, I'll put you in danger. I can't do that again. I—I have something for you. And then I have somewhere to be. I'm sorry, OK?"

Masha had said she wanted him for a job, offered him a pardon and more money than he'd even been able to envision. But he wasn't nearly enough of an innocent to believe he'd ever see a single credit of the fabulous sum she'd promised. Maybe he'd been that innocent once, but five months in prison, and the weeks leading up to it, had taught him a lesson he hoped he'd never forget again.

And so he'd pretended to agree, on one condition: he get a cut of the reward upfront. And she'd simply looked at him with those sharp eyes, shrugged, and handed him a chip with more credits on it than he'd ever seen in his entire cold, miserable existence.

And then, because he wasn't a plaguing innocent, he'd slipped away and run for his life.

She'd come after him, eventually. He was certain of it. But it couldn't be worse than if he didn't run. If he didn't run, he'd end up dead or in jail, because no one paid their debts to a street kid.

He pulled the chip out of his pocket. "Caz, I know you have a chip. Give me your com."

Caz held out his wrist mutely, and Tae touched the chip to it, counting off the credits.

He'd give them as much as he dared. As much as he had left. The rest were to buy him a passage out of this miserable city and off this miserable planet.

Caz and Peti were still staring at him.

They were only a couple years younger than he was, but they looked, somehow, much younger now.

"You're just leaving, then?" asked Peti. "You're just going to leave?"

The hurt confusion in her voice was going to make him sick. But he'd thought this through a million times.

"Listen. I have to do this. Didn't you see? Even getting here I was followed by a police drone. I've put all of you in danger enough times already. The others are just kids. They don't deserve this."

Caz and Peti didn't deserve it either. Caz was maybe two or three years younger than Tae, but he'd always been just a kid. The last five months seemed to have toughened him up, but he still looked young and somehow helpless.

"What happened to you, Tae?" asked Caz at last. Under the worry and the hurt in his voice, he sounded almost pitying.

"Maybe I was an idiot!" Tae exploded. "Have you thought of that? Maybe I was just wrong."

"What? Sticking around us was wrong?"

"No," he muttered. He looked down at the street to avoid seeing the hurt on their faces. "Not that. But what I did that landed me in jail? That was stupid. And it could have hurt all of you. Now that I'm out, I'm not going to do that again."

They were both looking at him now, and there was something in their expressions that cut him.

They didn't get it. They weren't the ones who'd been thrown in jail, and put the people they cared about in danger. Almost destroyed everything.

"But what you did I mean, the guy offered you a job and then stole your tech. What should you have done?"

"Nothing," he said bitterly. He couldn't meet their eyes. "I should have done nothing. I should have got out and gone home and licked my wounds. That's what street kids do. That's what we're meant to do."

"But you didn't," Peti said. "You didn't just let them walk over you."

"Out of all of us, you were the only one brave enough to fight back," Caz said softly.

"Yeah?" This time he did meet their eyes. "Well then listen to the rest of it. After I hacked his system and took him down, they threw me in jail a week later. I turned myself in. And you know what would have happened if I hadn't? They would have come in and burned us out. All the street kids. They would have killed you all and not thought twice about it. Now do you think what I did was a good idea?"

They stared at him, wide-eyed, faces stricken.

"I can't change the system, OK? Nor can you. Nor can any of us. All I can do is stay away from you so that the rest of you can stay safe. Go back and tell the others, OK?"

"Yeah," said Peti finally, turning away. "We will." She paused. "Did you know Mila is sick again?"

He frowned. Mila was still only six, the youngest member of their little street-gang. "She's sick? What with?"

Peti shrugged. "I don't know. Fever. Luca is going half-crazy. He— when I told the rest of them I'd seen you, he—he almost started crying. He was sure you'd know what to do for his sister."

Tae gritted his teeth. "You have credits now. You can get her medicine. You don't need me for that."

"Sure." She didn't even look at him.

"Tae," said Caz, his voice quiet and bitter. "I can't blame you for leaving. But don't say we don't understand. You have no idea what's been happening."

"What do you mean?" He tried to keep the sudden panic out of his voice.

Caz turned to face him finally, and for the first time Tae noticed how thin his face was, the lines of strain etched into it.

"The city mayor's been coming after the street-kid gangs. You know that place we used to sleep? They cleared it out. Levelled it.

We all made it out, but we lost everything. Do you know what it's like, trying to get all the kids through the winter without blankets and coats? There were a few mornings I woke up and thought one of them was dead, they were so cold."

It was Tae's turn to stare. "I—"

"So go ahead. Go off-planet. Another six months and there won't be any of us left here anyways."

Tae stared blankly at the back wall of the building across the alley from him, sickness rising inside him.

He'd thought just maybe, for once, he'd be free. He'd finally have options, finally be able to leave a bad job rather than take every desperate chance just to stay alive.

But he'd been fooling himself.

He'd never be free.

One look at Caz's anxious face, Peti's much-too-skinny frame, even under all the ragged street-clothing, told him it had always been impossible.

Peti had already turned to go, but Caz gave him one last look before he followed.

"Wait," said Tae, the word half-way dragged out of him. The two street-kids paused.

"Wait," he said again. Caz turned back to him, unable to hide the painful hope in his expression.

Why did they think he could solve all their problems? Why the hell did they think he had all the answers?

"I—Here. Give me your chip."

Caz took a step towards him and held out his wrist again, his eyes never leaving Tae's face. Tae touched the chip Masha had given him to the younger boy's com, and, swallowing down the bitter taste of disappointment, let the rest of the credits click over.

Caz's eyes widened as he saw the numbers, and Peti, who had turned as well, came to look over his shoulder. She whistled softly, then stared up at Tae.

"But—how are you going to pay for your ticket off-planet?" she whispered at last.

He took a deep breath, fighting down the knot of despair in his stomach.

"I changed my mind. I'm not going off-planet."

"Aren't you worried they'll catch you?" asked Caz finally. Tae shook his head, jaw clenched grimly.

"No. They won't have to. I'm going back."

"Going back? Where?"

"I … listen. I didn't escape from prison. Some government high-up broke me out to help with a job. I told them to pay me a cut upfront, and I ran."

They were staring at him.

"I—but listen. She offered me a pardon. And," he paused. "And enough money that maybe, if I pull the job off, I could get all of us out of this garbage-dump of a city. Off this garbage-dump of a planet."

The words tasted bitter in his mouth. He'd never imagined he'd be a sellout.

Although selling out probably required you to get paid, and they'd probably just kill him and dump his body somewhere, or throw him back in jail.

Still, there was nothing like being out of options to force you to be an optimist.

"Tae," said Peti. She put a hand on his arm, her face grave. "Listen. You don't have to—"

He shook her off. "I didn't know what was happening to the rest of you, OK? You need blankets, and some coats for the younger kids, and I had money on my chip."

"And now you don't," she whispered.

"Yeah. But I go back there, pull that job—maybe we all get out of here. Maybe we go somewhere off-planet, somewhere warm. Somewhere they aren't hunting street kids, somewhere Mila doesn't keep getting sick."

"You could do that?" Caz asked at last. The desperate hope in his face almost hurt Tae to look at.

"Maybe. If I can pull this job off."

"And if you can't?"

"I will, OK?" he said at last. "I'll come back. I promise."

Caz and Peti nodded, faces stricken.

The noise was so faint his ears barely caught it. He grabbed Caz and Peti by the shoulders and shoved them forward.

"Go!" he hissed.

They didn't stop to ask questions, just took off down the narrow alley, Tae on their heels.

"It'll follow me," he whispered. "Get back to the others."

"But—"

"Go! Tell them I'll see you all soon. Once the job's done."

He'd done it again. Put them in danger again. He cursed himself.

They were approaching the end of the alley.

"You go left," he panted. "Duck into the first alley you see. I'll lead it right."

"Tae—" Peti sounded scared.

"I'll be fine! Go!"

With one last look back at him, they obeyed. Tae darted to the right as they slipped down the street to the left.

Sure enough, the dark shadow of the drone came after him.

41

The street the alley opened up onto was wide and deserted, and the place between his shoulder blades itched as he bent low and sprinted up the street.

He had to lose the thing before he got back to Masha's.

He dived into another alleyway as a heat-blast sizzled off the concrete behind him, ran down it, and came out into another street. He looked around wildly for a moment, then flattened himself into a doorway.

A moment later the drone emerged. Not just a regular police drone, either. An armed tracking drone.

He groaned inwardly. Just his luck.

He hardly dared breathe as it rotated, scanning the street.

And then, finally, it disappeared back into the alley.

He was lightheaded with lack of breath, but even now he scarcely dared to make a sound. He counted slowly to five, then to ten, and then, at last, he gasped in a long breath and leaned against the doorway.

Caz and Peti were smart. They were street kids. They'd find a way to survive, and keep the others alive, until he got back. Until he could break them all out of this deathtrap of a city, that ground you down and ripped you up and spat out the pieces.

And, despite everything, he would come back. He had to.

He shook his head and peered out of the doorway.

All clear.

Still, he couldn't help looking over his shoulder as he made his careful way back to Masha's eclectic office. The place he'd never intended to return to.

He reached her door, and paused.

His last chance to run.

No. No wonder Masha hadn't been worried about giving him an

advance and letting him slip off. If she knew half as much about him as she seemed to, she'd have already known—he'd never have been able to run after all.

The bitter taste of anger almost choked him as he pulled open the door.

But at least here there was no one trying to kill him, for the moment.

He only had a moment to take in the fact that the composition of the room had changed before someone lunged at him.

He cursed and jumped back, but Ysbel was faster, grabbing the new figure, a lanky young woman with tawny skin and tousled black hair, around the waist and holding her in place.

Tae glared at her in disbelief as she struggled, gasped, swore, and finally collapsed into a chair, glowering.

This must be Jez. The pilot. Who apparently believed he had crashed some stupid ship, and wanted to kill him for it.

He'd never been on a ship in his damn life.

But then, everyone wanted to kill street kids. Reasons hardly seemed to come into it.

He watched her for a moment. The black eye and the bright, angry bruise that stood out in sharp relief across her cheekbone should have made her look a little pathetic. Instead, it made her look dangerous and unpredictable.

But he wasn't afraid of her. She may be dangerous, but she'd made it abundantly clear that her thought process went from her gut straight to her muscles, bypassing her brain entirely.

He stalked to an empty seat in the corner and scowled at the lot of them. The people who, apparently, he'd be working with. The people he'd somehow have to survive.

Lev, with his easy manner and sharp eyes, had the potential to be much more of a threat than the pilot. But as intelligent as the man certainly was, he looked like the type who would hesitate to step on a bug.

Ysbel was another matter. He was no Lev, but it had taken him about thirty seconds to refresh his memory on the dour, muscular woman. The mass murderer. Five years ago, and people still talked about it. Thirty-five people at once, and the foundations of a massive new launch and docking station blown to rubble. No one knew why, and she had never spoken a word about it, just sat through the trial as if she'd blown off her tongue along with the bloody ruins of workers and surveyors and officials and tons upon tons of construction material. No anguished guilt, no apology, no apparent regret. Every picture from the trial showed her with the same stoic, expressionless look on her face she was wearing now.

He shivered.

She made him nervous.

But there was only one person who he was actually afraid of.

The pleasant, friendly woman in the long pilot's coat, with the sharp glint behind her dark, compelling eyes.

Masha.

Despite her friendly smile and unassuming air, Masha left him utterly terrified.

# 5

Ysbel sat back in her seat, closing her eyes for a moment.

*Olya's three-year-old face was set in a mixture of pride and determination, and she clung to her little brother's chubby hand, the shadows of their small cottage dappling her skin. "Mama! Mama, I found a place where I can get across the stream without getting wet. And I even brought Misko with me. Look!"*

*Ysbel smiled as her wife's arm slipped around her waist. Tanya must have just come in from the fields, because she smelled of earth and sunshine.*

*"Did she get wet?" Ysbel whispered. Tanya's blue eyes sparkled with amusement.*

*"Look at her. This is after I wrung her clothes out and hung them in the sun for the last hour. Her shoes are still out there." She smiled, that wistful smile that still made Ysbel weak in the knees, even after seven years of marriage, and Ysbel leaned in for a kiss.*

"Alright." Masha's voice was brisk and businesslike, and Ysbel opened her eyes with a start.

Finally. What she'd been waiting for. Even if it meant putting up with those two brawling idiots. After five years in prison, Ysbel was accustomed to a much quicker, much more effective, and usually much more permanent form of dispute resolution.

45

But she had a decision to make, and she wouldn't be able to make it until after Masha was finished.

"I promised you details," Masha continued, "and now that you're all here, I'll give them to you." She glanced around at them. Ysbel narrowed her eyes. There was an intelligence glinting through the woman's pleasant expression, like a knife-blade through a cushion.

Masha was something more than she appeared. But then, Ysbel had known that from the moment she met her.

Really, it hardly mattered.

"As most of you know," Masha continued, "I work for the government. In various capacities. Recently, it has come to our attention that technology we thought lost twenty years ago still, in fact, exists. We've located it, and they tasked me with gathering a team to extract it."

Ysbel sighed and raised her head slightly. "What sort of tech?"

"Let's just say it would revolutionize both flight and weaponry."

Ysbel narrowed her eyes at her. "That's not enough. If you want me to help you, I need more than that."

Masha gave a pained shrug. "Our knowledge of it is somewhat limited, but it is an item that, if reverse-engineered, would allow us to create cloaking devices that are essentially impenetrable by today's technology, as well as a form of high-speed near-space travel that approaches ten times the speed of anything we currently have. And on top of that, apparently a hyperdrive technology that would negate the need to travel through wormholes."

From across the room, the crazy pilot-girl sat up straighter.

"It would create a super-ship," said the street-boy, Tae, the sullenness in his voice shot through with a mixture of interest and loathing. "Not to mention what it would do for warfare. Or policing."

He looked like he'd had plenty of run-ins with the police himself.

Masha nodded. "You're correct. And it almost did, twenty years ago. In our system's last war with Halo system, a ship carrying the only prototype of this technology, and the only person who possessed the plans for it, was shot and disabled near an uninhabited planet outside system boundaries. Everyone thought it was lost, but it appears the pilot was able to maneuver the damaged ship through the planet's atmosphere before crashing onto the surface."

Ysbel leaned back, half-closing her eyes again at the irrelevance of the information.

*Tanya's head was tipped back as she laughed, her long brown hair cascading down her back. "Oh my Ysi," she said, finally recovering herself. "Have I ever told you how much I adore you?"*

*"You could tell me again," said Ysbel, grinning as she took her wife in her arms. "I wouldn't mind."*

"And who was this pilot?" asked the scholarly young man in his even, pleasant tone.

"The pilot was Sasa Illiovich. The ship was the *Ungovernable.*"

Ysbel looked up, interested despite herself, as Tae jumped and Lev swore softly.

"Is that supposed to mean something?" Jez asked, grinning and leaning back in her seat.

Ysbel raised an eyebrow.

The pilot was more stupid even then she looked. And she looked pretty stupid.

Tae glared at Jez with, if possible, even more hatred than before. "Sasa Illiovich? They were only the best inventor who's ever lived. When they were shot down in the war, we lost the most brilliant mind of the millennium."

The pilot grinned wider, making herself comfortable in the soft cushions. "Not much of a pilot though, I guess."

Tae almost jumped to his feet, his eyes glowing sullen murder. Ysbel turned her flat stare on him, and he dropped back, glowering.

The pilot-girl winked, and his face went momentarily apoplectic.

Ysbel let out a long-suffering sigh.

*Olya, crying. "It's not fair, Mama! Misko bit me!"*

*"Yes, well, your mamochka and I are still not going to put him on a ship for deep space. I'm sorry, sweetheart." She met Tanya's eyes. Tanya was holding the struggling Misko and fighting back a laugh, and Ysbel had to press her lips hard together to keep her face straight.*

"So we go to the planet, pick it up, and bring it back," said Lev, his voice still mild. "On the face of it, it would appear you're embarrassingly over-resourced for this mission. I've looked up the histories on everyone here. Jez, apparently, has a flying record that no one in the system has ever matched, at least not in anything I can access. Tae may say that Sasa Illiovich was the most brilliant technological mind of the millennium, but he's well on track to giving them a run for their money. And Ysbel is, besides her ... more recent history, the system expert on weapons and explosives. Probably several systems' expert. And me—" he spread his hands depreciatingly. "Well. So, Masha. Why don't you tell the others what we're really doing?"

Masha smiled, and the expression she turned on the scholar-boy was almost fond. "You're right. It was never going to be as simple as that. Since the ship disappeared, the planet has been terraformed and inhabited. We believe the planet's owner has found and retrieved the ship, but doesn't realize what he has. He certainly doesn't know of the existence of the technology. However, it's inevitable that he'll figure it out eventually. Any offer on our governments' part to purchase the ship would almost certainly trigger his suspicions, and if he were to find the technology, the results would be ... disadvantageous."

"Disadvantageous to who?" grunted Ysbel.

"Disadvantageous to our continued existence as a viable species," said Masha with an apologetic shrug.

There was a moment of shocked silence from the others.

Ysbel sighed and closed her eyes. They were there again, Tanya, Olya, little Misko.

She knew what she'd see next, but even so she didn't open her eyes. It was worth it, worth everything, to see their faces for even one moment more.

*A roar, a whoosh of flames that Ysbel still heard in her dreams. Their tiny cottage, flames leaping from the doorway, Tanya's anguished face at the window, the screams of the children. The sick panic in her chest as she fought to reach them, struggling against the armed guards restraining her, her hands cuffed behind her back, her eyes stinging with tears and smoke.*

Ysbel opened her eyes, blinking back tears.

*I'm sorry, Tanya. I'm so sorry.*

They'd said that she'd shown no remorse and no regret after what she'd done at the shuttle site. And, she supposed, that was true. But it wasn't true that she didn't have regrets, late at night in her prison cell.

One regret.

That the people at the top, the ones who had been responsible for bringing her there, hadn't been at the site when the explosives she set went off.

When Masha had found her in her prison cell and talked to her about freedom and money, Ysbel ignored her, because freedom and money meant nothing.

But then the woman had mentioned who it was who had ordered the job. Who they'd be reporting to after it was done.

And Ysbel had looked up at her and smiled, for the first time in years. And agreed to listen.

"Wait. Who is this person who has the tech?" Tae looked up, the sullen glare that seemed to be his trademark directed at Masha instead of the pilot for a change.

"Vitali Dobrev," said Masha.

Ysbel swore quietly.

Vitali the Butcher. The weapons dealer.

Even her father had been afraid of him.

He didn't take sides, and he didn't play favourites, and it was a badly-kept secret that he dealt to anyone—government, mafia, terrorist pod, paramilitary group—who had the cold, hard credits to pay him. His weapons were brilliantly, horribly effective, but you didn't even say his name in polite society. In any society. Because people who did tended to turn up floating in space with no space suit.

But—he wasn't invincible. And she was very, very good at what she did.

If she decided to do this job, she would do whatever it took for it to succeed. Because really, the job was only a means to an end. All she really cared about is what would happen afterwards. When they went in to report to their employers.

It would be a simple matter to plant a new set of explosives, slip the control into her palm, to depress the button. And the building would collapse hundreds of tons of rubble onto the calculating, unemotional heads of the last of the people who had killed her family.

"I think that about covers it," said Masha, surveying them. "I should warn you, though, for reasons I'm certain you'll understand, this mission is highly confidential. Based on your records, as Lev has so helpfully pointed out, your pardons by the government within a relatively short period of time would cause certain elements to sit up and take notice. Therefore, this whole thing is secret from everyone except a very small, select few. This does not, unfortunately, include the police. That means, as far as the local authorities are concerned, you are all very dangerous, very wanted, escaped prisoners."

The pilot tipped her head back and put her hands behind her head lazily. "Don't know about the rest of you, but I have all kinds of experience with being very wanted." She gave the room a lascivious look, and Tae snorted in disgust.

Ysbel didn't bother to react.

Behind her eyelids, a slender, brown-haired woman smiled.

Only a few weeks more.

The rest of the team would die in the wreckage, of course. When Masha had brought her here, she'd wondered, for a moment, if she'd feel bad about that. If somehow she'd hesitate to kill the people she'd be working beside. It was a faint curiosity, although she hardly ever felt curious anymore. She hardly felt anything anymore, really.

That was the decision she'd had to make.

But … she glanced around at the brash, irritating pilot, the sullen, long-haired street-boy, the smug, self-satisfied scholar. And Masha, of course.

It hadn't been that hard of a decision, after all.

# 6

Lev leaned back in his chair and watched the others.

Masha had done the equivalent of tossing a particle bomb in the centre of the room, and their reactions were instructive.

Tae's face was blank fear. Understandable.

Ysbel was—not afraid. Angry. He filed that away. Ysbel was an interesting case.

He knew about the murders, of course. Everyone did, except possibly the long-limbed, fidgety, resplendently-irritating pilot.

Jez.

He rolled the name around in his mind.

He'd guessed who she was when Masha had mentioned her—that had been part, although certainly not all, of the reason he'd agreed to come along. But when he'd seen her, he was certain of it.

She wasn't what he'd expected. He'd expected someone a little older, a little more hardened. She was clearly no babe in arms, but there was an innocence about her, like a puppy. A gawky, growling, biting, shoe-chewing puppy, but something you'd ultimately feel bad about kicking.

And he planned to ... do what? He wasn't quite sure. Kill her was the obvious solution, but he'd never liked the obvious solution. There was almost always something hiding under the obvious that was so much cleaner, so much more unexpected, so much more satisfying.

But after finally meeting her in person, he might have to reconsider.

How do you kick a puppy—drown a puppy, really—and not lose sleep over it? It was a conundrum, but there'd be a way. There was always a way, if you thought about it hard enough.

He'd lost enough sleep over Jez. Even before she'd landed him in jail.

He watched her curiously now. She'd been shocked. Maybe frightened. But she was clearly already distracted. She glanced around the room with that cocky, restless grin, then winced and swore loudly. Bruises stiffening, no doubt. Tae looked up and glared at her. She returned the glare with interest, and for half a moment he thought she would go for him again. But she glanced briefly at Ysbel and subsided.

He smiled to himself.

So she did have some capacity for reflection. He'd honestly wondered.

And Masha.

She was watching the others too, with her pleasant, bland expression.

Was she making the same calculations he was?

When he was led, a week ago, into the visitors room in his prison, he'd been surprised. He'd been locked up, after all, for knowing too much, reading files he'd never been meant to read, downloading information that he should have known—probably had known, if he was being honest with himself—was illegal. They knew, of course, that he had photographic memory, that he'd be able to retrieve the information forever. His family, all of them, his mother, father, two little sisters, and even his older brothers and sisters, who no longer lived at home, had been locked up as well, on the mere chance that he'd shared some of it with them.

So to say that his visiting hours, where he could converse freely with someone outside of the prison, had been severely curtailed, was an understatement.

But he'd been even more surprised when he'd seen this nondescript woman, with her friendly smile and sharp eyes, sitting at the table across from him.

She'd presented him with her proposal. He'd listened politely, then, just as politely, refused.

She'd come back again the next day, with a better offer.

He'd refused that as well.

Finally, on the third day, she'd laid her cards on the table.

A weapons and explosives expert. A tech genius. A pilot who could fly anything through anything, probably in her sleep—a pilot in whom, although Masha was almost certainly unaware of it, he had a personal interest.

And, crucially, a promise: he'd go free, and his family would go free, and they'd go free before he left the planet.

That was what he'd been waiting for. Because, to be quite frank, everyone currently in this room was almost certainly going to die, violently. He's known that from the moment in the prison visitors room when he'd deduced who their mark was. But Lev was the reason his family had been locked up. Well, Jez was, indirectly. But that aside, getting them out of this mess was the least he could do.

It was worth working with Masha.

It was even worth working with those other three idiots.

At least he wouldn't feel too bad about the fact that none of them would likely survive this.

"OK, so I have a question," said Jez, shifting in her chair and wincing slightly. "I know bastard over there is good with tech, and Ysbel can blow things up. But what about pretty-boy?"

There was a long moment's pause as everyone looked at her.

She didn't seem even slightly embarrassed under their combined gaze.

Lev raised his eyebrows and shook his head. It took a certain amount of something, courage or stupidity or just plain thick-headedness, to know so absolutely, vanishingly little about anything, and to have no qualms whatsoever admitting it.

Masha was the only one whose smile didn't falter. She just gestured to Lev.

"Would you explain please, Lev? And when you're finished, why don't you walk us through what we need to know. You've spent the last few hours studying it, unless I'm much mistaken."

He smiled reluctantly. Masha, at least, had him pegged, even if Jez was staggeringly ignorant.

He turned to face the pilot, who was jiggling her foot against the leg of the chair, apparently at the limit of her ability to sit still, and spread his hands.

"I am here because I'm smart. I'm very, very smart. That's all."

She was looking at him challengingly, and he was surprised at the spark of humour in her eyes, under the brashness and the swagger.

She knew exactly how ridiculous she appeared. She just absolutely didn't care.

He shook his head slightly, and the glint of humour in her eyes deepened, like they'd just shared a joke. Slightly discomfited, he turned to the others. He tapped his com and expanded the holoscreen until it was large enough that they'd all be able to see it easily.

Then he tapped the centre, creating a glowing, rotating sphere.

"This planet is Vitali's base," he said. He zoomed in slightly with two fingers. "And this, here, is Vitali's compound." He tapped the screen again, leaving a small mark on the glowing sphere. "I've done some research, and it looks like this is more or less what we'll be up against if we want to get that thing out. First," he traced a circle with one forefinger around the outside of the sphere, "there's a forcefield, around the planet and another around the compound. He's a weapons dealer, and he has access to tech the rest of us only dream about. So no one gets onto or off of the planet without his permission."

"I could take it out," Ysbel said. Lev glanced at her and nodded.

"I'm certain you could. However, you couldn't without letting him know something is coming. If he locks down, I doubt even you have an explosive that would deal with the fireworks he'd be capable of putting into motion."

She raised one shoulder in reluctant acquiescence, and Lev turned back to his holoscreen. "So. That's the first hurdle. Then there are the ground defences. He has a fleet of dedicated ships, and I think we can safely assume that there are weapons and tech built into them that we've never seen before. It's unlikely we'll have anything even close to matching it on a standard ship, and even if Tae or Ysbel could come up with something, we don't know what we'll be up against. There are also," he zoomed in again on the dot, "surface cannons. They can take out a ship pretty easily, if my sources are correct. So, that's getting on to the planet.

"Once we're on, the next step would be to get inside the compound. There are walls made of gilite, which, as Ysbel will be aware, is impervious to most chemical reactions and extraordinary hard to blow up. There are also guards, who, if accounts are correct, are both highly-skilled and highly loyal. Any sign of corruption that isn't immediately reported to Vitali and he shoots the guard and the guard's entire unit. So there's a pretty high incentive to stay on the straight and narrow. Besides the guards, the planet itself is not what you'd call hospitable. He terraformed it before he made it his base, but the terraforming has transmutated over the years."

"Meaning?" asked Jez.

"Meaning carnivorous plants, deadly animals, and anything that bites you is probably poisonous. Not a place you'd want to spend time."

He expanded the screen even further. "Once we're inside the compound, we'd need to get into the vault. It's right here, in the centre, and it's where he keeps his most important things—weapons plans that he hasn't yet sold, his credit cylinders, the best of his new tech, and here, in the back, personal items he finds valuable. It appears that the ship is one of those. There is a standard security system, alarms, and a secondary security system which I'd need more time to find the specs on. And, of course, once we get to the ship, it's a matter of finding and removing the tech. If reports are to be believed, Sasa Illiovich was ... eccentric. We have no idea what the tech looks like, where it's attached, and how to get it out, although I think we can safely conclude that if Vitali didn't notice it, it's hidden fairly well."

"So. Easy peasy," said Jez, grinning. "And if we get caught?"

He drew a finger across his throat.

There was a long moment of silence as the others digested what he'd said.

He'd tried to keep it simple. Heavens knew these people needed things as simple as possible. And besides, he didn't want to give away exactly how much he knew. Masha was right—he had spent hours researching Vitali's hideout. But he'd prefer to keep her and anyone else from the realization that he knew much, much more than what could be gleaned in a few hours' study.

Finally, Tae rose to his feet. "This is stupid. It's impossible. Trust me, I know."

He glowered around the room, daring anyone to contradict him.

Jez shot him a poisonous glare, then stretched luxuriously, the effect spoiled somewhat by a wince she couldn't hide.

"Hate to say I agree with anything that bastard says, but I'm going to be honest—he's right. This is crap. I don't mind slim chances. But this is flat-out suicide."

There were a few moments of silence. Masha didn't react, just watched them with that pleasant, unreadable expression. At last she said, "I won't ask you to stay, then, if you think you can't do it. I'm happy to escort any of you who wish to leave back to their prison cells, or," she flashed a quick grin at Jez, "back to their, ahem, apartments."

Jez glared. "I didn't say I couldn't do it, you—"

But he never heard what insult Jez had prepared. The door shattered, splinters spraying the room, and a circular drone slightly larger than his head, crossed with the three unmistakable black police stripes, appeared in the opening.

# 7

Jez vaulted to her feet and rolled to one side as a beam from a drone-class particle-gun sizzled through the chair where she'd been sitting.

Clearly they weren't here to talk.

She turned and smacked directly into Tae. He glared at her, and then they both dived behind a chair as another particle-blast scorched the air above them.

She could strangle him right now. Ysbel probably wouldn't—

The drone's electrolaser blast lit up the chair in front of them, and they rolled out in opposite directions like colliding marbles.

She glanced around the room.

Lev had taken the bare precaution of positioning himself behind his chair rather than in front of it, his forehead creased with a frown of slight puzzlement. Masha ... she raised her eyebrows. Masha had two small, serviceable-looking heat-pistols, and was returning fire enthusiastically.

Maybe she'd underestimated the woman.

She yelped as another blast dissolved the padding on the floor at her feet, and jumped back.

Time to focus.

No escape, except through the middle of the police drone. No back door. No weapons, except the makeshift knife in her pocket from the prison break.

She felt the adrenalin-grin spreading across her face.

What the hell.

She yanked out the knife, depressed the blade, and launched herself out from behind the half-melted chair.

Time slowed, as it always did. She had time to notice the moment whoever was controlling the drone realized what she was doing and brought the weapons to bear, and then she was on top of it, slashing down with her knife that was, to her delight, sharp enough to make a dent in the drone's armour. She jumped clear as it lit up with electricity, and as the particle-cannon swung towards her, she braced herself for the shot. And then, over the noise and the chaos, Ysbel's voice. It was flat and dangerous, and demanded obedience.

"Down," she barked, and, like a puppet with her strings cut, Jez dropped.

A spray of viscous liquid spattered over the drone. Something in the back of Jez's brain recognized the threat in the sharp, chemical smell, and she rolled out of the way, taking shelter under perhaps the last remaining chair.

Then the whole world turned white.

It was a while before colour returned to her vision. She blinked at the massive, smoking hole in the floor where the drone had once been.

She still couldn't hear anything, and to be honest, after what had been more of a physical blow than a sound, she wasn't sure she wanted to.

Masha had slipped the pistols back into wherever she'd had them concealed, and was standing a couple paces back from the edges of what could have been the entrance to hell.

She said something—or, at least, Jez assumed that sound was coming out of her mouth. But from the appearance of the others, no one could hear it.

Lev got up with a look of clear exasperation, brushed the scattered ash off his clothes, and tapped his com. The holoscreen appeared, and he brought the com to his mouth and spoke into it.

His words scrolled across the screen.

She raised an eyebrow at him. He was smart, after all. Maybe Masha'd been right to bring him—you never knew when you might need someone who could figure out how to communicate when you'd all been rendered temporarily deaf by basically the entire world blowing up two meters away from you. Probably happened frequently around here.

*What in the name of everything sane was that?*

Ysbel raised her eyes to the sky and slapped her own com.

*It was saving your stupid life, idiot. What did you think?*

Jez grinned and slapped her com. This was type of conversation she felt at home in.

*Room needed redecorating anyways.*

They both glared at her.

Then Masha turned. She watched them for a moment, then tapped her own com. There was something sharp and hard in her normally-pleasant expression that made all of them pay attention.

*Well. Whatever that was, you're committed now. Ysbel's blast may have destroyed the tracking, but I guarantee you, they saw each one of your faces over the drone's com. The four of you, with your skills and your records? In the same room? As far as the police are concerned, you're not escaped prisoners anymore. You're terrorists, and you're at war.*

Jez felt her grin slowly fade.

Masha was right.

*You do this job, or when they catch you, they don't just throw in back in your cells. They kill you.*

Masha glanced around at them with her sharp gaze.

*There's a place I can take you. I was going to wait until you'd made your choice of whether to come or to go, but now, it appears, the choice was made for you. I would suggest we hurry. Ysbel may have destroyed the tracking device, but they'll figure out fairly quickly where we are.*

Slowly, reluctantly, they followed her from the room, shooting poisonous glares at each other as they went.

# 8

At least, Lev thought as he shoved the push-broom across the oil-stained floor of the large, converted hangar-bay, everyone's hearing seemed to have returned. His ears were still ringing, but shockingly, the blast didn't seem to have done permanent damage.

Masha had brought them there the night before, after Ysbel's explosion. There had been small sleeping rooms prepared off the main hangar bay—it seemed Masha had gambled on their cooperation—but other than that, it seemed comfort had gone the way of their respective options.

Ysbel dragged in an armful of worn sitting cushions and dropped them in a heap on the newly-swept floor as Tae shoved the remainder of the empty crates out of the way.

Jez leaned against the hangar bay wall, arms crossed, smirking at them and making no attempt to help.

He sighed and leaned against his broom. "So, Masha. To be clear, you expect us to get into Vitali's impossible-to-penetrate compound, steal tech we have zero specs on, and then somehow get out again. Without being killed."

Masha turned, picking up a discarded oil canister from off the floor. "Yes. Without being killed would be the preferable option."

He narrowed his eyes at her. "Unfortunately, you're not being particularly helpful."

"I chose each of you specifically because I believed you'd come up with a plan that would be feasible," she said in her calm voice, the pleasant look never leaving her face. "I have no intention of getting in your way."

Tae shot Masha a glare, then turned reluctantly to Lev. "I may be able to get us through the security systems, if you can get me specs."

Lev nodded slowly, studying the former street-boy. "I'll see what I can do. What about the force field?"

Tae shrugged. "Possibly I could build something to get us out of it. I doubt I'll be able to get us in."

Lev nodded, turning back to his broom. "Ysbel? You're the one who knows explosives. Do you have something that would take out a force field?"

Ysbel glanced up. "Perhaps," she grunted. "Again, we would have to be on the inside."

"You know," said Jez at last, still smirking. "I could get us in."

They all turned to stare at her.

"This isn't just about flying things really fast," Tae snapped. "Some rudimentary thought process has to be present."

"Well, see, that's exactly what I'm saying." Jez grinned. "I know you're all a bunch of geniuses, but you couldn't find your bums with both hands and a map. But," she turned to Lev, "for my money, you're basically a weapons dealer."

He stared at her, panic clutching his chest.

She didn't know. She couldn't. One hint and he'd be off the team, and his family would lose their one chance of freedom …

"And Ysbel and Tae here, definitely hired muscle. Definitely."

Lev took a deep breath, recovering himself.

"Security is tight," he said after a moment. "If we fly up and just announce that we're weapons dealers, I somehow think he'd see through that."

She shrugged. "We steal a ship, steal some identities. I've done it before."

"Of course you have," muttered Tae.

Lev gave her a calculating look.

He'd taken her for nothing but a sparking, live-wire bundle of instincts and adrenalin. She apparently also had a surprisingly-sharp mind.

And kept it surprisingly well-hidden.

"And you?"

"Me? I'm just a pilot. I fly."

He nodded slowly, still studying her. "Not bad. Needs some refining, but it could work."

Masha smiled her pleasant smile. "Of course, as I'm sure you've already considered, Vitali isn't going to let a weapons dealer and his bodyguards wander in without an invite. Luckily, I'm privy to information that most of you," she cut a meaningful glance at Lev, "are not. And I've been following Vitali for the past several months, tracking his movements, watching for patterns. Whenever he has new tech, he invites a select few weapons dealers to view it. My sources say he has something new coming out in the next few weeks. It's possible that's our chance."

She glanced around at them. "He will have already issued invites. If Tae can hack into the system, we can figure out who he's invited, and then narrow down the list to who he doesn't know personally."

"And then we kidnap the mud-sucker, steal his identity, and put him on a ship with no oxygen reserves, headed for deep space," Jez finished. "Sounds like my kind of plan."

OK, so his initial impression of her had been mostly right.

"And, if we wanted, we could send Bastard over there to keep him company." Her grin had a dangerous edge to it now.

Tae turned, his face tight with anger, and threw his armful of prefab crate-slats to the floor with a clatter. "That's it! I'm done being insulted by this piece of space-crap."

Jez's grin widened. "Hey, anytime you want—"

"Enough!" Lev raised his hands. "Listen. If the two of you want to kill each other, fine. That's none of my business. But Tae, how good are your piloting skills? And Jez, you plan on bypassing the security systems and building a device that will break us out through the force-field?"

They stared at each other for a few moments, and he could practically feel the hatred sparking between them.

"Fine," said Jez at last. "I work with this dirty bastard for as long as it takes to finish this job, until I can to get back in the sky and away from all of you losers. And I'll keep from smashing in his stupid face for long enough for us to do this. But I promise you," she turned to Tae, and her voice was low and deadly serious, "if we pull this off and Vitali doesn't kill you, you'd better be damn careful that I never see your face again. Because I'll make you wish you'd never been born."

Tae didn't drop her gaze, and he didn't flinch. He just stared at her, as if memorizing something and storing it away.

"I may be just a street kid to you," he said at last, softly. "But trust me. If you want to try something like that, you'd only better hope you fly as well as you say you do."

Masha cleared her throat, and everyone jumped.

"Well, now that's settled," she said, smiling as if she didn't notice the tension crackling in the air, "let's talk about next steps."

Slowly, grudgingly, the two of them turned to look at her. Lev raised his eyes to the ceiling.

Lady grant him patience.

"So, Lev."

He gritted his teeth. "Yes, Masha?"

"Enlighten us on next steps."

Jez glanced over at him, eyes dancing, anger replaced with a sort of dangerous excitement. "My ship," she said.

He sighed. "Your ship."

"If you want me to put weapons on this ship, I'll need it soon," Ysbel grunted.

"Me too, if you want it to be able to fly out of the force-field," Tae muttered.

Jez leaned forward, and the intensity in her gaze surprised him. "I can fly anything, but if I'm going to be doing fancy flying, I have a list."

"No," Masha broke in. "I have a list. We'll need a ship that can realistically be flown by a weapons buyer."

Jez froze. "Which means?" she whispered at last.

"Which means a SRS 17 at least. Latest models only."

"Are you serious?" Jez's voice was soft with the sort of wonder Lev had always imagined would accompany the birth of one's firstborn.

Masha nodded.

For a moment, Lev thought the pilot was going to actually break into tears. When she'd recovered, she asked, in the tone of someone afraid to break a spell, "How are we going to get this ship?"

"Steal it," said Masha.

Lev found himself taking a step forward in case Jez fainted from joy.

She didn't, but it was probably a close thing.

He sighed internally. Killing this one would definitely be like kicking a puppy.

A really irritating, kleptomaniac puppy, with a penchant for destroying things.

He turned to Masha. "Can't you just buy one?"

"Yes," said Masha calmly. "I could. But it would leave a paper trail, and we can't risk that right now."

"And stealing one wouldn't leave a trail?"

"Not if you do it well enough. And if you can't do that, our chances for getting in and out of Vitali's compound are slim."

He shook his head in a mixture of disbelief and irritation. "I think we've already established that."

Masha gave him that helpful, pleasant smile, with just a hint of a bite to it. "Lev, if you would, we'll need you to locate us a ship to steal. I trust you understand what we need. Jez, this is your baby. You'll be in charge of actually extracting it and bringing it back here, hopefully without anyone on your tail."

Jez's grin was wider than her face.

"They could have a tracking device on it," Tae muttered.

"Which is why you're going with her. And Lev, you're with them."

Lev's amusement vaporized almost as quickly as the smile on Jez's face.

"Hold on just a minute," Jez blurted. "I told you, I'm not a team player. And I'm not—"

"You are now," said Masha, and the glint in her eyes was keen and slightly amused. "If you want your ship, that is."

Lev gave Masha a long look. She met his gaze and didn't look away, a small smile playing around her mouth.

He narrowed his eyes, ignoring the sputtering Jez and the apoplectic Tae.

He'd known Masha for less than a week. But he was already very certain about two things—she was also very, very smart. And she did nothing without a reason.

She had a reason for sending the people on the team who had the most reason to want each other dead on the same mission. Whether she knew about his history with Jez he couldn't guess, but Jez had made no secret of her feelings for Tae.

He raised his eyebrow slightly, conceding this round to her.

But she didn't know everything. And he was a quick study.

Ready for round two, Masha.

# 9

Jez scowled at the two men standing across from her on the floor of the hangar bay. There was nothing about this situation she liked.

But … on the other hand, they were going to steal her a ship.

OK, technically it would be everyone's ship. But it would be hers. She could feel it in her bones. It would belong to her in the same way her name did. In the same way as the air in her lungs did.

Her ship.

She could taste the freedom of it on her tongue.

And if getting it meant working with a sulky, sleazebag government sellout and an egghead scholar-type, fine. She'd deal with it.

"OK," she said. "Here's the plan. We wait until our guy's in the building. We scope out the ship, see who's watching and where, tech-boy there gets us inside and hot-wires it, and I fly us out."

They were both staring at her.

"That's it?" Tae asked incredulously. She smirked at him.

"What else do you want? A parade? A holo-display?"

"Maybe a way to get out without dying!" he exploded.

"I said. I'll fly us out. Won't be a problem."

Lev had two fingers pressed to his temples. "Jez," he said, in a tone of forced calm. "I understand your wish to keep this simple. But there are going to be tracker devices, alarms—"

"Why we're bringing him along, I thought," she broke in.

"—body guards, probably private muscle as well, and they'll all be shooting at us—"

"I told you. I'll fly us. We'll be fine."

"Where?" Even Lev's patience seemed to be stretching thin. She rolled her eyes.

"It'll be fine. Trust me. We'll lose them in the streets. If tech-boy can disable the trackers, there'll be nothing to worry about. I'll lose them, then we'll bring it back here. Easy peasy."

Neither of them looked convinced.

It didn't matter. If this didn't work, she wasn't sure how long she'd last anyways, grounded like this.

"Anyways, we'd better get going."

There were no deep-space ships here, or even shallow-space, but in some of the alcoves off to the side Masha had shown them what she did have.

It wasn't impressive. A couple skybikes, an enclosed 437 Bluewing beater. All crap. But she could work with it.

"We'll take the skybikes. Less noticeable, and we can come back and grab them later. You know how to drive skybikes?"

Tae gave a sullen nod.

Lev looked hesitant.

She shook her head and rolled her eyes to the ceiling. "Fine. You know what, Lev, you'll ride with me. Tae, you follow."

Without waiting for an answer, she pulled out the longest of the crappy bikes and threw one leg over the side.

"Get on," she said over her shoulder.

Lev complied with gritted teeth. Behind her, Tae had mounted his bike with the air of someone going to his death, but at least he looked like he knew how to start the thing and steer it. She hit the ignition and the bike rose gently into the air. Lev grabbed onto the sides of the bike as if attempting to wrap the sidebars around him like a blanket.

"Sorry, you'll have to hold on to me," she said over her shoulder, grinning at his obvious discomfort. "Unless you'd like to end up as a stain on the concrete."

He put his arms gingerly around her waist, like someone embracing a live explosive, and she hit the safety tether, clamping them to the seats.

She leaned forward gently, getting used to the feel of the thing. It was old and worn down, but the anti-grav seemed to work fine. Steering was a little loose, that was ok, nothing she couldn't handle, and despite its age, the bike seemed to respond to her movements decently well.

Alright. Ready to go.

She glanced over her shoulder and gave Tae a challenging grin. Then she leaned almost parallel to the bike and they shot forward.

Lev yelped, his grip tightening to a stranglehold, but she didn't care.

She was moving. Flying. Not deep space, not yet, but the freedom of finally being in the air again was like a drug. She leaned forward even farther and dodged between buildings for a while, just for the fun of it, the dirty white sides of them brushing her trouser-legs as she weaved in and out. Then she yanked back on the handles, and the bike pointed its nose to the sky. They shot out of the labyrinth, and Lev gave another strangled yelp, and she waited until the nose of the bike almost touched the force-field surrounding the city before she levelled out, skimming along the barrier.

"What—the *hell*—was that?" Lev gasped in her ear.

"That," she shouted over the sound of the wind, "is called flying."

Slowly she straightened, letting the bike ease back. A quick glance over her shoulder told her that Tae was behind her—far, far behind her—and she eased up more, until the bike was puttering along.

When Tae finally caught up, she didn't even bother giving him a disdainful look, just sped up enough to make him uncomfortable and headed towards the blinking dot on the bike's holoscreen that showed their destination.

They'd get there early. She preferred to run things on the edge, show up just in time. But the stick-in-the-mud and the sellout would probably have revolted, so she had, with much long-suffering sighing, informed them that they should probably show up fifteen minutes early. Lev had almost had a heart attack, and insisted they get there a standard hour early at the very latest so they'd 'be ready,' whatever that meant. She'd argued him down to forty-five minutes.

So here they were. Idling in on their bikes forty-five minutes ahead of when they needed to be there. If their mark even showed up on time.

She sighed, and brought her bike gently down in an alley a couple blocks away. She pulled off her helmet, shook her head, and yanked the shabby black toque down over her spiky hair.

Lev was clutching onto her as if he hadn't quite worked out how to let go.

A moment later, Tae came to a stop beside them, glaring deadly poison.

"Idiot," he muttered.

"Sellout," she shot back.

Lev finally seemed to remember how to unclasp his hands, and shakily leaned back.

"Come on, you two." He took a deep breath, shook his head, and slowly pulled off his helmet. His face was three shades paler than it had been before they started. He closed his eyes for a moment, took another deep breath, and said, "If I have to walk wherever I go for the rest of my life, I'll be fine with it."

"Come on. It was fun!"

He glared at her. "I don't think you understand the definition of 'fun.' I honestly thought you were going to kill me."

She laughed. "I told you. I know how to fly." She jumped off the bike and leaned it against the grimy alley wall, then leaned back against the wall herself.

Forty-five minutes. Damn these plaguing eggheads.

Tae was still mounted on his bike, and still glaring at her.

"Hey stupid, we're here," she said. "You can get off your bike."

He made no move to dismount, just narrowed his eyes at her.

She glared back. "What's your problem?"

"I've had about enough of your crap, pilot. It's time we deal with this."

She raised one eyebrow. Her anger was rising easy and hot, tightening her muscles, sharpening her senses.

"Really. You've had enough of my crap? Well. That's nice. I've had about enough of breathing the same air as you, you worthless sellout, so why don't we deal with it? Right here." She rolled her shoulders, hands tightening into fists.

"Jez," Lev began warningly. She ignored him.

"I'm not a sellout. I don't even know what you're talking about," he gritted through his teeth, clenching his own fists.

"Really? That EMP tech that you sold to the government? The one that overrode all the safety-loops and disabled my ship so I was flying blind? When I crashed my damn ship into an astroid, and I couldn't do a damn thing about it, and I got thrown into a tiny prison cell where I almost lost my mind? I almost got killed trying to escape, and you know what? At that point I didn't even care, that's how bad it was. I lost my ship, I lost my cargo, I lost my reputation, and I can't even get a damn job except in this clown-show. I. Lost. My. Damn. Ship." She was shaking with anger. "Was that just something they made up? You've never heard of that, right?"

Tae was staring at her, face slack with shock.

Like this *was* the first time he'd heard of it.

She glared at him harder.

There were tears in her eyes, and she blinked hard to shove them back. He sure as hell didn't need to see that. How much it hurt.

He opened his mouth, but nothing came out. Lev was looking back and forth between them with a slightly analytical expression, like he was confirming a theory.

"Is that what this is about?" Tae said at last, his voice a mixture of incredulity and bitterness.

She frowned at him. What the hell did he have to be bitter about?

"They stole that from me. Before they locked me up, they stole my tech. You think getting locked up because you were smuggling is bad? You have no idea. You didn't even think about that, though, did you? I'm a street kid, so of course I'm the one who's fault it is. Plaguing idiot."

He swung his leg over his bike and turned away sharply, and it was Jez's turn to stare after him.

Stolen tech. Was that why they'd been laughing after her arrest, when they said they'd send him a thank-you note?

She'd spent three weeks planning her revenge. Now she felt like the grav-controls on her ship had gone haywire before she'd buckled down, and she was floating free.

Lev was still watching them, and she could sense a quiet amusement from him, but she was too shaken to be angry.

It was a long forty-five minutes. She didn't look at Tae, and he didn't look at her.

She felt ever-so-slightly sick to her stomach.

When Lev's holoscreen showed the blinking red light that meant their mark, a low-level mobster, had started towards them, it was a welcome relief.

And then she peered out of the alley and saw the ship, and forgot everything else.

It was beautiful. Not in a showy way. It was deliberately understated, the sides a uniform muted silver, the shielding a modest tinted black. Its sleek body bore the faint score-marks of atmosphere exit and re-entry, and there were scuffs along the sides, like you'd get if you flew in-atmosphere fast enough that the air particles scratched the metal like tiny spikes. But it had clearly been taken care of, every inch of it buffed, every surface meticulously cleaned.

It practically glowed.

Jez was in love.

She barely saw the man exit the vehicle through the rosy haze that suffused her vision. She barely took note of the burly bodyguards who dismounted beside him. She only had eyes for the ship. And when it lifted off gently, to be raised to its parking station on the top of the building, she almost groaned out loud at the pang of loss.

She needed that ship.

"Jez!" Lev hissed in her ear. She started.

"What?"

"I said, does that look like something you can fly?"

She just stared at him for a moment, waiting for his words to make sense. He sighed.

"Alright. I'll take that as a yes. Tae, did you get a scan?"

She glanced over at the sullen street-boy, then remembered and looked away quickly. He'd pulled up his holoscreen on his com, and was rapidly scanning through pages of information. When he spoke, his voice was decisive and businesslike, with no hint of either his usual anger, or his usual sullenness.

"He's got good security on this thing. Must be his baby. There's the standard security, then there's an additional security overlay. That will be a little complicated. There's a control lock that pops up if any of the motion sensors get triggered without the override, and there's an all-systems shielding loop to short out any external control or EMP guns. There's a voice-control keyed to three specific people, and fingerprint and retinal scanners, and it's set to only respond to a specific weight parameter in the pilot's seat. Which I doubt is set for anyone in our weight class."

"So?" asked Lev.

"Give me a few minutes." He was still staring at his screen, frowning in concentration. "Let's see …" He swiped a couple more pages, then shook his wrist to re-set the screen, pulled it in front of him with three fingers, then began typing rapidly. Lev and Jez watched in silence.

Jez's foot tapped impatiently on the concrete, and she stilled it with an effort. No time to be in a hurry. They had to work this the right way. But … she bumped her closed fist against her thigh.

This had to work. She needed that ship. She'd die if she couldn't have that ship.

Tae smiled, and glanced up. "Good news. He bought factory-security, and he never bothered to get it modded. And besides, we're the zero day threat—I doubt he even knew about this vulnerability before I hacked it. So I was able to get in. I'm going to need to be closer to get through the security overlay, and I won't be able to work on the control lock until we're inside, since that's a physical system, but I don't think it will be too complicated. Shielding loop we can leave, although we'll want to take control of it. But, I'm through the main security, and I thiiiink …" he squinted at the screen and typed in a couple more rapid commands. "I think I've got control of the scans." He gave a soft laugh, and Jez's gaze flicked from the screen to his face in shock.

Tae laughed?

"Yes. Got it. That's why you never leave the factory settings." He was grinning, another expression Jez had never expected from him.

Lev took a deep breath. "You know, don't you, that once we do this, we're all the way in. Oleg may be low-level, but he has friends. The mafia doesn't like people stepping on their toes."

Jez turned to look at him. Anticipation tingled through her muscles, her whole body light with it.

Whoever this Masha woman was, whatever the job entailed, she'd be back in the sky. That was all that mattered.

Lev sighed. "Alright. Let's go, then."

# 10

Jez glanced around quickly as the three of them stepped out of the ancient lifts of the drab government building and onto the roof.

Two of Oleg's bodyguards, standing casually next to the ship, and four others on the sides of the roof, facing away from them.

"Lots of muscle for someone who doesn't re-set the factory settings on his security," Tae whispered.

A joke. From Tae. She was almost too shocked to react. Then she gave a snort of laughter that made Lev turn and glare.

"Sorry," she mouthed. She stepped behind the curve of a concrete barrier, pretending to be looking for her ship. There were only a handful up here, so that would only last so long before they looked suspicious. Already one of the guards had turned and was studying them.

"How long do you need to get past the overlay and get us inside?" she whispered.

"A minute. Thirty seconds if I'm lucky. I did the preliminary work in the street. All I need to do is hook it into the system."

She nodded, and pretended to be shuffling through her pockets for a chip. "Lev, I'm going to punch you."

He quirked an eyebrow. "Did I offend you somehow?"

"If we're both shouting loud enough, the guards should be look-ing at us. There's that ledge beside where they parked it. That close enough, Tae?"

He frowned and looked over, then nodded. "That should work."

"OK. Lev and I are going to wander this way, and then I'll start a fight. As soon as you're in, tap your com and I'll see if I can get the guards out of the way for long enough for you to get inside."

"Then what?"

"Then hold the door for us. I assume it'll have shields?"

"Yeah."

"Good. Because they'll probably be shooting at us."

Lev heaved a deep sigh and muttered something about having a serious talk with Masha when they got back.

Tae nodded, and meandered in the opposite direction. Jez took a deep breath, grinned, and shoved Lev as hard as she could. He stumbled backwards on the bare concrete surface, barely catching his balance.

"You lost my chip?" she shouted at him. "You dirty mud-sucker!"

Only she could see him roll his eyes upward. He straightened, and his voice, when he spoke, was loud and strident. "I've had about enough of this! I'm your assistant, not your slave. I never touched your chip."

She grinned at him. "You plaguing scum-sucker! Don't you talk to me like that. You're out of a job tomorrow. You're out of a job today! Now! This moment!" The guards were looking in her direc-tion, but more in curiosity than anything else.

Well. They wanted a show? She'd give them a show.

Lev must have come to the same conclusion, because he threw his arms in the air, turning away. "Good luck getting your ship off the lot then!"

She grabbed him by the shoulder and yanked him back around. "Don't you dare! You're going to march yourself back into my office, and you're going to find my key chip, and I don't care if you have to go through the whole damn cockpit on hands and knees."

Lev's eyes twinkled slightly. "Cockpit?" he mouthed. She rolled her eyes. Then he reached out and shoved her back. It was a delicate sort of shove, and she bit back a snort of laughter.

Something flashed on her com. Tae had the system down.

She screamed and fell backwards, the rough concrete jolting her bruises unpleasantly as she landed. "He's trying to kill me! Someone help! My assistant's trying to kill me!"

One of the guards rolled her eyes, but the other started forward. Jez signalled frantically to Lev with her eyes. He frowned in confusion, then caught on, and reached down to help her up at the same time as the guard did. As they both bent down, Jez lunged upward with a vicious sucker-punch to the guard's gut. The man dropped, choking and sputtering, and Jez screamed, "He's killing this man! Somebody help!"

The guard by the ship and two of the others sprinted over, pulling out their guns as they ran, and Jez grabbed the fallen guard and hauled him upright by the arm, screaming and cursing and somehow, almost casually, managing to keep his bulk between them and the other guards.

"Is he in?" she hissed to Lev. Lev shook his head, face pale, and she glanced over. Tae was struggling with the mechanism to open the ship door, frantically. He yanked out a wrench and slammed it into the door, and she winced.

The guard from the ship reached them, and Jez threw the fallen guard bodily at her, knocking her back into a second guard.

"He's in!" Lev hissed.

"About time!" She shoved Lev towards the ship as the third guard started firing. Lev ran, and she dived behind one of the ships as heat-blasts glanced off the side, scoring red-hot scars across the plates.

Someone was going to have a really bad day when they came back into the parking station.

She crawled around to the other side and peered out.

All the guards were back on their feet, walking towards her hiding place slowly, and they were firing at the ship she was hiding behind with the concentrated focus of people willing to melt their way through solid metal to get to her.

Which meant … they weren't looking at the ship. She tapped her com and whispered, "Get the door open, and be ready to shut it. I'm coming in hot."

"Wha—"

She didn't wait for whoever it was to finish, just took a deep breath, rolled to her feet, and ran, zig-zagging back and forth as heat-blasts whined and hissed off the concrete on either side of her.

The door was open. Lev was holding it just a crack, and heat-blasts singed off the side of the ship. He shoved it open as she reached it, she rolled in, and he slammed it shut behind her.

"Lock it down!" he shouted to Tae, and there was the *hiss* of the locks engaging.

"Scoot over!" she panted. "Let me in the seat."

"I haven't got the control lock off yet," Tae growled through gritted teeth. Jez glanced outside.

The guards had reached the ship and were wrestling with the doors. One of them stepped back and spoke into his com.

"Any time you feel like it," she said.

"Give me a minute!"

"We don't have a minute!"

Outside, one of the guards fired up what looked like a metal-cutter. It flamed white hot, and Jez yelped.

"They're cutting my ship! They're going to cut my ship! Hurry it up!"

Tae blew out an exasperated breath. "I got the basic controls working, but there's still a choke I haven't taken off."

"That's fine! I can work with that. Move over!"

Tae slid out of the pilots seat, and she slid into it. For half a second she closed her eyes, luxuriating in the moment.

"Jez," said Lev, in a voice that was trying very hard to be calm.

She smiled, eyes still closed, and touched the starter button that Tae had hot-wired.

The ship moved gracefully into the air.

She opened her eyes. Below them, the guards were still shooting, shouting into their coms.

"Hold on," she whispered. Then she bumped the throttle, ever so lightly, and her beautiful ship shot forward with enough speed to leave her insides behind.

Tae swore, loudly and creatively, and Lev made a noise like he was about to throw up. Jez sighed in sheer ecstasy, and pushed the throttle harder.

They skimmed across the tops of the buildings, dodging between the other ships that had clearance in the city's bubble. She could feel the choke straining through the controls, but here, under the city force-field, it would hardly affect them.

"They're after us," Lev said through gritted teeth. "Five ships. Coming in on your three o'clock, five o'clock, and eight o'clock."

"Got it," said Jez, flipping up the com screen with her other hand.

There were five flashing red lights, and they were coming up fast.

She grinned.

"You kids secured?"

There was a sound like two people searching desperately for harnesses.

"Well, too late now." She dived out of the ship lane and into the space between the buildings.

This was life. This was everything. She leaned back in her seat, eyes half-closed, feeling what she needed to do long before her brain could process what she was seeing. The skimmed past buildings, short wings millimetres away from the windows. She flipped them on their side and skinned them through an alley, then another. People, windows, buildings, streets flashed past so quickly she couldn't take them in. If she stopped to think for even one second, they'd all be dead, but she didn't need to think. She didn't need to do anything but fly.

The dots hadn't followed them down into the labyrinth, opting instead to trail them at a safe distance over the rooftops.

"You have the tracker on this thing disabled?" she called over her shoulder.

"Focus on flying!" Tae ground out.

"I said, do you—"

"Yes! I just finished it."

"Perfect. Then I'm just going to—" she yanked back on the controls, and the ship rocketed out of the maze of buildings like a swamp rat with its tail on fire. There was a moment when the red dots seemed to freeze, too shocked to react, then the heat-cannon blasts warped the air around them. She kept the nose pointed at the sky for long enough that it looked like they were going to make a suicide dash for freedom through the force-field, and then she flipped on her side, pivoted around, and streaked straight for the ships. They scattered, and she dove back in between the buildings.

"Like I said. I'm just going to fly us out."

Lev's voice sounded strained. "That would be great, except looks like we miscalculated. They're coming in with reinforcements."

Tae was typing furiously on his holoscreen, and then more red dots popped up on her screen.

A lot more.

"He's got the police in his pocket, apparently," Lev finished, unnecessarily.

Jez swore.

They were surrounded. The police ships had joined the mob ships above the buildings, but now there were smaller yellow dots that must be police bikes making their gingerly way through the buildings towards them.

Disabling the tracking device wasn't going to do them any good if there were enough of their pursuers to keep a visual on them.

Damn.

She glanced over at Tae and Lev. Judging from their tense expressions, they'd come to the same conclusion.

She sighed deeply. Yes, they were a couple idiots, but there was no point in getting them killed too. It was her ship, after all.

"Tell you what. I'll fly low, shut down, and you jump out. Then I'm going to take as many of these scum-eaters with me as I can."

Tae gave a grunt of annoyance.

"No," said Lev slowly. "How long can you keep us flying?"

She glanced back at the screen. "They're going to have cables. And nets. But none of them fly as well as I do." She shrugged. "A few minutes?"

"OK. Keep us in the air, then. I need to think."

"Well, I was thinking about crashing us, but since you asked so nicely—" She jammed the accelerator and pulled up, bringing a herd of smaller police ships and bikes after them like a school of space squid. The ships on top of the buildings converged on them, and a few magnetic cables hit the ship and stuck, but she pulled into a tight roll. The following ships cut the cables to avoid being pulled into each other, and she dived down again, the cables trailing behind them like some sort of outer-rim parasite.

"Tae, listen," said Lev. "Can you reverse the field on the shielding loop?"

"What?"

"Can you—"

"Yeah, OK. I've ... never tried it before, but theoretically—"

"How long would it take you?"

A drone had picked up on their tail, and it was following so close behind that it was practically glued to the ship.

"Hold on," she called, and flipped the ship on its side millimetres away from an office building. The drone, caught between her wings and the building walls, exploded loudly in a blossom of flame that vanished behind them.

"Five minutes?" Tae said, sounding sick.

"It'll have to be less."

"Listen, kids, I can't hold them much longer. Last chance to get off."

"Jez. You need to do exactly what I tell you." Lev's voice was still strained, but it had regained some of its usual calm.

That did not sound like a good plan. Especially since she trusted him about as much as she trusted Masha.

She glanced at her screen, the flashing dots converging on their position from all sides.

That being said ...

"Fine."

"Alright." He maneuvered himself into the copilot's seat and flipped on his com screen. "Ready?"

She nodded.

Behind them, three bikes were coming up, harpoon-launchers held ready.

"Left. Now," he snapped. She turned, and they shot through a narrow alley.

"Right, then straight past the next three buildings."

"Where are you taking us?" she said through her teeth.

"There are a few back streets that don't show up on the maps. Which means they won't show up on their ship screens, which means it will buy us time. Just trust me. Left! Then right, then two streets down and left."

Their ship careened down the narrow openings, pedestrians diving for cover as they shot past overhead.

The dots were milling about, confused.

"Right! Now left. Right. There's an arch, you want to go—"

She dived under it, and he gripped the seat-arms. "I was going to say over."

She grinned. "No point in giving them extra visuals. Where you taking us?"

"Either out of the city-field, or into the biggest explosion of our lives. Left, then the next right, then straight. Tae, how's it coming?"

"Working on it," came Tae's voice from the back.

"You've got about—" he glanced at his screen. "Forty-five seconds." He looked forward. "Right! There!"

She yanked on the controls, turning the ship up on one side and practically man-handling it through the narrow opening, the side of the ship scraping sparks off the apartment walls flashing past. She glared at him.

"Sorry," he said. "Now left. At the end of this street it forks. Take the right one."

"We're getting close to the end of the city." She straightened out. Ahead of them, through the warehouses and in-atmosphere docking ports, she could see the faint distortion that was the edge of the city's force field.

They hit that at this speed, they'd be nothing but a ball of flame and a bunch of drifting ash.

"Tae?" asked Lev.

"Got it!" he said, his voice triumphant. "It's reversed."

"OK. Jez, up there. Between those two warehouses and that docking port. That's a weak spot in the field. You'll have to hit it at full speed."

She had a split second to decide whether he was crazy or brilliant.

Hell. She'd always liked living on the edge.

"On it, genius-boy," she said, grinning. Then she popped up above the buildings and punched the accelerator. The ship flung itself forward like it had just been warming up. The speed flattened her to her seat, and she was grinning like a maniac at the sheer joy of it.

If you were going to die, this was the way to go.

They hit the shield. The ship vibrated, shaking itself almost out of her hands, and they slowed and time slowed as if they were traveling through a strange, transparent flow of stretchy, sticky molasses.

And then the ship popped free, and they were out.

"That should not have worked," Tae said shakily. "Even with then loop reversed, that should not have worked."

"Weak spot in the force-field. They've been working on it for a couple weeks, they just keep it on the down-low." Lev sounded almost smug.

Jez pointed their nose at the sky and did a celebratory loop. Lev frowned at her. "Jez. They're still behind us."

She glared at him. "That was some good flying, OK? Give me a minute."

"It's not me who you need to worry about giving you a minute," he ground out.

She glanced at the screen again.

Of course. The police ships had the tech to slip through the shield. Not much use otherwise.

"Well, can't take us up with the choke still on. I guess we try to outrun them."

Not much hope of that, really, not with their speed choked down. But it was the best she had to offer at this point.

"Wait. Tae. The ships behind us are B73 models, from the look of it. I'm pulling up the specs on them right now."

"Give them to me."

Lev swiped his fingers across his screen, and in the back she could hear Tae typing steadily.

"I'm setting them into the blocker," he said.

"And then you'll reverse it?"

He must have nodded, because Lev sat back and smiled.

Whatever they were doing, she didn't have time to worry about it. Shots glanced off the ship's armour, and she twisted and dodged to get clear. She hit the accelerator, but here in the open air, they weren't going to outrun this. Their pursuers were closing in.

Just a few more seconds. Then they'd be caught.

Damn. Not much even she could do, in the wide open with a choked ship.

Well, it had been a good run, anyways.

"It's OK, baby," she said softly, patting the ship's sides. "You did your best."

"Done!" Tae shouted, and Lev shouted, "Jez, hit the blockers!"

She did.

The dots on the screen flickered and died, and a quick glance over her shoulder showed a fleet of police ships, slowly drifting towards the ground as the officers inside frantically fought with the controls.

She whooped and punched the accelerator, and they shot out over the deep forests that surrounded the city, the frost-tipped tangle of evergreens crisp and sharp against the setting sun.

Lev watched her as she brought them out in a wide, lazy loop. In the back, Tae was frantically scrubbing any traces of tracking from the ship. When he was done, they should be able to come in through the main entrance. No one checked with visuals any more, and they wouldn't be expecting anything like this, considering it usually took days to completely scrub a ship. Unless you happened to be the sullen prodigy currently sitting in the back of the ship, swearing softly to himself. Even then, it would take an hour or so.

Jez was giving Tae the time, and, more surprisingly, not insulting him or hurrying him along.

So Masha had been right after all.

Lev shook his head slightly. He'd never in his life seen anyone fly like that. He wouldn't have believed it, if he hadn't been there. And when she thought they weren't going to escape … she'd offered to let them out, and lead the police away.

Not what he had expected.

She was smiling to herself with a sort of intense, intimate joy that seemed to light her from the inside. Her face had a peace to it that was unexpected, and for half a moment, he thought maybe he understood her love of flying.

It was a sort of freedom. A serenity. He got it from an unlimited source of books and information. She got it from being in the air.

She must have felt his gaze, because she turned, and again he caught that flash of intelligence, that sparkle of humour, as if they were sharing a joke.

"Bet you've never flown like that before."

"Honestly, Jez, I doubt anyone has flown like that before." He made no effort to hide his sincerity. She gave him a slight frown, as if trying to figure out the insult. Then she shrugged and grinned.

"Was that a compliment? From genius-boy? I'm impressed."

He smiled, despite himself.

"Hey. You did good back there too," she said at last, turning forward again.

He watched her. There was something about her that caught his gaze and held it, a vitality, an intensity of life that took him by surprise. It was strangely magnetic.

He looked away quickly. Nope. Nope, nope, nope, nope, nope.

There was unfinished business between him and this pilot. Get the job underway, get his family free. Then he'd have to figure out a way to deal with her.

# 11

It took Lev the entire rest of the day, all that night, and well into the next morning before he stopped feeling like the floor was spinning under him, and that he might possibly throw up.

It wasn't that he'd never been on a ship before. It was that he had never been on that particular ship, with that particular pilot, before.

He much preferred his current occupation, which consisted of holing up in his room going through pages and pages of documents which were entirely illegal and completely classified.

Masha had handed him the download chip the day before.

There was a tap at the door, and he blinked and glanced up from the holoscreen document that was scrolling rapidly downward, the tracking matching his eye speed as he scanned.

"Come in," he called cautiously.

The door swung briskly open, and Masha stepped inside, as immaculate, if slightly-disheveled, as always. He wondered how she did it, that perfect mix of competence and self-effacing forgettable-ness.

"So. What do you have for me?"

He sighed and shoved the holoscreen away. "A better question would be, what don't I have? I have enough problems, holes, weaknesses, impossibilities, and potential disasters-in-the-making to sink this project eternally. This is not a survivable heist, Masha, and you know it as well as I do."

She sat in the chair across from him, without waiting for it to be offered, and leaned forward. She was still smiling that slight, bland smile, but her eyes sparkled.

"I know it would not be, if I were to plan it. Or if you were to fly it, or Jez tried to manipulate the tech or get us the weapons we'll need. Thankfully," her grin sharpened, "that is not necessary. So." She leaned back into the chair, crossing her boots in front of her casually. "What do you have for me?"

He met her eyes. "You played the ship job well," he said, keeping his tone neutral. "I'm impressed."

"And I'm flattered." A dimple appeared, then disappeared, on her cheek. "What do you have for me?"

"How to get us to work together, that's the real puzzle for you, isn't it?" he continued. "You didn't have any doubt I could come up with a plan, or that between Jez, Tae, and Ysbel, we'd have the knowledge and the skills to carry it off. But getting us to work together, that was the rub. A hothead pilot, and angry street-boy, a mass murderer, and an introverted and likely-insufferable scholar. So you throw the pilot and the street-kid, who you know want to kill each other, on a possible death-mission, with the scholar along to keep the hostilities to a manageable level, and you let the hothead plan it. And from there, we have enough near-death experiences together that we come back, if not friends, then at least colleagues. Not bad for a first foray."

He didn't know if she knew his history with Jez, and he wasn't about to reveal it if she didn't.

She considered him for a moment, smile serene. "You missed the part where the scholar learns that the hothead is pretty good at coming up with strategies that are surprisingly effective, if unsubtle, and the street boy can improvise on the fly. And then he uses that in his plans to pull off the heist. So. I'll ask again, what do you have?"

He sighed. "Fine. I think I've put something together that has a chance of success. Not a large chance, but a chance, and with what we're working with, that's more than should be possible. I also went through what you sent me, and put together a list of weapons buyers who received an invite to Vitali's latest technological debut. I struck out the ones who were obviously well-known to him, and the ones who it would be impossible to impersonate. That leaves us with a list of about seven mid-level, relatively-unknown but still wealthy buyers. I'll give that to you, and you can narrow it down further." He gave her a piercing glance. "But after seeing the names on that list, I am curious why the government, which apparently is impotent in tracking down weapons buyers, has this information, and has done nothing to act on it. There are mob bosses in the system who could take out a small army. We've never gone after them, because the information is impossible to track down. Except it isn't. It's sitting in government vaults. Read by people like you, Masha."

Her gaze sharpened as she watched him, expression calculating. "That, Lev, is a very good question. One which I expect you will come to understand in time," she said at last. "Explain the plan to me."

After Masha left, Lev gave a long sigh and reluctantly closed down his holoscreen.

Interacting with people had never been something he looked forward to. And yet, here he was.

He pushed himself to his feet and made his way out the door and down into the hangar, which he had been meticulously avoiding.

Ysbel was underneath the ship, tinkering with something. Jez was on the opposite side of the ship with her own battered tools, grease smeared across her forehead and liberally staining her mechanics overalls. Her black toque was shoved down over her disheveled black hair, and she was humming to herself softly. She popped off one of the panels, and gasped in ecstasy.

"Oh you beautiful, beautiful girl. This thing is going to be amazing, Ysbel. I can't even tell you. I thought she was beautiful on the outside."

He waited for the inevitable "Piss off," or possibly an explosion, but a second quick glance at Ysbel showed the woman was working with explosive-test-level ear protection.

Tae glanced up from where he was sitting on a thin cushion in the corner. Lev raised an eyebrow and tapped his ear questioningly.

Tae pulled one of his own ear plugs free. "Trust me," he whispered, giving Lev a meaningful look, "it's better this way. I honestly thought there'd be a second mass murder here this morning before she went and got them."

A holoscreen glowed in front of him, and the floor around him was littered with wires and chips and at least three complicated-looking circuitboards.

Lev walked over and pulled up a cushion. "Tae."

The young man looked wary. "What?"

"I've gotten more detail on the security inside the compound."

Tae pulled the other ear plug out of his ear, with an expression like that of someone awaiting a death sentence. "And?"

Lev tapped his com to bring up the holoscreen. He swiped a few times, bringing up the information screen he'd complied, then expanded it until it was large enough they could both see the details.

Tae leaned forward, squinting at it. Then he raised his eyebrows and whistled softly.

"This guy's not kidding around, is he?"

"He doesn't usually," Lev murmured, then he glanced up quickly.

Tae didn't seem to have noticed his slip.

"I have a feeling nothing here will be left on factory settings," Tae murmured to himself. "The one security system on the vault is close enough to standard that I can pre-write a hack for it, and then modify it when I get there. But the other is like nothing I've seen before. I'll study it and see what I can come up with. And the physical one—that's going to be tough."

"I may have a solution for the physical system. Just worry about the digital side."

Tae was still frowning at the screen. "Bring up the specs on the security for the walls and gates," he said at last. Lev complied, and Tae studied them in silence for a few minutes. Lev glanced around.

Jez had pulled something out of the ship, then apparently got distracted, because now she was juggling three wrenches and carrying on an entirely one-sided conversation about the last time she's seen someone fly an SRS class ship.

"Is she just going to—" Lev began. Tae glanced up and gave a long-suffering sigh.

"She'll put it back together, eventually. She's a half-way decent mechanic, from what I've seen. Attention span of a space squid, but she'd die before she let something happen to that ship."

That Lev could believe.

Tae turned back to the screen. "The whole thing is a closed loop, which means it's next to impossible for someone from outside to hack in."

"Yes. But I was talking with Masha earlier. She thinks she may be able to get you in as a guard. Would that do it?"

Tae frowned in thought. "Maybe. Any password on any system would get you into the loop, and the guards will have to have access to at least the basic systems."

"Perfect. So, you'll have your tech, and, assuming Masha can do what she says she can do, you'll have a password. What else do you need?"

Tae shook his head. "Even if I get things prepared beforehand, and even if I can find a way to smuggle my tech in, hacking through to reset the systems will take me at least ten minutes. Maybe longer. I'll need a distraction."

"I thought you might." He stood. "How do you attract Ysbel's attention when you want to talk to her?"

"I don't," he said. "I'm trying not to get blown up."

It was a fair point.

He walked over to where Ysbel was working and knelt down where he should be in her peripheral vision.

She glanced at him, almost ignored him, then, with clear reluctance, removed an ear plug.

"What do you want? I'm busy."

"I need some information from you on explosives."

She sighed, and pushed herself out from under the ship. "Has that idiot pilot talked herself to death yet?"

Lev glanced up. Jez had put down the wrenches, crawled into the cockpit, and was now carefully removing some wiring. She caught his glance and grinned.

"You thought this thing was fast before. Wait until you take a spin in it after I'm done."

His thoughts must have shown through on his face, because she laughed. "Oh come on, genius-boy. You know you liked it."

"You're an uncommonly good pilot, Jez. That doesn't mean I want to ride in your ship ever again."

She hopped out of the cockpit and wandered over. "Whatcha doing? I thought you'd decided to hide out in your room for the rest of your life."

"It's been less than twenty-four standard hours," he said, hearing the slight exasperation in his own voice. Her eyes twinkled, and he sighed internally.

She was extraordinarily good at this.

Ysbel was standing now, her expression one of grim foreboding. Jez's grin widened, and she opened her mouth.

"No," said Ysbel. "I am not going to tell you how many guns I am putting on your ship. I am not going to give you an extra two or three. I am not going to let you make suggestions. I am not—"

"All I was going to say is, if you put the main gun there it'll cut into my vis-field while I'm flying," said Jez, still grinning. Ysbel's scowl deepened, and for a moment Lev understood Tae's concern about the entire hangar being blown up.

"Why don't you—"

"I know, I know, piss off," Jez said, turning back to the ship. "I'm right, though."

"Jez. Wait." He paused. "I'd … like you to join us for a moment, if you would," he said quickly. She turned and stared at him. She looked almost … shaken. Like she'd never heard those words before in her life.

"I need your opinion on something."

She kept staring, then raised an eyebrow and tried to smile. "Sure."

He found himself wondering what her life had been like, outside of being a pilot.

They joined Tae, Ysbel still scowling dangerously. Lev pulled up a couple extra cushions, but Jez settled herself on the floor in a loose-limbed slouch.

"Ysbel," Lev said, when they were all settled. "We have at least some of the specs on the weapons, and I'll run those by you shortly so you know what we're up against. But Tae has told me he'll need a distraction. Considering the security we'll be going through before we get into the compound, will you be able to give us one?"

She nodded. "Security will not be a problem. Maybe for my traditional explosives, but I have gel explosives that are impossible to detect. What kind of distraction do you need?"

"Tae will be already on the inside as a guard, and we'll need to give him at least ten minutes standing outside the vault doors, which are pretty central to the compound. So it'll have to be somewhere on the periphery, and big enough or extended enough to draw every-one's attention."

She cocked her head, frowning in concentration. "I could set up a chain reaction, so the explosives go off one after the other. I believe I could keep them busy for at least ten minutes. But the issue will be getting something big enough that would keep their attention with-out having them evacuate the compound."

"Unless," said Jez slowly. They all turned to look at her. "Unless, that was the point all along. Ysbel sets off something big enough that everyone panics. Tae does whatever crap he does while the guards are running around. If the explosions are consecutive, eventually Vitali will start evacuating everyone, because that will be the only option. Lev and Ysbel and Masha get escorted out—right back through security, easy peasy. It takes a while to get a crowd of people out of an enclosed place like that, so Tae gets into the vault, gets the tech, and slips out of the compound in the confusion. Or gets shot, whichever. I fly us out, we drop off the tech, and then while you losers do whatever it is you do, I take my ship and my credits, leave atmosphere, and never come back."

Lev nodded thoughtfully. "Not bad. That could work."

"Still the problem of the physical security," said Tae. "I can deal with the digital systems, but the physical one will take at least two people."

"Which is why Jez is going to be in there with you."

Jez and Tae both stared at him, then glared at each other.

Ysbel looked like she was biting back a snicker.

"Jez, you're the one who, I understand, broke out of prison and piloted an escape pod from the prison ship down to the planet with your hands cuffed behind your back. We need someone with the agility to deal with the physical aspects of the system while Tae deals with the digital."

"What kind of physical aspects?" Jez asked warily.

Lev spread his hands. "Still working on that. I'll get you the specs as soon as I can get them."

"So what? I just walk up to the gates and tell them that Mr. Weapons Dealer Lev forgot his glasses and I'm here to drop them off?"

Lev bit back a smile. "No. Tae will let you in the back entrance."

"Hold on just a minute," Tae began.

"He'll give you a guard uniform, which he'll have stolen, and you'll change into it. Then the two of you will get into the vault, grab the tech, and get out."

"Or get shot," Tae said, glaring at Jez. She grinned back.

"That sounds like my kind of plan."

"It was your plaguing plan."

"See, that's why I like it."

Lev held up a hand before Tae could respond. "OK. What do the rest of you think? Is this workable?"

Ysbel who had been frowning and biting her cheek in concentration, looked up and nodded briefly. "I can do that."

"Tae?"

He gave another long-suffering sigh. "So now I need to find a way to steal another guards uniform and get past the security on the back entrance."

"Can you do it?"

Another sigh. "Fine. Why not? I'm already working half-a-dozen miracles for you, why not make it a full dozen?"

"Can you do it?"

"Yes! Yes, I can do it."

"Jez?"

She smiled lazily. "I can do basically anything."

"As long as it doesn't involve sitting still or shutting up," Tae muttered.

"Other than those things," she amended.

"Alright, alright," said Lev, holding up his hands. "That's all I needed. I'll go back and keep searching for more details. I'll send you the weapon specs on your com, Ysbel, and Jez, I'll get you and Tae as much information as I can find on the security system."

Jez gave him a mocking salute. "Yes, cap'n." Tae rolled his eyes, and Ysbel got to her feet and stalked back over to the ship. Lev stood, and Jez stood as well as Tae deliberately shoved his earplugs back in. Lev watched them for a moment.

"Why, Jez?" he asked.

She looked at him. "What? You have a problem?"

"Why do you go out of your way to irritate them?"

She gave a snort of laughter. "Why the hell not?"

He studied her. "You're smart. You act stupid, but you're one of the brightest people I've met in a long time."

"Besides you, you mean."

"Besides me." He smiled, and she smiled back reluctantly, not her trademark cheeky grin, but a genuine smile.

"So why do you do it?"

She considered him a moment, and her eyes, for once, were serious. "Look, Lev. Masha thinks she knows all about me. All of you think you know all about me. But you don't. I'm not a team player. I don't want to be. I want to get this done and get the hell out of here. Why should I care what they think of me?"

"That's what I'm wondering," Lev said softly. "Why do you care so much that everyone hates you?"

"It's a natural process," she said, reverting to her snarky grin. "Just helping it along." She showed her teeth. "Gotta run, genius-boy, got stuff to do and people to annoy." She sauntered off, whistling, and, picking up a wrench, skimmed it across the floor so it bounced noisily on the concrete, flipped end-over-end, and fell lightly into Tae's lap. He jumped and swore, then spun around to glare at Jez, who'd turned back to her work on the outside of the ship.

Lev watched them thoughtfully for a few moments, then at last headed back to the blissful quiet of his room.

# 12

Tae stepped into the hangar-bay with a sigh of relief. He pulled the balaclava off his head and laid it neatly in the corner, then peeled off the filthy, over-sized shirt that blended him in with every other street-kid out there and rolled his shoulders, trying to release some of the tension.

In fairness, he was the best one to get the black-market supplies—he knew where the sellers were, he knew the street code. Still, every job had him peering over his shoulder, double-checking for another police drone.

He just wanted this over with and to get himself and the other kids who were depending on him out of this plaguing city. That's all.

He heard the faint sound from behind him as he was in the process of lifting the bag of supplies off his shoulder.

He dived to the ground, throwing off the bag, as a booted foot kicked hard through the space he'd only just occupied.

"Damn it, Jez!" he growled, jumping to his feet and stumbling backwards as she let loose another kick, then a quick one-two punch. "This isn't a good time!"

She was grinning.

Plaguing idiot.

He faked a blow at her head, then slid forward with a vicious sucker-punch. She twisted aside, but he caught the flash of surprise in her eyes.

You couldn't be a street-kid without knowing at least a little about how to fight.

She came in close and brought her knee up, aiming for his groin, but he jumped out of the way, then grabbed the front of her shirt and slammed his forehead into where the bridge of her nose should have been. Somehow, though, she twisted out of his grasp, and she circled him, a little more warily this time. He wiped a sleeve quickly across his forehead and turned to face her. Then, with a movement that was almost too quick to follow, she slid inside his defence with two knock-out punches to his temple.

Or they would have been knock-out punches, if they'd landed. She pulled back at the last moment, grinning widely.

"Not bad, tech-head," she said. "Took me almost two minutes to finish you that time."

Tae shook his head, panting heavily. "Consort's frozen blue balls, Jez," he grumbled when he'd caught his breath enough to speak. "I hadn't even finished unloading Ysbel's supplies."

"Good practice," she said. "At least I wasn't shooting at you this time."

He glowered at the pilot, who grinned back without the faintest hint of remorse.

Ysbel poked her head out of the small, padded room she'd turned into a weapons manufactory. "Did Jez wreck any of my materials?" she growled. "If she did—"

"I know. You're always looking for an excuse to get your hands on me," said Jez.

"Yes, but believe me, it's not in the way you're thinking," Ysbel muttered darkly.

"I got them, Ysbel," Tae said with a long-suffering sigh.

"Good." She turned away. "Bring them back. I want you in here for a minute anyways."

"Can I watch?"

"Jez. Go away," grunted Ysbel.

"You'll miss me."

"I will not miss you. I never miss."

Jez laughed, although Tae was pretty sure it hadn't been a joke. "Maybe, but I'll bet you hard credits that you wouldn't out-draw me."

This time, Ysbel turned and gave Jez the benefit of her full, emotionless stare. "Listen to me, pilot-woman. I would not have to out-draw you, because if I wanted to kill you, I would only smear a few drops of explosive gel on your boots. Then I would activate it, and you would turn into a fine red mist that we would all be breathing in for the next three days."

Jez raised her eyebrows suggestively, still grinning. "A lot of people have called me fine. And wanted to breathe me in."

"Trust me. None of them wanted you blasted into particles small enough to make that happen nearly as badly as I do. Now piss off."

Jez straightened and sauntered back towards the ship, winking at them over her shoulder.

Tae locked eyes with Ysbel, and for a moment they shared a look of awestruck exasperation.

Jez was honestly unbelievable.

He shook his head, hoisted the bag back over his shoulder, and followed Ysbel into the weapons room.

The weapons room was small and crowded, the walls thickly

padded with non-reactive material, the air thick with the smell of burning chemicals. In the corner, a small, battered test dummy stood despondently. He'd lost count of how many Ysbel had melted, burned, or simply vaporized already, and this one would almost certainly follow in its predecessor's footsteps before long.

And he was working with her.

He generally tried not to think about that too hard.

Ysbel took the bag from him carefully and laid it on her worktable. She glanced inside and gave a grunt of approval.

"Good. You got what I asked."

"Do I ever not?" he muttered. She looked at him, and for half a second he almost thought she'd smile.

"You always do. That's why I don't trust anyone else with it. Those other lunatics run around in pilots coats waving their little guns and punching people, but you and I, we know what we need to make these things work. Pilots coats and punching people doesn't make good weapons, and it doesn't make good explosives. But in fairness, I am stuck in the same building as the pilot woman all day, so you'll excuse me if I check everything."

He chuckled reluctantly. "If she'd just stand still for two consecutive seconds, she'd be a lot easier to handle."

"If she didn't have a mouth that opened, she'd be a lot easier to handle." She straightened. "So. Masha's taking you in tonight, yes, to apply as a bodyguard?"

"I—think so," he said. Even the thought sent streaks of ice through the pit of his stomach.

Masha had done—something, he wasn't clear on the details. But the upshot of it was, Vitali was now hiring guards. He'd been training for over a week now, between everything else he was doing. Jez insisted the best way to learn to fight better was to have her personally jump him at every opportunity. Lev kept pulling him aside and talking about strategy, which was almost as irritating in its own way as Jez's methods, although less likely to leave him with a bloody nose. And Ysbel had drilled him on target practice until his eyelids felt like they were filled with sand and he was ready to collapse with exhaustion.

Tonight they'd find out if it had been worth it.

Or else, tonight he'd die.

Masha had warned him that the trials would be rough.

Ysbel handed him a heat pistol, and he inspected it quickly—you could never assume that anything Ysbel handed you was a simple pistol—raised it in both hands, then, exhaling slowly, squeezed the trigger. The shot sizzled through the air and slammed into the bullseye on the target painted on the mannequin's chest, turning it momentarily a brilliant orange.

"Not bad," said Ysbel. "You've been practicing. Do it again."

He shot twice more, and twice more hit close enough to the bullseye that Ysbel seemed satisfied.

Lev appeared in the doorway. "Tae. There you are. You've got about a standard hour before you need to be in place. Why don't you change, and then we'll—"

"One more test," said Ysbel. She pulled a pouch out from under her shirt and reached into it. Whatever she had, she hid in her hand, twisting it carefully. Then she tossed it at Tae.

"It's an ion-bomb," she said, "and I just activated it. You have twenty seconds to disarm it before we all go up."

Lev's eyebrows shot up, and from the other room, Jez yelped.

Tae scowled at Ysbel, not even bothering to look at the tiny, deadly sphere in his hands.

He was about done with being tested.

His fingers explored the mechanism gently. Easy enough. It was almost insulting, actually. With a deft twist, he pulled the thing apart, reached inside, and twitched a wire free.

Lev sucked in a breath, and Ysbel gave a grudging smile.

"Well done. Now go change."

He was ready long before the standard hour was up, pacing restlessly in the hangar. This must be how it felt to be Jez, except all the time.

She wandered over and clapped him on the shoulder hard enough that he winced.

"You'll be fine, tech-head," she said. "Not great, but fine. I mean, I doubt they'll actually kill you in the trials. If anything, they'll let you in, and then murder you in your cot. But they probably won't suspect anything."

"Thanks a lot," he muttered sourly.

"Anytime," she said with a grin. She paused a moment. "Good luck," she said at last. "I—I mean, you're doing really good work on my ship. I don't want to have to do it by myself."

She sounded ... serious.

He stared at her, but before he had time to sort through what had just happened, there were footsteps from the stairway behind them, and they both turned. Jez gasped and went for her heat pistol, and Tae instinctively reached for his own holstered weapon before the stranger smiled, and he recognized her.

Masha.

He frowned, and looked closer.

It was uncanny, really. She'd done nothing to change her unremarkable features, and her disguise was no more and no less than a frayed street-smuggler outfit, with the cropped pants, thin boots, and long, disreputable overshirt in faded greys and blues. She had a short-brimmed cap on her head, pulled low over her eyes, and her hair shoved up underneath it. But her face was no longer mild. Instead there was a haunted intensity to her expression, an unhinged look in her eyes that was slightly terrifying. Her posture was tense, her muscles tight, like a touch on her shoulder would send her into a killing rage.

Was this who she'd been all along, is that what she was hiding?

Then he caught a gleam of amusement in those deadly eyes, and her face twitched for a moment into its familiar bland smile.

"Are you ready, Tae?" she asked.

He nodded. The old clothes from his street days were all he needed for no one to give him a second glance.

She led the way out of the hangar, and he followed, his unease at the prospect of the upcoming test mingling with the unease of being within grabbing-distance of a Masha who looked like a crazed smuggler-slash-serial-killer.

They left the warehouse district through dirty back-alleys that he'd probably slept in once or twice in his life. The streets were quiet at this time of the evening, the cold damp seeping through clothing and jackets and wrapping clammy fingers around the bare flesh underneath. Peti and Caz and the other street kids would be huddled together in their shelter now, trying to keep themselves warm under a nest of dirty blankets.

Somehow Lev had figured out where Vitali's thugs hired guards, and Masha said she'd be his owner. He bristled at the term, but she was right. If he went in there on his own as a street kid and they thought he was any good, they'd grab him and drug him and he'd wake up in Vitali's compound with his freedom permanently forfeit.

When they reached the place Lev had shown them on his holoscreen—a dirty back entrance to a decrepit building, stained with unrecognizable substances, with chunks of the pre-fab blocks falling despondently from corners and the edges of doorways.

Three or four burly individuals lurked around the doorway, not close enough to be called guards, but not far away enough to be called comfortable. Masha walked through the middle of them, ignoring them completely, and tapped on the door. Tae hurried after her, suddenly preferring to be close.

"What do you want?" asked one of the hooded figures, his voice husky and rough.

Masha turned her unnerving eyes on the speaker, and he took a step back.

"I'm here because I have a proposition. I know Vitali's people are here tonight looking for guards. I have a candidate."

The man turned to Tae for the first time, looking him up and down.

"Not much to look at."

"No. But he's a genius with tech. I want to throw him in the ring."

"What are you looking for?"

"Five-year contract, I get twenty percent of the pay."

The man shrugged. "Standard enough. I'm warning you though, we offer no guarantees. He gets hurt in there, that's on you. We don't give any recompense for injuries."

"I know, I know." She brushed the man out of the way with an impatient hand. "Let us in. I've got a lot of confidence in this one."

The man stepped in front of her and shoved the door open. He called inside, "One here for the guards. Send them down to the basement."

Two more figures materialized inside the room, and in the flickering lights Tae could make out neither their forms nor their faces.

"Come on," one of them said, beckoning them forward. They

followed, Tae staying so close behind Masha that he almost stepped on her heels.

When they reached the dimly-lit basement, the flickering industrial lights illuminated a space that was almost the size of Masha's converted hangar. A tall woman, with muscles that made Tae swallow nervously, planted herself in front of them.

"Here for the guard applications," one of their guides said. The woman ignored him, and glowered at Masha.

"How'd you know about this?"

"Friend of a friend," said Masha.

"I need more than that."

Masha's eyes darted about nervously. "Don't really like to say. If she found out I came here—"

"Right now you should be more worried about what I'm going to find out." The woman's voice was soft with menace. "So I'm going to ask you one more time. How did you know about the tryouts?"

Masha paused, and the woman took a threatening step forward. Tae held his breath.

"Fine! It was Nadia," Masha gulped. "We were doing business, and she mentioned it. One of her people made it through the trials a year ago, and the payout was good. I got her drunk and got the location out of her, but if you tell her that, she'll slit my throat."

The woman relaxed slightly. "Joke's on you. We told her she could pass the word on, if she was discrete. You'd just asked instead of getting her drunk, she'd have told you straight out."

Masha looked slightly sulky. "Anyways, we're here. I got one I think you'll like."

She grabbed Tae and shoved him forward, and even though he'd been expecting it, he found himself stiffening in anger at the arrogance of her hand on his shoulder.

"Street boy. I found him a couple years ago. He's a decent fighter, but he's really good with tech. You need to see him in action. He's good."

The woman looked him up and down, and again he felt himself stiffening at her gaze. All the helpless anger of his life on the street bubbled up in his chest, and he had to remind himself this was all a ploy. He wasn't helpless anymore.

At least, not as helpless.

"Fine," the woman said at last, gesturing dismissively. "Not very impressive, but if he knows tech, like you say—"

"Oh, he does—" Masha began ingratiatingly, but the woman rolled her eyes.

"Get him in the pit then." She gestured them through a set of large doors on the opposite end of the room.

He followed Masha across the room, his shoulders twitching uncomfortably at the weight of the guards' eyes on his back. The bright lights momentarily blinded him as he stepped through the heavy doors, and he blinked, staring around in disorientation.

This room was small, and smelled of sweat and the distinctive scorched-air scent of a recent heat-blast. There was a handful of seating cushions in a roped-off riser on the far side of the room, a person-sized black door in the far wall. The rest of the floor was covered with a thin layer of white sand, with detritus scattered across it—overturned chairs, a half-smashed table with a thick scorch-mark cut down the middle of it. Two men and a woman, dressed in the same navy-blue uniform as the man outside, waited on the riser, not bothering to rise as he and Masha entered.

"Good evening," the shorter of the two men said, nodding at Masha. "This one yours?"

She nodded back, her smile obsequious. "Yes. Street boy. Been working with him for a while. Genius with technology. Best kid I ever had."

The man gestured her to a seat on the riser, then turned to Tae and smiled a cold smile. "Alright, boy. Let's see what you can do."

Before Tae had time to read his meaning, a heat-blast scorched the ground at his feet. He leapt back, and ducked away as another heat-blast seared the air over his right shoulder.

His instincts took over, and he rolled behind the shelter of an overturned chair as another heat-blast melted through the thin metal.

He had no weapons—but then he usually didn't when Jez attacked him either. He scooped up a handful of the bare sand and peeked out through the melted hole in his makeshift shelter.

A figure stood in the centre of the ring. They must have come through the smaller back door. They were dressed in black, and they were wearing heat-dispersion body armour. And they were levelling a heat-pistol directly at him.

He swallowed down the panic in his stomach and jumped to his feet, hurling his pathetic handful of sand at the figure's face. Then he flung himself forward, grabbing the overturned chair and swinging it at them like a bludgeon. He managed to hit his attacker in the leg, and as they stumbled, he bent and kicked up at their gun hand.

The pistol went flying end-over-end. He let out a quick breath of relief, but it was cut short as the figure recovered and yanked another heat pistol from their belt.

From the corner of his eye, he saw Masha shift slightly.

"You said your boy's good with tech?" the guard beside her said, his voice cold and amused. "Here, boy. Catch."

Something flew through the air towards him, and he snatched it out of the air.

His attacker was bringing their weapon to bear, and Tae kicked out again, hitting them in the stomach. They staggered backwards, then whipped their weapon around. The butt of it hit him across the bridge of the nose, bringing tears to his eyes as he stumbled.

What was in his hands? He ran his fingers over it quickly. A pistol. He brought it up quickly, bracing himself, and fired.

Nothing happened.

Damn.

His attacker had recovered and was moving towards him in a crouch. He bent down to grab another handful of sand and they fired again, leaving a scorched hole in the ground by his hand. He jumped back and swung the chair up, and they paused.

Broken. The pistol was broken. They were trying to test his tech abilities. OK, that he could do.

He twisted, and, with all his strength, flung the broken chair at his attacker. As they ducked out of the way, he slid his hand down the pistol.

He'd heard the firing mechanism click when he pulled the trigger, so it wasn't that. The heat sink—there. There was a connector missing. If he could just—He dived to the ground and rolled as a sizzling bolt of heat distorted the air where he'd been standing.

Just one connection. If he bent this piece here—

He straighten and fired. The blowback heat seared his face, and his attacker's body armour sparked as it dispersed the blow. He took a quick breath and made ready to squeeze the trigger a second time, but the guard who had been watching stepped forward, raising his hand.

"That's good enough," he said, and the black-clad attacker stepped back. The man held out his hand for the weapon, and grudgingly, Tae handed it over. The guard inspected it quickly, and raised his eyebrows at the other two guards. Then he turned to Masha.

"Your boy did well. Bring him back in a week. We'll ship him out with the others."

Masha's expression was a greasy mixture of fawning and greed. "Thank you. You won't regret taking him."

"I hope not," the guard said, voice cold. "He'll be getting in right before a big event. Not normal protocol in general, and Vitali takes his security seriously." He gestured another guard. She stepped forward, pulling out a wand and passing it up and down in front of Tae.

"What are you doing with him?" Masha asked, voice shrill with alarm. The guard laughed.

"Relax. Just a scan. You're lucky—usually you have to pay for a full database search, but since we're running a full search on everyone at the event in a couple day's time, we can slide the new recruits' scans in there."

A full database search.

Tae didn't let himself glance at Masha, but his palms had turned sweaty.

A full database search would turn up exactly who every one of them was, and even if he hacked in, he didn't have the tech to wipe the database.

Masha turned to him, her expression unreadable. "Come on, boy, let's go."

She didn't speak to him again, and he found himself trotting humiliatingly at her heels as they left the building.

His muscles were shaking. They would have killed him. If he'd messed up once, he'd be dead right now. The thought brought a sick acid taste to his mouth.

They were almost back to the warehouse district when Masha tripped, falling into him hard enough to knock them both back into the entrance to an alleyway. He opened his mouth, but Masha put a finger to her lips, and he froze. For a long time they were silent, staring out at the entrance. At last she shook her head with a depreciating smile.

"Sorry about that," she whispered. "Just hoping to catch sight of whoever's following us, but I suppose that was asking too much."

He frowned at her, but she shook her head. "Later," she whispered.

They waited a while longer, and finally Masha led them out a back way and through several more alleys before they reached the street where the abandoned hangar bay sat.

Once they were inside she shook her head and rolled her shoulders, and now he could see the tension in her expression.

"Well. I guess our timetable has moved up. I'd best let the others know."

He nodded without looking at her, and she paused, contemplating him for a moment. At last she pulled a thin pistol out from her pocket. "Do you know what this is, Tae?"

He glanced at it, curious despite himself.

"This is a little something that Ysbel made for me," she said. "Cuts through heat-armour like it's not there. You did well in the ring. You did an excellent job, in fact. But if for one second I'd thought you were in trouble, every guard in that room would have died."

He stared at her. She gave him her bland smile.

"I think the others would have killed me if I'd let anything happen to you. Ysbel threatened to blow me up, Lev wouldn't shut up about potential issues with the plan, and even Jez said she'd dump me out in space without a space suit if I showed up back here without you."

He blinked at her, dumbstruck. "Jez?"

"Why do you think she's been training you so hard?"

"I—assumed it was because she liked punching me in the face."

Masha smiled. "Go get some sleep. You earned it. And after what we just heard, sleep might be in short supply for the next few days."

# 13

Ysbel pressed her mouth into a tight, disapproving line as she handed out the weapons.

She would have preferred much more time to train the rest of these idiots.

The weapons weren't anything special, just heat-pistols that she'd added a couple of mods to. Still, Lev looked distinctly uncomfortable with his, and Ysbel was distinctly uncomfortable at the sight of it in Masha's hands.

Masha looked all too comfortable with it.

"Don't use it unless you have to," she said. "It looks like an ordinary heat-pistol, but it's much more destructive. It will be noticeable."

"How noticeable?" asked Lev.

Why anyone had thought it would be a good idea to dress this professor-boy up as a weapons dealer was beyond her. He was currently watching the weapon in his hand as if afraid it would turn around and snap at him. She sighed, and pulled out her own pistol with a practiced movement.

They should probably all know what they were getting into.

They were in her weapons room, the walls pitted and scarred from explosions. She took aim at the battered and vaguely-humanoid target dummy in the corner and fired. The air shimmered with the reflected heat of the bolt. For a moment, it appeared that nothing had happened. Then the target dummy collapsed in on itself gently, its lining twisted and melting, its core vaporized. There was a soft, 'drip … drip' of melting material puddling on the floor.

Lev's face held a kind of sick fascination. "I thought the dummy was made of non-reactive fiberstone," he said finally.

"It is. If you'd done that to a person, there would be nothing but a black grease spot on the concrete," she said. "If you miss the person, you find out at what temperature concrete burns."

Masha was looking at the weapon thoughtfully. "Very impressive," she said at last. She holstered hers with a practiced motion. "Alright. Are you ready?"

She wasn't ready. The thought of leaving the hangar made her feel almost sick.

She'd thought she hadn't cared about being imprisoned. Certainly it hadn't driven her half-mad, like it had the crazy pilot girl. After spending almost a week in close proximity to her, Ysbel wasn't certain how anyone—Jez, the guards, or innocent bystanders—had survived three weeks of Jez being confined to a bare cell.

Unlike the restless, snarky hothead, though, she'd thought prison had meant nothing to her. But it wasn't true. She'd wanted it. Needed it. Somewhere where nothing would be expected of her but silence, and she would get nothing but distain in return.

And now, instead, she was here. Trapped in a converted hangar-bay with these idiots. A sulky street boy, whose quiet brilliance she'd come to appreciate and even admire. An introverted genius, who had probably forgotten more than the rest of them combined had ever known, and whose dislike for the company of others and need for privacy matched even her own. A goofy, hot-headed, gangly pilot, who was so intensely irritating that it almost beggared belief, and who was trying so hard to be annoying while at the same time so obviously crushing on her, that, even though Ysbel hated to admit it, it was very nearly endearing, in a sort of puppy-dog way. And Masha. That bland, average woman who was so very clearly not average, and who neither she, nor any of the others, knew the first thing about.

Masha was playing a long game. Ysbel was no Lev, but she was smart enough to see that. But what the long game was, and where it would end, she had no idea.

"Ysbel?" asked Lev.

"I'm ready," she said, shoving the pistol back in its holster. "Let's get this over with."

They walked out through the hangar, and Jez looked up from the cockpit and called cheerfully, "Don't get shot! My ship doesn't have its weapons yet!"

Then Masha opened the door, and the three of them stepped out into the street.

Ysbel swallowed hard and stared at the pavement.

It had been a long time since she'd felt the sun on her skin.

"You alright?" Lev whispered. She glared at him. He noticed too much for his own good.

Masha was already striding on ahead, and they hurried to catch up.

"Remind me why we didn't take the bikes or the Bluewing?" Lev asked as they came up with her. Masha smiled at him.

"Two reasons. First, people are more likely to remember vehicles than they are to remember pedestrians. It will be easier for us to keep our heads down like this. And second, as I told you from the beginning, there are only a very few people who know about this operation. My colleague would be in danger of being asked questions that would be quite difficult for him to answer if people saw a vehicle that the government records indicate belongs to me, with two people who fit the general physical description of two highly-dangerous escaped criminals-turned-terrorists riding inside. So, we walk, and we go in the back way, and no one notices. At least," she turned to smile at them, "that's the plan."

It wasn't a long walk. She and Lev followed Masha's example, pulling up their scarves to cover their heads and staring at the pavement, like everyone else around them. On this miserable planet in this miserable city, where everything was grey and musty and just a little bit too cold, it was a perfectly natural thing to do.

Back home, there had been sun. The rich smell of dirt in the summer, the hot rays on their bare necks and shoulders when she and Tanya worked in the fields together ...

No. There was no point thinking of that now. That world was so far away that she could almost imagine it didn't exist.

By the time they left the warehouse district and entered the city proper, Ysbel could almost feel an itch between her shoulders.

Someone was watching them. Following them. She glanced at the others, but they didn't seem to notice.

She grunted and shook her head. Typical scholar and—whatever it was that Masha was.

Masha led them from the busy street down a small alley behind one of the ubiquitous government buildings. A small man waited at a doorway. When he saw them, he beckoned them in nervously, and gave an audible sigh of relief as they passed through the doorway. He cast uneasy sideways glances at her the whole way down the bare, unpainted prefab-block hallway.

She'd heard once that the government had chosen to manufacture all prefab blocks white because coloured walls would distract the government workers from their tasks. And the thing was, she believed it. If there was anything she'd learned about this government in the past five years, it was its mindless worship of busy-ness as an end in itself. It had been simple to design and rig the explosives that had taken out the shuttle station, because no one had noticed when her production went down and her tasks weren't completed on time. She looked busy, and that was all that mattered.

The man stopped and gestured them into a small office space, packed with various medical gear.. When he'd shut the door behind them, he leaned against the wall in relief.

"Masha," he said, turning to her. "I wish you'd chosen someone else to help you with this."

She gave him a look of bland innocence. "It wasn't me, Yokov. The powers that be decided you were the person for the job."

"With no input from you, I'm sure," he said bitterly. She smiled and shook her head.

"You got the directive, didn't you? They'll protect you if things go badly. I'm taking this risk on my own head. And since they're going to let me take the fall if anything goes wrong, you'll be easy to rehabilitate. Everyone knows how vicious I am when I don't get what I want."

"I don't supposed I much of a choice now," he said, tone a mix of irritation and nervousness. He turned and looked at the three of them. "Well then. What do you need from me?"

"I need five profiles wiped completely, and three new blank ones made up," she said, in a brisk voice. "It needs to be done today, no later. I've got the information for the other two on this chip, but

Ysbel, Lev and myself will need to pass a fairly comprehensive security check. I'll need the new profiles to show up on every database. Can you do it?"

He sighed heavily. "Of course I can do it." He paused, giving her a sharp look. "But if I do what you're asking, I won't be able to retrieve your old profile."

She hesitated for just a moment. "I know," she said at last. "I understand. The powers that be believe this mission is worth whatever cost it might entail."

"And do you believe that?"

Another slight hesitation. "I believe that they are working in the government's best interest," she said in a level voice. "And I began working for the government because I believed certain things. The government asking me to make a sacrifice doesn't change that."

He raised his eyebrows. "I never took you for an ideologist."

"People's motivations go deeper than you might think," she said quietly.

Ysbel watched them in silence, and wondered yet again what the government had offered Masha in exchange for pulling this off. Or was she simply an ideologue, like she'd professed?

Yokov studied Ysbel and Lev for a few moments, frowning absently.

"Ysbel," he said at last, "I knew your name the moment Masha mentioned it. I followed your career since you came to work for the government. Until the, ah, accident."

Accident.

For a moment, she was so angry she could hardly think.

*Grey-masked people grabbing her, shoving a gag over her mouth, cuffing her hands together, dragging her to the ship. Flames licking from the windows of their cottage, Tanya's frantic face at the window, Ysbel screaming their names through the gag until her voice was raw ...*

*Packing explosives into the hollows of the massive blocks that were about to be laid for the shuttle station, tucking them into the foundation just so, waiting for the day the officials would come to inspect.*

Accident. So that's how they'd spun it, in the end.

"It was no accident," she said coldly. She'd thought her voice would be shaking from anger, but somehow it was steady. "And I did not come to work for the government. They asked me over and over and over, and each time I refused. I had my own life, and my own family, my wife and my children, our little farm. We were happy. But they wanted me, so they came in one night and took me against my will. And in the process they killed my wife and my babies. I watched our house burn down around them. My daughter was three, my son was eighteen months. I watched them burn, and I could do nothing. So believe me when I tell you that explosion at the shuttle site was no accident."

Yokov had gone very pale. "I—I had no—I didn't know that. I had nothing to do with it, I swear."

"I know you didn't," said Ysbel, voice still deadly cold and deadly calm. "If you had, you would have been dead before we reached the end of the hallway."

Beside her, Lev's face had gone pale too, though whether because of the story or because of the threat, she wasn't certain.

It didn't matter. If he hadn't known what this government was capable of, he needed to grow up quickly.

The man took swabs and measurements, and sat them in a chair where a compact scanner did a quick circuit of them. He took digital impressions of each of their faces, and asked them to stand on a mat filled with a viscous material that formed to their feet beneath the soft surface. He pulled up his holoscreen and checked his measurements, then he nodded.

"I've done everything I can. By the time you get home, none of the five of you will officially exist. By tomorrow, I'll have constructed new identities for the other two, and I'll have the blank profiles done up for the three of you. As soon as you send me your new identities, I'll plug them in. But I'm warning you, you'll never get your old life back. Once it's gone, it's gone forever."

"I understand," said Masha, businesslike once again.

"And Masha," he leaned in, lowering his voice. "I know who you're up against. If you're not frightened, you should be. I've seen what Vitali's done to people who cross him. Out on the outside-rim planets, there are whole villages he's wiped out."

"I understand that too," she said. "I'm not concerned."

But one look at Lev's face told Ysbel that he was.

Was she?

She shouldn't be. The only outcome worse than dying before she could get her revenge on the government officials who had ordered her extraction was living past it.

But she couldn't escape the sense of foreboding as they made their way out of Yokov's office and into the street.

They were half-way home when she stepped up next to Masha and whispered, "We're being followed."

"I know," said Masha, her voice neutral.

"The last time we were followed, it ended in all your comfortable chairs being melted, and a hole blasted through the floor," Lev said in a low voice, coming up beside them. "I'd prefer not to do that again."

"It will be fine," said Masha. "It's not the police."

"If not the police, than who?" asked Lev.

"Our employers," she said quietly. "They're keeping an eye on me."

"And are they going to try to kill us again?"

"I hope not," she said, and there was something grim in her tone that made Ysbel glance at her sharply.

Masha was worried.

This was something she'd need to think on. Masha was clearly unconcerned about Vitali, and had seemed hardly phased by the attack by the police.

Whatever it was that had Masha worried was likely something that should concern the rest of them as well.

When they reached the hangar, Lev excused himself and walked quickly back to his small room, closing the door firmly behind him. When he was certain he was alone, he sank down on the narrow bed and put his head in his hands.

That operation. The extraction. That had been Ysbel.

He'd had no idea. They'd told him they needed a plan to extract an operative who had gone rogue, and who was hiding on a remote agricultural planet, on the outskirts of the system. They'd given him the details, and he'd come up with an operation.

He'd never been told what had happened, and he'd never asked. To be honest, he'd hardly thought about it since, except for the occasional niggling curiosity about who it had been.

And now he knew.

Her daughter had been three, her son eighteen months. That hadn't been part of the plan he'd given them. Murder had never been part of the plan. But, that nagging voice in the back of his mind said, he could have foreseen it. It would have been obvious, in hindsight, that the operation he'd designed would likely end up with non-target casualties, if the target tried to fight back and the operatives had to subdue her.

He felt sick to his stomach. An innocent woman, a three-year-old girl and an eighteen-month-old boy. Burned to death inside their own home, with Ysbel looking on in horror. Restrained. Kidnapped. Unable to do anything.

And the thirty-five dead on the shuttle site, he'd been indirectly responsible for that as well.

He closed his eyes and shook his head.

She couldn't know. No one could know, not now. She'd try to kill him, and almost certainly succeed, and his family wasn't free yet. He needed to free them, at least. Other innocents caught up in something they didn't understand.

But that wasn't the only motive—deep down he knew it, even if he didn't want to admit it.

He was a coward, and he didn't want to die.

He sat like that for a long time, guilt scalding his throat and his stomach like coals from a burning house.

Three years old and eighteen months.

There was a soft tap on his door. He took a deep breath, ran his hands over his face, and glanced in the small wall-mirror over the sink in the corner.

He was paler than usual, but he'd managed to plaster a calm expression over the guilt and horror roiling inside him. You wouldn't be able to tell, if you didn't already know, that he'd learned just minutes before that he was a mass murderer, a killer of innocents and children. A coward.

He gave his reflection a bleak smile, and crossed to open the door.

Masha and Ysbel stood there, as he'd expected.

"Are you alright?" Masha asked, giving him a searching look.

"Fine. I … didn't know Ysbel's story before today, and it was more than I had expected."

Too much? Had he given himself away? Still, he'd learned the closer to the truth you were able to stay, the easier it was to lie.

Ysbel gave him a sharp look, but under her usual expressionlessness, he caught a hint of something else. Suspicion?

No. Pity.

He thought for a moment he might throw up.

"Come in, please. What do you need?"

Masha and Ysbel entered and took their seats on the sitting cushions. He resumed his former place on the bed.

"I've decided on the identity we'll need to steal," Masha said, tapping her com. A light flashed on his own com, and he pulled up the message as Ysbel did the same.

He raised his eyebrows at the portrait that appeared on the holoscreen in front of him.

It was a young man, with a smooth, cruel face. He was staring straight ahead in the image, so he seemed to be looking directly at Lev. His hair was a light blond, smoothed down in the latest style, his eyes a pale blue.

"Mikail Yanovik," Lev said quietly. Masha nodded. He flipped quickly through the other two screens—Mikail's bodyguards. For herself, Masha had chosen a woman of medium height and sharp features, her eyes cold and green, her skin a few shades lighter than Masha's own. For Ysbel, it was a stocky man with dark hair and eyes and startlingly-pale skin.

"You think we can pull these off?"

"We no longer exist, Lev. And once we take Mikail and his bodyguards out of commission, we will be them, on every database in the system. I chose people with each of your basic body type and age. Colouring and physical features can be altered, but body type is more difficult."

He flipped back to the young man and studied him for a moment. He looked cold. Like a killer. Appropriate, then. Slowly, Lev nodded. "Very well. I suppose the next thing to plan is how we'll go about getting the identities."

"Yes." Masha stood. "I'll leave you to study on it. We have until the day after tomorrow. If we don't have then identities by then, Vitali will have done the scan, and will kill us on sight. We'll reconvene in the morning."

They nodded, and Ysbel stood. As they left, and before she closed the door, Masha said quietly, "And, as always, whatever you find on Vitali, we'll need to know."

"Of course," he said, closing the door behind her.

When they left, he sat on his bed for a few moments.

They all had secrets. That was clear enough. But now the secrets he was keeping had gone up in number and importance.

No one could know about the extraction. No one could know he'd been the one to plan it.

And no one must know how closely he was connected to Vitali.

If either of those secrets got out, he was as good as dead.

# 14

"So, we're going to go in and kick this guy's butt. That's basically the plan, right?" Jez tapped her foot against the hangar floor and rubbed her fingers up and down the holster of her pistol.

This was the test. She'd been working on the ship for days now, practically sleeping in the hangar bay.

She was going to go crazy. She thought she might honestly go completely mad. Crammed into a tiny space, around other people every minute of every day—this was not what she was good at. This was not something she could do.

But it would be worth it, as long as her ship did what she wanted it to do. What she needed it to do.

She needed this ship, and she needed to fly.

And this was her chance.

The others looked unaccountably grim as they stood around the hangar bay waiting for Masha. Lev checked his weapons, but she could tell by the look on his face he had very little confidence in his ability to use them.

She could have told him that Ysbel had given him the ones that you basically just had to point in the general direction of the enemy and depress the mechanism, but she wasn't certain that would help.

Ysbel and Tae stood quietly, Ysbel with a stoic expression, Tae with his trademark scowl. It didn't irritate her as much as it had a few days ago. The bruise over his eye was fading slightly, but it gave him character, at least.

Masha had explained what they were doing, but to be honest Jez had been a bit distracted—OK, more like tearing-her-hair-out desperate. Staying on the ground did that to her. But she'd caught enough to know that this was going to be dangerous. Although probably any time you tried to kidnap a murderous weapons buyer and two of his bodyguards, it was probably not going to be a jaunt to the moon.

"Are we ready?" Masha had come in quietly, dressed in her usual generic uniform and battered pilot's coat. Lev gave a tight nod.

"Alright," said Masha. "I guess it's time to see what this ship can do."

Just climbing into the cockpit was a bit like a drug. Jez could feel the calm settling over her mind, the sharpness in her senses, the adrenalin pulsing through her.

She'd be flying.

"Harnesses," Lev said over his shoulder, climbing in beside her with noticeable reluctance. "You'll need them." His face looked, if anything, even more grim than it had a few minutes ago, when he'd been trying to figure out which end of the pistol was the dangerous one.

She waited until she heard the click of the three harnesses in the back. Then she held her breath and hit the ignition.

The cockpit lit up, and the ship purred to life, just the tiniest tremor of motion. Something you wouldn't feel if your hands weren't on the controls.

It felt alive. It felt like breathing in finally, after holding your breath for ages.

When the bored official at the city entrance waved their ship out through the barrier and into the clean night air, she leaned her head back for half a second, revelling in the freedom of it. Then she punched the throttle, ignoring the yelp from Tae, the grunt from Ysbel, and the sound, from beside her, of someone trying not to vomit.

They shot out over the forest, skimming the tops of the trees, and then she turned the ship heavenward and fired up the boosters.

"Going up," she called over the com. "Hold on."

The ship gained speed as they went up, pressing her back into her seat, and as they got higher and higher, it began to shake ever-so-slightly. She looked out, watching the planet falling away below them, and the ship was louder now, and ...

They were through. She cut back on the throttle and stared out the cockpit window at the stars around her.

She blinked back tears

It felt like it had been years. Lifetimes.

Beside her, Lev's holoscreen glowed to life.

"I'll send the coordinates on to the ship com," Lev said, in a voice that sounded slightly sick. She nodded and pulled up the screen with one hand. A glowing set of coordinates appeared, and she squinted at them.

"We're going to have to do a wormhole jump."

"I know." He did not sound enthused by the prospect.

"Anything I should know before I head in?"

He sighed. "We're heading here. The pleasure planet. Mikail's booked to stay there until he leaves for Vitali's. Tae got far enough into the security that he could nudge a guard rotation, so Mikail will be bringing along the two guards we're after. Once we're there, we follow the plan we discussed last night."

She turned. "Which was?"

Lev blew out a long breath, and from the back, Ysbel muttered something that was probably meant to be insulting.

"Jez. Seriously?"

"Fine, don't tell me." She turned back to the controls. "I'm good at improvising."

Idiot.

"I'm going in with Masha and Tae." Lev was speaking through gritted teeth. "When Mikail lands, Masha is going to convince him to come back to the ship, where we'll drug him. You'll fly us out, Mikail and his guards go to prison under fake names, and Masha's contact plugs our blank profiles over theirs before Vitali does his scan."

"So basically, I'm not expecting anyone shooting at me when we come in," she said, rolling her eyes.

Lev and his pointless details.

"No. I don't think so."

"Good."

The wormhole blinked on her holoscreen, and she could feel the • tug of its gravity through the controls.

"Hold on, kids," she said, grinning. She hit the throttle.

The trick was to get enough speed that the ship would skim around the outside of the wormhole and be spat out the other side, rather than crushed. She half-closed her eyes as they were sucked in, feeling the ship talk to her as they skimmed the edge of the hole, the crushing gravity grasping at them as the they danced lightly along the knife-edge of destruction. Almost there ... almost there ... There! She jammed the accelerator, and for half a second the ship's engines fought with the gravity and they teetered on the edge—and then the ship popped free.

From behind her and beside her came the sounds of four people letting out a long-held breath. She sighed blissfully, and opened her eyes.

There was a planet in the distance—that must have been the one Lev was talking about—but it was surrounded by gunner ships.

"So," she said quietly. "No guns, eh?"

Lev had gone slightly pale, and was staring at the planet. "There wasn't supposed to be guns."

He pulled open his holoscreen and typed something rapidly. At last he shook his head and swore. "Looks like a bigwig mafia type came in unscheduled, and brought his army."

He looked worried. Really worried.

She shrugged. "Just a few guns. Not a big deal."

"It is a big deal," Lev said in a strained voice. "There's no way they don't notice us now. There'll be a record of us going in and out. Our whole plan is shot."

"Then you're going to have to think of a new one," she said reasonably, steering them in a slow arc.

"She's right." Masha's voice came over the com. "This is our only chance."

"I don't know if I've ever mentioned this, but I actually hate getting shot at," Lev grumbled.

"It's kinda like getting hit in the face. Not so bad once you get used to it, right Tae?" Jez said into the com. She was met with an icy silence.

"We could blow up a pleasure house while we're down there," Ysbel grunted after a moment's pause. "That should help."

Lev turned in his seat to stare at her.

"Lots of people want to do it," she said.

Slowly, he raised his eyebrows and nodded. "So they have a record of us going in and out, but as saboteurs, not kidnappers." He paused a moment. "Do we have the supplies to do that?"

"I brought my explosives. I always bring my explosives."

Jez grinned. "See, Ysbel's my kind of woman."

"Piss off."

Lev was staring straight ahead out the cockpit window, chewing on his bottom lip.

"So—" said Jez, not bothering to hide her impatience.

"So we go in," said Lev quietly, turning to her. "Masha's right. We don't have much of an option. But I'm worried about our chances."

Jez grinned in relief. That sounded more up her alley. "Good. Nothing I hate more than a boring job."

Lev shook his head.

Kid needed to learn how to lighten up.

She winked at him, and turned to her controls.

They came up on the back side of the planet. Even so, the guarding ships didn't seem excited to let her through, until Masha called in over the com, "We're bringing in some new entertainment for the Strani House. Please move aside."

Grudgingly, the ships did so, and Jez passed between them. They hit the planet's atmosphere, and the air outside glowed and the ship shook slightly as they passed through it.

"What's the Strani House?" she whispered to Lev. He was frowning, his expression dark.

"It's … not a place you'd want to spend time in, Jez."

She glared at him. "What kind of an innocent do you think I am? You can tell me."

He sighed, and told her, and she felt vomit rising in her throat.

"They do that? To people?"

"Yes."

"And when Masha said we were bringing in new entertainment, she meant—"

"Yes."

For a moment, she thought she might throw up. She hit the com. "Where in the hell did you learn about this, Masha? I'm not flying a slave ship."

"Would you rather they have shot us?" came Masha's calm voice from the back.

"Actually, yes!" She shut the com off, a little more violently than she had to.

For half a moment, as Lev was talking, she'd been a kid again, caught in the breathless, hopeless horror of a key turning in a lock, closing her in, her father's footsteps walking off down the hallway. Not knowing when he'd come back. When he'd let her out. What her punishment would be when he did.

And it was worse than that. Because these people knew exactly what would happen when their door was unlocked.

The adventure had suddenly taken on an ugly tinge. She felt dirty, and not certain if she'd ever be able to wash it off.

"There," said Lev, pointing. "Put the ship down there."

She set them down carefully in a dip between two of the bare, rolling grass hills of the planet. The city was in view in the distance before they sunk down below the hills, maybe a fifteen minute walk away.

Lev didn't seem to realize they'd landed until after she'd pulled off her harness.

"We're on the ground, folks," she said over the com. "Not sure if you were planning to get out at any point."

There was the sound from the back seat of harnesses releasing, and a few moments later they gathered at the door.

"The air here is breathable," Masha said in a low voice, "so there's no need for helmets. We're going to get in, get the goods and get out. You might see things that will … disturb you. Leave them. There's nothing we can do about them right now. We're not here to start fights, we're not here to make friends. Get what we came for and get out, understand?"

They all nodded. Jez's heart was pounding harder than it had been, and for once she didn't feel like grinning.

"Are you sure we can't just—"

"No." Masha's voice was sharp. "We can't 'just' anything. We can't break anyone out. We can't stop any of this, not right now."

"I—"

Masha turned to face her. Even through the disgust and horror twisting in Jez's gut, there was something in the woman's eyes that made her pause.

Masha hated this as much as she did.

"This is not the right time. Please, Jez. Trust me."

Jez wasn't used to trusting anyone. But for some reason, she nodded slowly.

"Thank you," said Masha, her voice so low Jez doubted the others could hear it.

Lev glanced around at them grimly. "I'm going to stay back to coordinate. Masha, Tae, you follow the original plan. Jez—" he paused. "Go with Ysbel. We'll meet back at the ship."

Ysbel nodded, and handed out the weapons. "Don't use these unless you have to," she said.

Lev depressed the door lock, and the door swung aside, and they stepped out onto the planet surface.

It was bright and hot, and the sun glared off the ship's paneling, half-blinding her. Masha pulled her thin scarf up over her head, and the others followed suit. Jez's stomach was clenched, her hands sweaty.

She felt dirty just standing on the planet surface. She wanted to burn this place to the ground.

They made their way across the brilliant, short-cropped green grass towards the city that shimmered in the distance, the five of them strung out in a line, and the hot, decadent smell of strong sunlight on growing things filled Jez's nostrils. She fell behind Lev, and he stepped forward until he was walking beside Masha. He probably meant to be whispering, but she caught his words, the strain in his voice.

"This is no good, Masha. We're not ready for this."

"We're going to have to be."

He blew out a breath. "You heard Jez—she wasn't even listening to the plan. She's a grenade with the pin pulled. She'll get everyone here killed."

She stopped walking abruptly, and Tae almost ran into her. He glared at her and muttered something under his breath, but she hardly heard.

Damn Lev. What the hell did he know?

Something small and accusing in the back of her mind, though, whispered that he was probably right.

There was a reason she worked alone.

She swallowed hard.

When they reached the entrance to the city, Lev and Masha paused until the others caught up.

"You all know what you're doing?" Lev asked quietly. Ysbel and Tae nodded. Jez scowled.

"Good," he said. "Tae, Masha, leave your coms on so we know when you have Mikail." They nodded, and Tae followed Masha through the arched gateway and into the narrow, cobbled streets. Ysbel turned to Jez.

"Come on, pilot. Let's go."

She followed Ysbel down another street in the opposite direction. It was crowded with people, stifling and noisy, and she heard shouts and moans and screams from inside the brilliantly-coloured walls of the pleasure-houses surrounding them. She kept her gaze fixed on the smooth cobblestones under their feet as they wove their way through the throngs of people. If she looked around, she was afraid she'd throw up.

When Ysbel stopped, Jez almost ran into her.

"This is the one we're going to blow up," Ysbel whispered. This time Jez did look up. The holo-sign over the door glowed garish yellow letters that spelled "Strani House."

She swallowed. "Won't—won't that hurt the ... the—"

Some of what she felt must have shown on her face, because Ysbel gave her a grim smile that was almost sympathetic.

"Don't worry, pilot-girl. I'm good at what I do. I'll set the explosives in the lobby, where the patrons wait."

Jez nodded, not trusting herself to speak.

Over the ear-piece in her com, Tae swore suddenly.

"There's more than two guards, Lev," he whispered.

"How many?"

"Five."

Jez and Ysbel exchanged glances.

In the background, she heard Masha's voice. "Yes, sir. I was sent by my House to come find you. We have a lovely garden, and the widest variety of entertainment. You will not come away unimpressed."

"I already have reservations booked," came a cold voice. "Don't think I'm some gullible traveler. You'll regret it."

Masha sounded shocked. "Heaven forbid! I know exactly who you are. And, I know …" her voice lowered, and Jez couldn't hear the rest of what she said.

"We need backup," Tae whispered. "They're not going to come. Masha's working on them, but it's not what we expected."

There was a short pause, then Lev said reluctantly, "Jez. Can you —"

"On it, genius-boy."

She hoped she didn't sound as sick as she felt.

"Take this." Ysbel tossed something in her direction. Jez snatched it out of the air, looked at it, then started down the street through the crowds of people at a light run.

A scream came from one of the pleasure houses.

Her feet stopped moving, almost of their own accord. She was here, and she had a gas-bomb …

"Coordinates on your com," Lev whispered.

*She'll get us all killed,* he'd said.

*Trust me on this,* Masha had asked.

They were counting on her. Tae, and Masha, and that damn idiot Lev.

And Masha had been right—a gas bomb wouldn't do anything for whoever it was who had been screaming.

She closed her eyes, swallowing down the bile in her throat, and glanced at her com. Then she turned and started down a back street at a sprint.

"Gas-bomb coming in at your six o'clock," she whispered into the com.

"What?" came Tae's alarmed voice.

"Let Masha know. We're dragging them out of here."

She reached the back of the dock where Mikail had landed, twisted the bomb, and tossed it lightly over the top of the docking wall. Then she dropped to the ground as it began to hiss.

"What—" she heard from inside, and the thumps of bodies hitting the floor. She slid the thin mask Ysbel had given each of them over her mouth and nose and strode into the dock.

"Everyone out," she said. "Get everyone out of here. We have a pressurizer leak. Move aside please, we're coming in for search and rescue."

Tae and Masha had already pulled the masks over their faces, and they strode into the grey cloud alongside her.

"What are you doing?" Tae hissed through the mask. She grinned, even though she knew they couldn't see it.

"Being brilliant." She reached down and grabbed the pale young man under the arms and hoisted him on her shoulder. "Let's go."

"There's six of them. I'm positive you heard me say that." Tae was clearly furious.

Jez reached down to two of the guards and snapped a magnetic cord around their ankles, then pulled a third beside them. "So we take six. I thought you brought an anti-grav."

Tae sighed and pulled a tiny device out of his jacket pocket. "This isn't going to look suspicious at all, us dragging a bunch of unconscious bodyguards like some sort of pet on a leash."

She shrugged. "There was a gas leak. We're getting people to safety. Now, where are the other two?"

"I think," came Masha's calm voice, "that that may be our problem."

Slowly, Jez turned.

Two bodyguards were standing at angles that made it impossible for her to keep her eyes on both of them at once. Both had face-masks on. And both had their weapons drawn.

Jez hit the button on her com with the palm of her hand as she turned slowly.

"What are you doing?" Masha said, her voice brusk. "Are you here to help evacuate?"

The bodyguards didn't speak, just made an all-too-understandable gesture. Jez sighed, and lowered the young man she had hoisted over her shoulder onto the ground.

"Now, step away," said one of the guards. "I'm going to give you the benefit of the doubt and not shoot you right now. But this is an ion-gun, so one false move and there won't be enough left of you to sweep up in a pile."

Slowly, Jez straightened, hands in the air. Beside her, Tae did the same. Masha was already standing, hands raised.

"What these two doing? They're representatives of a House, or at least that's what they told us," one of the bodyguards growled.

"I grabbed them," Jez said sullenly. "I'm trying to save your boss, and I don't think he's going to be very happy that you stopped me. They were here, and they had masks, so I told them I'd need a hand."

"And they just came?"

"They're very helpful."

This was going sideways fast.

"On the left." Lev's voice was barely a whisper into her com earpiece. "I checked their weapon stores. He's got the ion gun, but it's a narrow-beam long range. It's not going to be much good in close quarters."

She glanced at Tae out of the corner of her eye. He gave her a quick look that told her he was hearing this too.

"The one on the right has a standard heat-gun with some mods. Close-range weapon. But she's not going to want to use it in here until the gas has cleared, because it doesn't look like they have the tech on their masks to get the chemical composition. She's not going to want to risk sending everything up."

The bodyguard on the right was openly sneering at her. "Ah. I see. You all just happened to be walking by when there was a gas leak, and the three of you out of the goodness of your hearts came to help." He raised his wrist towards his mouth, other hand coming up to tap the transmit button.

She gave Tae a meaningful look. Then she yanked her modded pistol out of her belt, tossed it at Masha, and threw herself towards the guard on the left.

Everything seemed to happen at once.

The woman lifted her pistol, then hesitated. Jez hit her at full speed, knocking her off her feet and rolling them both across the floor. They grappled for a moment, each trying to grab for the other's mask. There was the crackling hiss of a heat gun, and from the corner of her eye she saw the com spark and melt off the wrist of the guard on the left. He screamed, then Tae's foot connected with his crotch and he grunted, doubling over. Tae snatched the mask from his face, and he gasped, choked, and went down.

The guard Jez was grappling with was smart—as soon as she'd seen Masha's shot, she grabbed for her own weapon, and was struggling to bring it to bear on Masha. Jez hit her in the face, and she blinked, disoriented, then brought the butt of her gun down on Jez's shoulder. Jez yelped, and then a hand grabbed the front of her mask. She gasped in desperately as the mask tore from her face, not daring to breathe as she struggled with the woman. Masha was sprinting towards them, and kicked guard's gun hand just as the woman kneed Jez in the stomach. Jez doubled over, stars dancing in front of her eyes, fighting not to suck in the breath that would put her on the ground—and then something was shoved over her face. She gasped in a breath instinctively and realized she was breathing oxygen. She sucked in the sweet air in desperation, then looked up. Tae was holding a mask to her face, his own face uncovered and his lips going purple. She pulled in a final breath, yanked the mask off her face, and shoved it back onto his. He gasped, colour coming back to his cheeks.

Masha tapped her on the shoulder and handed her the guard's mask, and she slipped it on gratefully.

"Well," she said, once she'd caught her breath. "That was exciting."

Masha looked grim. "We have to get out of here. I think he got off word before I shot his com."

"Negative," said Lev over the com. His voice sounded smug. "Tae hooked a blocker up to your coms, if you recall."

They all turned to look at each other. Jez felt a slow smile spreading across her face.

"So, we're home free?"

"If we get them out of the city without anyone noticing," said Tae. "There'll be people at the dock any second now. Lev? How are we doing?"

"You have three dock-workers coming up from the west," Lev said. He paused. Then Ysbel's voice came through the com.

"In about five seconds, you'll have all the distraction you need. Are you ready?"

"Let's go," said Masha. She shrugged off her pilots coat and shoved it at Jez, then slung one of the guards over her shoulder. Jez frowned, and Tae pointed impatiently to the two guards floating gently, the anti-grav strapped underneath them. She grinned and added the third guard to the top of the pile, making it sag slightly, and then threw the coat over top of them. She pulled off her scarf and threw it on to of the pile, Tae added his own outer clothing, and Jez grabbed the end of the cord that was attached to what now looked like a pile of luggage and loose clothing, and pulled it along behind her. She slung the young man over her shoulders again, and Tae knelt and lifted the final guard, staggering slightly under her weight.

From far off, a 'boom' echoed through the city.

"Let's go," said Masha, and they ran.

Ysbel and Lev were waiting for them outside the walls of the compound.

"We've got to get out of here," Lev said, grabbing the magnetic cord from Jez. He reached into his pocket and pulled out another anti-grav. "Let's go."

They made a pile of the weapons dealer and the other two guards and tied them together, then started for the ship. When they reached it, Tae and Ysbel loaded their cargo into the hold while Lev checked his screen.

"They've noticed us," he said, voice tense. "They're coming out to investigate."

Ysbel slammed the hatch. "Let's go, then."

They piled into the ship, and Jez started it up and lifted them gently up over the dunes. In the distance she could see a group of speeders headed towards them.

She pointed their nose towards the sky and hit the controls.

She'd never been so glad to leave a planet.

As they cleared the atmosphere a flurry of bolts whizzed around them, but Tae's shields worked a dream. A couple ships broke off to follow, but when she jammed down on the accelerator, they quickly disappeared behind them.

She pointed them in the direction of the wormhole, grinning.

"Jez. Um." Lev didn't meet her eyes. "You—did well back there."

She glanced at him and raised an eyebrow.

"I—wasn't sure you would. I'm sorry."

She swallowed down something in her throat. "I wasn't sure I would either, genius-boy," she said softly. He turned, and gave her a quick smile.

"You surprised both of us, then," he said.

She stared at him for a moment, then turned back to the controls. But for some reason, there was a warmth spreading through her chest.

She wasn't a team player, never had been. But this—this actually hadn't been that bad.

# 15

Once they'd made their drop, Jez docked the ship carefully in the hangar and released her harness. "I'm going for food," she announced.

There was a moment's pause, then Tae said, as if the words were being dragged out of him, "The rest of us are hungry too, you know. I'll come."

She turned to stare at him.

He was glowering, as usual, but under his glower, there was a reluctant expression that looked almost like—the beginnings of a smile?

Masha pinched her lips together. "We have plenty of—"

Jez rolled her eyes. "We just pulled off the last job that stands between us and this heist. Your buddy wiped us from every database in the system. We don't exist anymore. So I'm going out." She hesitated, and took a deep breath. "The rest of you coming, or not?"

"Alright," said Lev, with a fake reluctance that couldn't hide his own smile. "We'll come. Right Ysbel?"

"I suppose," she growled.

The four of them stepped out into the cool evening air. Jez

couldn't hold back a shiver at the chill.

She glanced behind her at the others.

She'd invited them to come with, sort of. At least, she hadn't protested. She wasn't entirely sure why. It was a strange feeling, this almost-camaraderie.

But—they'd made a pretty good team back there, all things considered. Even her.

They'd left the warehouse district and were almost to the main thoroughfare when Jez caught a movement from the mouth of a dark alley beside her.

She spun, but someone grabbed her from behind and a heavy hand clamped over her mouth. She turned her head wildly, searching for the others.

She caught a glimpse of Tae's boots, disappearing around the side of the street.

The others had vanished.

Her stomach dropped.

She'd been stupid. Again. It only took so long for people to get sick of her and throw her out. It was her own damn fault, she knew it, but she couldn't seem to help it.

She'd been dumb enough to think that maybe this was different.

"Jez." The hand on her mouth loosened, the voice in her ear sickeningly familiar.

Antoni.

"It's so good to see you again. We were worried you were off getting into trouble all by yourself."

"I have the money coming, Antoni. I'm in the middle of a job. Give me two weeks. Then Lena gets her ship back, and you never see me again. Win-win."

"Oh Jez." His voice was almost sympathetic. "You still don't get it.

I warned you she wanted her ship. I let you go. I trusted you. And how did you repay me? You disappeared. Wiped from every database. What are we supposed to think about that, Jez? It takes cold hard credits to do that. For what it cost you to wipe yourself, you could have put in a pretty down-payment on a ship." He pulled her closer, his massive arm squeezing her ribs. She could feel them cracking and protesting under the pressure.

"I wasn't—"

"Funny thing, Jez, but she doesn't trust you much anymore."

"Let me go." Her voice choked with the effort of trying to draw in a breath.

"So we're putting the deadline forward. You pay up now, with wherever you found the credits for your database wipe. Or, we use you as an example. You can't say that's not fair."

"I—" She could feel tears gathering in her eyes. It wasn't fair. She'd been so close.

Then, abruptly, the pressure on her ribs loosened. She dropped to the ground, barely catching herself on her hands.

"That's right, let her go," came a familiar calm voice.

Lev stood behind Antoni, holding one of Ysbel's snub-nosed heat pistols to his ribs. She spun.

Tae had two of the thugs at gunpoint, and Ysbel was holding another in a headlock.

They must have circled around through the back of the alley.

She felt a slow grin spread across her face.

"You OK, Jez?" Lev asked.

"I'm good," she said, brushing herself off.

"Good," said Lev, his tone full of meaning. "Because if you hadn't been, these people here might have gotten into an accident."

"Still time for that," Ysbel grunted. "No one tries to kill this pilot but me. I get very angry when people try to deprive me of my rights."

"You heard her," said Lev. "If I were you, I'd think about leaving. She kills people for fun."

The man Ysbel was holding in a headlock tried to speak. She tightened her hold, and he choked.

"He can't run when you're holding him like that," said Lev. His voice was tinged with a hint of amusement.

Antoni's thugs didn't look amused.

"Good point," Ysbel grunted. She let up on the headlock, then planted her foot in the small of the man's back and shoved him forward. "Better start running, then."

He stumbled forward, picked himself up, and ran for his life. Tae gestured with his gun, and the guards he had at gunpoint started after their fleeing companion. Lev kept his gun where it was.

"Leave Jez alone," he said, his tone carrying all sorts of levels of menace. "If we see you around here again, you'll be the example. Got it?"

Antoni scowled. Lev twisted the gun harder, and the muscle-bound man winced.

"Got it," he muttered.

"Good," said Lev, removing the pistol carefully.

"Now," said Ysbel, pulling an explosive from the pouch around her neck. "Let's see how fast you can run."

Antoni took one look at them, and took off after the others.

"Tell Lena I said hi," Jez called after him.

When they were gone, they stood in the street, looking at each other. Lev holstered his pistol, and Ysbel gently placed the explosive back in the padded bag.

"Well," Tae said at last. "Shall we get food?"

Lev started off, and after a moment, Jez followed.

She wasn't sure what to think. But there was something light and unfamiliar glowing inside her.

It felt kind of good, actually.

They laughed and joked on the way home from the food stall. The food had been warm and greasy, and it sat comfortably in her stomach. Even Ysbel had cracked a smile once or twice.

It wasn't until they were close to the hangar-bay that she saw the smoke.

"Is that—" Tae started. They looked at each other in wordless horror, then started towards the hangar bay at a run.

She slowed as they reached it, not quite able to believe what she was seeing.

The hangar was a ruin. A hole had been blown in the roof, and flames still flickered out of the hangar doors.

"Stay back," Ysbel grunted, pulling the padded bag of explosives from her neck. She handed them to Tae, who looked like she'd gifted him a live snake, pulled her scarf up over her face and head, and strode into the smoke.

"Wait—" Jez started after her, but Lev grabbed her arm.

"Leave her. Her clothes are fire-retardant. She works with explosives, she'll know how to stay safe."

She stared after the woman, chest tight.

Was this Antoni? Had this been her fault?

Tae moved the padded bag gingerly into one hand and tapped his com. "The fire retardant is the button to the left of the hangar door," he said. Ysbel grunted in response. A few moments later, there was a *hiss*, and the flames flickered and died.

"It's safe to come in now," she called at last.

Slowly, they walked through the ruined doors.

Jez knew what she'd see, but when she actually saw it, it felt like someone had dropped a lead weight into her stomach.

"My ship," she whispered.

It was still whole, but the beautiful finish was blackened and blistered from the heat.

"They burned my ship." She had to swallow hard against the tears.

The inside of the hangar, too, was blackened. Tools lay twisted and melted, and Tae's stack of half-finished tech was a smoking pile of wires and warped metal.

"Who did this?" Lev asked quietly.

"I have a guess," came a voice from behind them. Jez jumped and spun around.

Masha stood there. Her face was blackened, her expression grim.

"This was a warning. I think our employers wanted to let me know they were watching. I think they wanted to make sure we didn't get too cocky."

"Our—" she started, but a glance at Masha's face made her fall silent.

"Let's get this mess cleaned up," Masha said, voice still grim. "The sooner the better. We have a lot to do."

Silently, they nodded and went to get the brooms.


Cleanup took all that night and well into the next morning. By the time they fell into their bunks, exhausted, the sun was high in the sky, and Tae's eyes were sandy from lack of sleep.

When he rolled groggily out of his bed to a knock at his door, it was late evening. He felt like he'd slept no more than five minutes.

Yawning, he dragged himself into fresh clothes and splashed cold water on his face, then staggered out to join the others in the hangar deck.

Everyone else looked just as tired as he did, except for Jez, who looked not only just as tired, but three times as jumpy.

She didn't give him any sort of insulting greeting when he came in, but whether that was because she was too tired to think of one, or too distracted, he wasn't sure.

Or maybe it had something to do with what had happened in the alley last night.

He'd seen the look on her face. She'd thought they were all going to leave her.

He did kind of hate her. She was the most irritating, exasperating person he had ever met, and she had a knack for getting under his skin. But that didn't mean he was going to leave her to get beat up, any more than he would have one of the street-kids he'd grown up with. You just didn't do that to people.

Maybe she didn't know that people didn't do that to people.

Lev stepped forward. There were dark circles under his eyes, but he looked like he'd been awake for some time.

"Listen," he said, voice rough from lack of sleep. "We have a problem."

"What, you mean besides getting our hangar blown up?" asked Jez. She was drumming her fingers nervously against her hip, and the tip of her toe was tapping out a rhythm on the hard hangar floor.

"Vitali added some new security measures," Lev said. His expression was grim. "Genotyping. Vitali's outfitted the guards with DNA sensors. They collected samples from each person he invited, and they're setting them into the system."

Tae stared at him. "They have DNA scans? How did they do that?"

"Not as exact as DNA scans. But they'll be able to tell with relative accuracy if we match who we say we are. I doubt they'll bother with the bodyguards, since they may change up to the last minute. But the guests will be typed as they go through the gates."

This wasn't good.

"How accurate are the scans?" Tae asked after a moment.

"Accurate enough. If it was a parent and a child, it probably wouldn't catch it. But me and Mikail? That's a guaranteed mismatch."

Tae ran a hand over his face.

This wasn't something he could hack, not with no lead time. This was tech he'd never heard of.

Hell.

"So what do we do?" Jez broke in. Ysbel was still just standing, staring stolidly straight ahead, as if none of this affected her in the least.

"My contacts could possibly get us a patch that would get us through," said Masha from one side. "But it would take them a minimum of ten to twelve days. We'll need to be leaving the planet by the end of the week."

Lev sighed, and Tae groaned internally. He already knew what was coming next.

"Tae. I hate to ask this of you, but it's all I have. You'll have to get in from the guards' quarters early. You'll need to get there before we arrive, and make sure you're either the one letting us in the gate, or that you've tampered with the gate guards' equipment so it will let us through. We only have a week left, and we don't have time to deal with it any other way."

Vitali's guards had been ready to kill him just to see if he'd pass their test. He shook his head reluctantly, his shoulders tight. "I— don't know if that will work. I doubt they use new recruits as gate guards, and if I sneak out, it won't take them long to notice I'm missing."

"You'll have to figure something out," said Lev. "Unless you can come up with another plan."

Tae paused.

He couldn't. Lev knew it as well as he did.

"You'll have some time," said Masha. "I checked—they'll be bringing you and the rest of the trainees into the compound a day or two before we're set to arrive. Give you time to recon the ground and figure out the best way to get around."

He nodded reluctantly. Somehow, every complication that came up in the plan seemed to be solved by 'Tae, can you—'

He was liking this plan less and less the closer it got.

"So," said Masha again, "As Lev was saying, we don't have much time to prepare, and after the attack on our hangar we'll need to be extra cautious. With that in mind, I'm forbidding anyone to leave the hangar without my explicit permission, which will be given only for absolute necessities. Do you understand?"

"I—I can't just stay in the hangar for a week," Jez blurted. "What am I going to do? You can't keep me locked up. I might as well have just stayed in prison."

He glanced over at her. It should have been laughable, but her eyes had a frantic pleading in them that somehow wasn't funny at all.

"I'm sorry, Jez," said Masha. Her voice was implacable, but Tae thought he could catch a hint of sympathy in her eyes. "It's the only way to make sure we can pull this off. And we all need this, even you. Tae, I believe Lev has sent the new specs to your com. You'll need to have them memorized."

Tae sighed and nodded. One more thing. He couldn't even keep count anymore. He turned and made his way over to the corner that had once been his stash of tech.

He'd spent hours on it. Days. Reduced to a stain of melted plastic and metal that they'd been unable to scrub off the floor.

He was too tired to be angry right now, but the sight set something ugly bubbling up in his chest.

No matter where he was, no matter what he was doing, someone always stepped in and took it away from him. Always.

He wasn't sure how much longer he could take it, and not lose his mind. And he wasn't sure what would happen if he did.

# 16

Lev watched the others move slowly away to their preparations.

For an attack, the fire had been singularly ineffective. The door to Ysbel's weapons room had been closed, and it was completely fire and heat resistant. Jez's ship, which had almost reduced her to tears the night before was, on closer inspection, not too badly damaged—mostly just the outside body work and some of the external modifications. Tae's equipment had suffered the most damage, but in honesty, the things he'd been spending the most time on were either inside the ship itself, uploaded to his com system, or packed in his upstairs room for storage.

"Masha," he said quietly, "I'd like to speak to you for a moment, if you would."

She turned, raising her eyebrows, then nodded and followed him to his room. He opened the door and beckoned her to a comfortable cushion on the floor while he took his customary seat on the bed.

"We were lucky last night," he said, once they'd both settled themselves. "For damage that looked that extensive, it had a relatively small effect on our plans."

She nodded, her eyes piercing. "Yes," she said in a non-committal tone. "We were lucky. Although I think if you tell the others that right now, someone will probably shoot you."

He allowed himself to crack a smile at that.

"It seemed a bit odd to me," he continued, "so when we finished cleaning up this morning, I decided to look into it a little more. I checked through the rubble we'd cleaned out, and I did a quick scan on the material they'd used to light it up. Oddly enough, I was able to trace it back to a batch that had been purchased some time ago. It had gone through several shell companies, obviously, and had been purchased under an assumed name. But at the end of the day, I was able to track down the material to the organization who'd bought it." He leaned forward. "It was the mafia."

He paused, studying her reaction. She didn't seem to react at all, just sat watching him, her eyebrows raised in polite interest, but he knew her well enough to see that there was something behind that bland gaze, something sharp and intelligent. And worried.

"I thought to myself, why would Masha tell us that it was our employers who'd left this little gift for us? Clearly you work for the government. You've proven that to my satisfaction, and as you might have suspected, I searched all my files and records to which I had access to make sure you were who you said you were before I accepted this job. So I know that that part of your resume wasn't a lie." He paused again. "So when did you start working for the mafia, Masha? What's the end game here? Are you planning on selling us out when we get home with the tech?"

She watched him for a long, long time. Finally she gave a weary shake of her head, and he realized with a jolt that she must be just as tired as the rest of them. For some reason, he'd never thought of Masha as getting tired, or hungry, or stressed. She'd seemed as much as an automaton as the ship itself.

But now she looked weary, and fully human, and even a little frightened.

"Who have you talked to about this?" she asked quietly. He shook his head.

"No one, yet. But it's in my com, and if you kill me, it's programmed to send a message to all the others immediately."

The hint of a smile appeared at one corner of her mouth. "I see I didn't overestimate you when I chose you for this heist," she said. "I admire your preparedness. However, I have no intention of killing you." She paused, studying him. "Believe me when I say I have no plans to double-cross you, or to put you or the others in any danger. But what I'm doing with the mafia is vital."

"Vital to our mission? Or to yours?"

Her face was, as always, impossible to read.

She shook her head slowly. "I'm sorry, Lev. I will have to ask you to trust me, and to believe that you will get a fulsome explanation when the time is right." She studied him a moment longer, then stood. "I can't stop you from telling the others, if that is what you choose. But if you do that, you know as well as I do that they are unlikely to continue with this. Unlike you, they have no way of verifying that I am indeed who I told them I was."

"And something else as well," he murmured.

She nodded. "And something else as well, but certainly what I told them I was. But I can say that I have a motive to pull off this heist that matches any one of your own." She gave him a last piercing glance, and stepped out of the room, closing the door behind her.

Once she'd left, he sat on the bed for a long time.

The thing was, he did trust her. At least, he wanted to. There was something about her that inspired trust. But it was exactly that that made him wary. Did he trust her because it was the right thing to do, or because he'd fallen prey to her admittedly impressive powers of persuasion?

And how would he tell the difference?

At last he sighed and stood.

He wouldn't tell the others, at least not yet. The attack on the hangar bay had clearly shaken her. It had been a warning, and she'd taken it that way. So she wasn't necessarily in the mafia's good graces.

That didn't mean whatever it was she'd gotten herself into wasn't going to hurt the rest of them. It just meant she probably wasn't going to do it on purpose.

He'd see where this strange path took them. And when the time came to it, he'd decide what to do. It wasn't like he wasn't keeping his own secrets.

It wasn't like any of them weren't keeping their own secrets.

The week simultaneously crawled by at the pace of a lazy tree-slug, and sped past in the blink of an eye. Lev went over and over the plans, combing through documents to find something—anything—more than he had about the security measures. He'd managed to drop a few possibilities about the physical security system onto Jez and Tae's com. Tae had gone through it with him piece by scanty piece, but he wasn't certain Jez had even looked at hers.

Something about Masha's direction to stay in the hangar seemed to have kicked her over the edge. She paced the hangar bay all day and long into the night. She'd have frantic bursts where she'd spend an hour buffing the outside of the ship with polisher and a cleaning rag, then she'd sink down into the corner in despair. Then she'd jump to her feet, as if driven by a motor, and go back to pacing.

He was starting to realize, for the first time, how bad her three weeks in prison must have been.

Ysbel was almost silent, her face creased in a permanent scowl. When he asked her what was wrong she snapped at him to piss off, but he gathered from her muttering that she was worried about the weapons tech on the ship after the fire. She'd been going back and forth between fiddling with the ship and working in her shop, but since they couldn't take the ship out to test anything, and since her weapons room was far too small for it, she settled for making the rest of their lives hell if they got in her way.

Tae was almost as bad, huddled in his corner and working long into the night to replace the tech that had been burned. He'd taken the loss particularly badly. Lev wasn't sure why, and it bothered him not to know. And Tae would be flying out to Vitali's compound soon. Masha was to bring him to the rendezvous place in two days' time.

Which meant, on the bright side, that the last of the pieces had fallen into place. And on the other hand, meant that Tae had to replace all of his tech and train them on it in a matter of hours that seemed far too short.

To top it off, when they discussed the heist, Jez couldn't seem to focus for long enough for him to get through a sentence, and the last time Tae had tried to train her on some of the tech it had ended in a shouting match where Ysbel almost had to put Jez into a headlock, like she'd done the first day they'd all met.

When Tae's rendezvous date arrived, and he and Masha slipped out the door long after nightfall, Lev almost breathed a sigh of relief.

Without Jez and Tae fighting, he might actually get a few minutes of peace and quiet to finish memorizing the biographical information of Mikail. Security was going to be thorough, and Vitali was no idiot. Masha and Ysbel were bodyguards, so below Vitali's notice, but he would have to be very well prepared indeed.

Ysbel seemed just as eager to take advantage of the peace and quiet—he heard the door to her weapons room click shut as he made his way up the stairs, and he smiled slightly to himself.

It wasn't until hours later, when he heard the shouting, that he realized what a bad idea leaving Jez alone had been.

He pounded down the stairs, and arrived in the hangar at almost the same time as Ysbel's door banged open.

Then he stopped and raised his eyes to the ceiling in complete exasperation.

Jez must have snuck out after Masha was gone. How far, he didn't know, but far enough to procure herself copious amounts of sump, and probably several other substances as well.

She was laying back in the cockpit, her eyes dilated and unfocused, her body relaxed, smirking at Masha.

Masha was anything but relaxed.

"You have one last chance to tell me," she said, her voice low and dangerous. "Where did you get that?"

"Rained from the sky, probably," said Jez, her words carefully over-enunciated. Lev winced.

There was a lot he didn't know about Masha, but he could guess that talking to her like this when she was in this sort of a mood was not a good idea.

"Where did you get it?" Her words snapped out like a whip.

"Dunno. I haven't been allowed to leave this prison, sorry, work-shop, for an entire week now. Have no idea where this came from."

Masha raised her hands in exasperation. "What were you thinking, you idiot? We're flying out tomorrow night! What have you been taking? We can't fly into Vitali's compound with a drunk pilot."

"I," said Jez, straightening herself with an effort, "can fly anything into anywhere any way I want to. You know that Masha. Why'd you think you came after me like you did? Know I'm good looking and all, but I'm the only one who can do what you want me to do. And I did it. I did everything you wanted me to do, and now you've locked me up. So fine. Today Tae went off to his … his …" she waived a vague hand in the air. "To whatever it is he's doing. We're free and clear, and you get what you want. So I'm going to celebrate. What you going to do, throw me out?"

Masha's eyes glinted, and for half a moment Lev thought she might. Finally, though, she gave a sigh of exasperation. "Ysbel," she said, through gritted teeth. "Would you please take this idiot out of the cockpit?"

Ysbel, who hadn't moved through the whole exchange, stepped forward, but Lev thought he caught a hint of amusement in her eyes.

"Come on stupid, up you go," she said, climbing into the cockpit beside Jez. Jez waved her hand expansively.

"Got lots left. Help yourself. You're a good woman, Ysbel. Not like that crazy one over there."

"Come on. Get out."

"I know, I know. Pees oaf, right?"

Ysbel didn't bother to respond, just hoisted Jez bodily up and lifted her from the ship. She leaned her against the side, and Jez promptly collapsed. Masha drew in a breath through her teeth.

"I can't believe this," she muttered.

"You might as well start," said Jez, from where she'd somehow managed to prop herself up against the side of the ship. She pulled a bottle of sump from somewhere, and put it to her lips. She managed one swallow before Masha strode over, snatched it from her hands, and broke it on the hangar floor.

"What'd you do that for?" Jez grumbled, trying and failing to get to her feet.

"You," said Masha, leaning over her, "are a disrespectful, drunken
—"

"Useless, no good, unreliable solo player. I know. Heard it all my
life."

"You'd better start worrying about where that will leave you,"
Masha hissed.

Jez studied her for a moment, then said, enunciating her words
very clearly, "I'll tell you where that leaves me, Masha. That leaves
me somewhere that I don't get locked up in a hangar bay. That
leaves me somewhere that I can fly a ship, all on my lonesome, out as
far into deep space as I can go. That leaves me far, far away from
petty little women who think they can run my life."

She pulled out a smaller flask, but Masha snatched it before she
could even get it to her lips and emptied it onto the ground.

"Get to your room, and get sober. I'll be damned if I let you mess
this up."

Jez's passion seemed to have drained with the remaining sump,
and now she was watching the pool of liquid on the floor sadly.
Masha shook her head, lips pressed tight together.

"I'll take her to her room," Lev said. The words surprised him.
He hadn't thought to say them.

"Fine," said Masha, still tight-lipped. "Take her up. But make sure
she doesn't have any more sump on her first."

Lev came over and knelt beside the inebriated pilot. She grinned
up at him drunkenly. "Hey genius-boy. You want some sump?"

"No, Jez," he said gently. "And I don't think you need any more
either. Come on, time for bed."

"I'm not tired," she said, sounding a bit like a sulky child.

Ysbel grunted. "You are tired, and your bed will feel better than
the concrete. Which is your next option."

Jez turned her head vacantly. "Oh, Ysbel's here too. Does she want some?"

"Come on." Lev hoisted Jez up and led her, in a staggering weave, across the floor and over to the stairway. Getting up the stairs was a bit of a nightmare, but they managed, and by the time he got her to her room, her eyelids were already beginning to droop.

"Don't know why I'm tired. Not nearly late enough yet," she mumbled. He rolled his eyes and sat her on the bed, doing a quick pat-down for contraband bottles. He found one more flask in her pocket, and removed it before she could see.

"No reason to be tired," she muttered again, slumping back against the wall. He looked at her sternly.

"To be honest with you, Jez, I'm not certain how you're still conscious at this point, with whatever it is you have running through your system. If I cut you, I think you'd bleed straight sump."

"You think so?" she murmured, yawning.

He watched her for a moment.

He shouldn't do this. He knew he shouldn't.

But he couldn't help himself.

"You said you worked for Lena once," he said quietly.

She nodded. "Yep. Sure did." She laughed. "Wasn't the best decision of my life."

"Why?"

She stared at him blearily, trying to focus her eyes. "Why? Mistake, mostly. Parents threw me out when I was fourteen. I was a stupid kid, and no one would hire me, because they don't hire fourteen-year-old pilots. You know? Stupid if you ask me. I was a good pilot. Hell, if they'd just given me a chance, they'd have known. I could out-fly ..." she faded off, seeming to loose her trail of thought.

"Lena," Lev prompted. "Why did you fly for her?"

"Oh, Lena? You know her? I don't like her."

"Why did you fly for her?"

She cocked her head at him. "Why? Told you. I was fourteen. She was the only one who would hire me. 'Course, it was because she was a smuggler and a damn thief, but I was just a kid. Had no idea. So I flew jobs for her. Five years I flew jobs for her, and I was so dumb I didn't realize she was a smuggler and a ... a whatever you call it, until the last year."

She was slumping farther and farther down against the wall, her words growing more slurred.

"Didn't ... didn't want ... Never wanted to be a smuggler, you know. Not in my plans. But thing is, once you start, you're not going to get an honest job. That's the thing, no honest job for a smuggler. So I stole her best ship and took off. Never looked back."

"You never looked back?" Lev asked softly. "And what about the people you stole from when you were flying for her? Because you were the best, weren't you? You could take jobs no one else could. You should have known, even if you didn't."

"Probably right," she murmured. Her eyes were all the way closed now, her head shoved uncomfortably up against the headboard.

"Do you think they ever look back? The people whose lives you ruined?"

She opened her eyes suddenly, startling him.

"You know," she said, her words once again enunciated. "I think they do. I used to have nightmares about someone I ruined finding me. They'd kill me, I figured. Or maybe they'd do worse. Maybe they'd just make it so I couldn't fly anymore. Ground me. I don't know. Used to scare me so bad."

She stared at him with those bright, over-dilated eyes for a moment, and he found himself unable to look away. Then, like a string had been cut, she slumped back again, eyes drifting shut.

"Do you ever worry about that now?" he asked softly. His heart was pounding in his chest, his palms sweating.

He'd never thought he'd be this close. He never thought he'd be here, and she'd be lying helpless in front of him.

"No," she whispered, grabbing a handful of blanket and resting her face against it like a pillow. "Not any more. Got you. Got my team. You'd keep 'em away from me. Not scared at all anymore."

She nestled her head into the handful of dirty blanket, and a moment later began to snore.

He watched her for a long, long time.

His family had never been rich. All his siblings had left to work for the factories once they'd hit eight, just to keep food on the table. He'd been terrified of that, his whole life, and when he managed, at seven, to earn himself a scholarship to one of the top schools, his parents probably should have told him no. They'd been counting on the income he'd bring in. But they'd said yes, and he'd gone to a paradise of books and teachers and learning. He'd devoured the knowledge they offered like a starving desert-dog, and when he'd graduated at thirteen and been offered a scholarship to university, room and board included, his parents hadn't had the heart to say no. The same when he'd graduated at sixteen and been offered a place in a graduate program, with a small stipend. And at nineteen, he'd been the youngest person ever to be offered a professorship.

It was the life he'd always dreamed of. The pay wouldn't be high, but it would be enough for him to live off, and send a few credits home to his family each month. His parents had managed to put some money into investments that should pay enough that they could feed themselves and the rest of the children without him getting a high-wage job.

And then the news had come. The trading they'd invested in, on a ship that should have been impossible to steal—it was gone. All of it. The entire cargo that represented his family's home, their livelihood.

His dreams.

What could he have done? He declined the professorship and went to work for the government, at a wage that would keep his family at least in their home, with food on the table. He'd never said anything to them about the nights he'd stay awake staring at the walls, too sick with despair even to cry, as he watched his professorship go to a middle-aged woman and his dreams fade away.

And he'd looked up how someone could have stolen that cargo.

They couldn't have. There was no way. Except that there was a smuggling cartel, led by one Lena, who had a pilot who could defy the laws of physics.

A young kid. A girl named Jez.

He looked back at the bed.

She was snoring loudly now, clutching the blanket, a thin trail of drool dribbling from one corner of her open mouth.

There were so many small things he could do. So many delicate nerves and arteries, in her hands, her fingers, her throat.

Just a tiny nick with a razor to kill her, or leave her unable to fly. Her worst nightmare. Her dream, snatched away like she'd snatched his dream so many years ago.

Life had seemed so simple, once upon a time. Before he'd given up the thing he'd wanted more than he'd ever wanted anything. Before he'd planned Ysbel's extraction, and murdered her family. Before he'd sent his own family to jail. Before he'd lost everything, including any hope for the future.

There was nothing left of his old dream. But there was this.

He took a deep breath. His palms were sweaty, his heart beating too fast. Slowly he reached out to the sleeping pilot, and gently, he lifted her head.

She didn't even stir.

He let out his breath and pulled the crumpled pillow from the corner, tucking it under her head. Then he spread the blanket over her sprawled limbs, and pulled the trash bucket beside the bed in case she needed to vomit. He straightened and looked at her wryly, shaking his head at himself.

"Sleep well, Jez," he said softly, and slipped out the door.

# 17

Jez didn't wake until half-way through the next day. When she did, she felt like someone had taken a hammer, climbed in through her mouth with muddy boots, and was currently trying to break his way out through her forehead.

She blinked painfully, squinting her eyes and trying to figure out where she was and what she'd done to make whoever it was so angry.

Slowly, fragments of memory came drifting back, and she groaned.

Then she vomited into the bucket someone had left beside her bed.

She alternated between these two activities for a few minutes, and finally decided she'd see if all the limbs sprawled out on the bed actually belonged to her.

They did, but it took her longer to sit up than it should have.

Damn.

She felt like absolute crap.

Anyways, it was Masha's fault. What did she expect, keeping people locked up? Mostly, if she'd admit it, she'd gotten roaring drunk to teach Masha a lesson. However ... she pressed her hands to her aching eyes. There may have been less-painful ways to do that.

Damn, she felt like crap. Something must have crawled inside her mouth and died, and then slid down into her stomach to rot.

The thought sent her grabbing for the puke bucket again.

At least, if her memory could be trusted, which it probably couldn't, Masha had been angry.

On the other hand, that probably meant yelling this morning.

She wasn't sure if she was up for that.

Finally she managed to stagger to her feet and stumble to the shower. She let the cool water stream down her face, closing her eyes against the bracing pain of her headache, and leaned against the shower wall.

Unless she'd slept a lot longer than she'd thought, today was the day they left.

Today was the day they found out if everything they'd done over the past three weeks had been enough.

Tonight, she'd take the ship up. And by the end of tomorrow, they'd either have the tech and return home heroes, or they'd all be dead.

Her hands were shaking slightly. She rubbed her wet fingers through her hair, let some of the water from the tap drip into her mouth, and finally, feeling mildly more human and mildly more alive, stumbled back into her room to get dressed.

There was a knock on the door. "You up, you dirty drunk?"

She winced. It was Ysbel.

"Yes," she muttered sullenly.

A small white packet was thrust under the door.

"I thought you might need these. For your headache. I've never seen anyone drink that much and not die."

"Kinda feel like I died," she said. From outside the door, Ysbel laughed.

"You probably look like it too. And you might wish you had when you see Masha. She's not very happy. You're supposed to stay in your room until it's time to go, and I'm supposed to put a lock on the door. But I'm not going to do that, and you're not going to come out. OK?"

"Fine. OK." She bent down, sucked in a gasp at the wave of pain, and took the white packet gingerly. There were two tablets inside, and she swallowed them dry.

"Good," said Ysbel, then her footsteps moved off.

In the time it took for the tablets to kick in, Jez briefly thought about lying down and letting sweet death take her, but since that would mean no more flying, she reluctantly decided against it. When her headache finally dimmed, she sighed and pulled up the holo-screen, opening the file Lev had sent her.

She hadn't looked at it yet. She'd figured she'd have plenty of time, and anyways, when she was locked in somewhere she found it hard to concentrate.

OK, she always found it hard to concentrate. But more so when she was locked into places.

The diagram was dense, and her head still ached dully, so after a few half-hearted attempts to read through it, she flopped back onto her bed, squeezed her eyes shut, and prayed to the god of hangovers to leave her well enough alone.

Her stomach was still roiling and her head still felt stuffed with manufab when the sharp, impatient knock rapped against her bedroom door.

Somehow even the knock managed to sound angry.

She winced and got to her feet, and pulled the door open.

Masha stood there. Her lips were pressed tightly together, but all she said was, "I hope you're ready."

"Ready, cap'n," said Jez, with a mock salute. Masha didn't bother to respond, just turned on her heel, and Jez rolled her eyes, then winced.

She grabbed her bag of toiletries and stumbled down the stairs to the ship. But once she climbed into the cockpit, the soothing feel of the controls under her hands and the sweet exhilaration of knowing she'd be outside this hangar, outside this city, and outside the atmosphere on this stifling planet, flowed over her like a soothing balm.

"How's your head?" Ysbel whispered as she climbed in. She was actually grinning. "Does it feel like it's going to fall off yet?"

"Piss off," Jez muttered, and Ysbel gave a low laugh.

Lev climbed in next. He had an odd expression on his face when he looked at her, and for the first time she realized that he was actually not bad looking, in a nerdy sort of way. His face had a sort of gentleness to it that was strangely attractive.

She turned away quickly.

That was a nope from her. She wasn't going to get soft over some stupid scholar-boy who looked like he was going to puke when she did some basic flying, and who had a hard time figuring out which end of the gun was the dangerous end.

Nope, nope, nope.

Masha came in last, and slid into the back beside Ysbel. The anger steamed off her like liquid nitrogen, almost tangible in the close air of the cockpit.

Jez grinned. That, at least, was a familiar feeling. She still wasn't sure about the joking, or the tentative sympathy from the others. But absolute loathing was something she was good at.

"Buckle up, kids," she said, and pressed the starter button. Even through the stuffing in her head, the feel of the engine was clean and perfect.

This was what she was born for.

The door to the hangar opened, and she pointed the throttle forward and didn't look back.

The sky outside the atmosphere of the rapidly-fading planet was the dark, midnight colour of freedom, and she closed her eyes, revelling in the feeling of it.

Space. Shallow space, yes, but space.

Tomorrow this time, it would all be over. Tomorrow this time, she'd have her ship and her credits and her freedom. Or she'd be dead.

She'd prefer the first, to be honest. But after three weeks on that prison ship, and three more weeks land bound, she'd take the second if the first wasn't available.

As they approached the wormhole jump, Lev cleared his throat nervously.

"Are you—certain you can handle a jump? After—"

She grinned at him. "I could have done this jump last night in my sleep."

He didn't look convinced.

She hit the throttle, and the ship leapt forward into the yawning black nothing that was the wormhole.

He was a bit pale when they shot out the other side, but then, that was pretty much par for the course.

The rest of the flight was long. She set the controls and lay back in her seat, letting the sweet feeling of flying wash over her. In the back, the two women had folded back the seats into beds and tethered themselves down, and beside her, Lev had fallen asleep leaning back in the co-pilot's chair. She smiled to herself, and lowered the seat controls until he was lying flat and his head no longer flopped uncomfortably against the window.

His shaggy hair was clipped shorter now, the same icy blond as the weapons buyer they'd kidnapped the week before, and his long, dark eyelashes were now pale. But he still looked innocent in his sleep.

How had he ended up in jail? It was something about reading classified information, she remembered that. I mean, what else would she have expected? But still, watching him, she wondered what more there was to the story.

She'd never bothered to care before. She wondered why it mattered now, somehow.


It was almost seven standard hours later that she saw the tiny green planet in the distance. She nudged Lev.

"Wake up," she whispered. "We're coming in."

He yawned and stretched and sat up, blinking. "How you feeling?" he asked, his voice rough with sleep. "You OK?"

"Fine. I'm used to pulling standard-day runs. I'll be fine."

He shook his head to clear it, then propped his seat back up and turned to the back.

"Masha, Ysbel. Wake up. We're getting close. Be there in a couple standard hours. We should get into our seating arrangements."

There was yawning and a groan from the back seat, and then Masha said, her voice still icy, "Jez. Why don't you sleep for a bit, I'll take the controls. I'll switch out when we get closer."

It was clear from her voice that she was not doing this out of anything other than a sense of self-preservation, but that was fine by Jez. Honestly, she could use a cat-nap.

At least the hangover was pretty much gone.

She climbed out of her seat and stretched out in the back, and was asleep before Masha had finished putting her hands onto the controls.

When she woke to Lev's hand shaking her shoulder, she blinked and sat up quickly.

The planet had come much closer.

She slid around Masha and took her place in the pilot's seat, while Masha took co-pilot, and Ysbel sat beside Lev in the back.

A few standard-minutes later, a voice came over the com.

"Identify yourselves."

Masha pressed the com. "Mikail Yanovik. We were invited. Requesting permission to land."

There was a moment of silence from the other end, and out of the corner of her eye Jez saw five ships fall into line around them, blocking off every avenue of escape.

She tried to ignore them, tried to ignore the clammy feeling in her palms and the sudden pounding in her chest.

She wasn't trapped. This was all part of the plan.

But if felt like being trapped.

Once again, she felt that icy hand reaching inside her chest, that feeling of flying a ship where the controls weren't under her command.

"Permission granted. Please follow the pilot ship to your docking station," the voice came over the com.

Jez swallowed hard as another, smaller ship flew down in front of her cockpit window. She pushed the throttle gently forward and followed it through the break in the planet-shielding, and then down through the atmosphere, the outside of both ships glowing a bright orange as they descended. Then the pilot ship levelled out over a thick green jungle, and she followed it to a clear-cut break in the trees.

"Hangar-bay is down there," the pilot-ship called back. "Follow me in, and you'll be in docking bay four."

"Copy," Masha replied, and Jez did as she was told.

"Any word from Tae yet?" Lev whispered as the ship swooped into the hangar bay. Masha shook her head.

"We're just going to have to hope he's alright."

Lev nodded grimly, and Jez turned to face front.

She placed the ship down lightly on the landing pad, holding her breath for a moment. Then she turned and glanced at the others.

"This is it," she mouthed. Lev gave her a quick smile, Ysbel a quick scowl. Masha ignored her completely.

She hit the door controls, and with a hiss, the doors slid open.

For better or for worse, they were in.

# 18

"Tae."

The navy-uniformed guard read the name from a piece of paper, his voice bored. Tae stepped forward quickly.

The guard looked him over with ill-concealed distaste. "Over there with the others. Get your standard equipment, then go to the change rooms and strip down. No personal belongings. If we find you trying to smuggle any in, you'll be shot."

He said it in such a bored voice that for a moment Tae almost wondered if he was joking. Then he looked at the man's face.

Definitely not joking.

He moved over to the crowd of other recruits in the corner. An older guard handed him a bag and pointed him in the direction of the change rooms.

"When you come out, you'll be directed to where you need to go," she said. Tae nodded, took the things, and walked into the change room.

He had no personal belongings, thankfully, except for one—he needed what he'd programmed onto his com. So Ysbel had given him a gummy plaster to stick it to the roof of his mouth. The coating was non-reactive, and she'd assured him it would pass through the scanners. Even if they picked up anything, it would read like a tooth filling.

He hoped she was right.

But it also meant that, even though he'd given the others concealed coms and ear-pieces, he'd have no access to a com until after he was down on the planet.

It was a risk they'd had to take. They didn't really have any other options. But it shouldn't matter. He'd be on the planet well ahead of the rest of them, and by the time they got there, he'd be inside the gates to let them in. Hopefully.

Unless someone killed him first.

He changed quickly, and left his belongings in a pile outside the door to be incinerated. Then he joined the other new recruits in their identical navy uniforms.

"Alright," called a man when they were all out. "To your bunks. There's a holoscreen on each bunk that will have your instructions on it. You'll have two days to memorize it, and I recommend that you do so. The day after that, we take you to the planet."

Tae stared at him, hoping he'd misheard.

"I thought we were heading out tonight," he said at last.

"You thought wrong," the guard said, glaring at him. "We're waiting on the last batch of recruits, and they got delayed. Be thankful you have extra days to memorize your instructions, because let me tell you, if you don't know them, you'll wish you had. Now get."

He turned away.

Tae stood for a moment, his feet rooted to the floor. Sickness sloshed in his stomach.

Two days. If he arrived before the others, it would be a matter of hours, not days. And he might arrive after.

For a wild moment, he thought about wedging his tongue under the pad of plaster on the top of his mouth and knocking the com chip free, calling in to Masha to let her know.

But if he did, he'd be caught and shot, probably before he could even link in. He'd been watching the systems they had set up here. Any communication out would be trapped and noticed.

"Recruit. Why are you standing there? Didn't you hear the orders?"

"Yes, sir. Sorry, sir," he said quickly. He turned and followed the others down the hallway, feeling like his insides had turned to ice.

# 19

Two navy-uniformed guards stood waiting as Ysbel climbed out of the plane and into the large, airy hangar-bay. Sunlight streamed through the window-panelled ceiling, glinting off the polished surfaces of walls and floor. She was no ship expert, like their crazy pilot, but the ships around them appeared to be at least as modern as theirs, and most of them were not in the least understated.

She took her place beside Lev, weapon at the ready, and stood stoically as Masha did the same. Lev brushed himself off haughtily and glared around him.

That boy wouldn't know tough if it spat in his face, but he was passible at haughty.

The uniformed guards gave him a quick bow.

"It's good to have you here, sir. Welcome planet-side. I understand it was a long flight."

"Longer than I'd like in this short-haul piece of junk," Lev said, his tone cutting. Jez, who'd been leaning up against the side of the ship, winced, and Ysbel almost cracked a smile.

Blowing up that crazy drunken pilot would be harder than she'd thought it would be.

Blowing up any of these crazies would be harder than she'd imagined.

Still, they didn't have the tech yet. She could worry about the rest of it when they got out of here alive.

"I'm sorry, sir," the guard was saying. "I'm sure you understand why we can't accept long-haul ships on the planet. Vitali puts the security of himself and his guests as a top priority."

Lev brushed a final imaginary piece of dust from his wrinkled coat and grimaced.

"Needs must, I suppose," he said, the distaste evident in his voice. "What will happen to my pilot and my ship while we're gone? As per the invitation, I was not permitted to bring my usual guard to protect my ship."

"No need to worry on that account, sir," the guard replied. "Our hangar is heavily guarded. Your pilot will be taken to private quarters to rest and recuperate while you enjoy the presentation."

Lev nodded brusquely. "See that she is. She's a good pilot, and I don't want her damaged."

"Of course not, sir."

As they spoke, Ysbel glanced quickly around again.

The hangar-bay was busy with guards, and there were only two entrances that she could see, the ship entrances and a smaller door to one side. Likely another entrance that she couldn't see, because she couldn't imagine Vitali would own a building with only one human-sized exit. Still, it would be a test of Jez's skill to get past this.

Lev would have given her all the specs on her com. Jez would be fine.

Best to worry about her own part to play.

She could feel the gentle lumps of gel, tepid against her skin, where she'd shoved them into the pockets of her undershirt.

Right under her breasts. No one checked there, and if they did, having a pocket of gel there was always explainable.

"Come. There is a room for a quick refreshment before we take you in. Sometimes after a long flight …" the guard gave them an understanding look. Lev nodded brusquely, and the three of them followed the guard. He opened the door to the small, comfortable room, beckoned them inside, and left them.

There were lounging-seats laid out around the walls of the room, with small tables for drinks. On one side was a modern, compact cleansing pod, on the other a table of various refreshments. Ysbel looked them over, a sudden tightness gripping her throat. She hadn't seen fruits fresh from a tree since the day her life had ended, since the day she'd watched from the window of a ship as her farm, her tiny cottage, her family—her whole heart—burned to the ground.

She wandered over, and picked one up.

Lev had splashed water on his face and taken off his coat to put in the cleanser. The noise of it was louder than she'd expected, a monotonous 'woosh, woosh,' that underscored her thoughts.

Lev stood watching it for a moment. Out of the corner of her eye, she could see his hands fiddling with the cuffs on his shirt.

He was nervous. She hadn't thought he would be. Oh, he didn't like to fly fast, and he wasn't used to weapons. That she understood. But he didn't seem the type to be afraid.

Still, whatever his thoughts were, they clearly left him deeply uneasy.

When the cycle was almost finished, he seemed to make up his mind, and crossed the room towards her. He paused, and she turned, keeping her movements respectful. They probably couldn't hear anything over the noise of the cleanser on the bugs that were certainly planted throughout the room, but they'd be able to see.

"Show me the weapons you brought," he said. "I want to inspect them."

She frowned at him, but pulled a modded heat gun from her hip holster, and a second from her thigh holster. He examined them, frowning.

"Ysbel," he whispered, without looking up. "Don't react to what I say. I just ... I'm not certain we'll make it out of here alive. And if we don't—" He took a deep breath, still pretending to inspect the weapons. "If we don't I thought you should know. I—was upset when I heard your story, and I've been looking up the files. It weren't easy to find, but I—found something. On the flight here. While Jez was sleeping"

He paused again, picking up the pistol, then replacing it in her palm.

Her hands were sweating. Whatever he was going to tell her, she didn't want to hear it.

And she was desperate to hear it.

"Your family isn't dead," he whispered. "They survived. A woman named Tanya, and two children. The government has them on a prison planet, but they're safe and alive."

He nodded, and patted her on the back. "Reholster your weapons," he said, as the cleanser ground to a halt. Then he turned away and walked quickly back to retrieve his jacket.

She stared after him. She couldn't feel the ground under her feet, or the weight of the weapons in her hands. Every sensation, every thought, had been suctioned from her.

She wasn't sure if she remembered how to breathe. She wasn't sure if her heart remembered how to beat.

"Dulik!" The shout shook her out of her reverie. She blinked, and holstered her weapons automatically.

"What's wrong with you?"

It was Masha. She managed to put some expression on her face, somehow. She wasn't sure what it was, but it seemed to satisfy the other woman, because she gestured impatiently for Ysbel to take her position. But there was concern in the woman's sharp eyes.

Ysbel's heart thumped in her chest, the intensity of it almost taking her breath away.

It had been so long since she'd felt anything at all. And now it was as if every sensation from the last five years had caught up with her, and was flooding over her, and she could hardly bear the pain of it.

They were alive. They were alive.

Tanya, Olya, Misko. They hadn't burned.

She followed Lev numbly, unable to finish a full thought in her head.

Somehow they'd survived.

What this meant, she wasn't sure.

But one thing she was sure of. She was going to survive this too.

She had to.


Lev glanced back uneasily as he followed the guards out of the small hangar bay door.

He shouldn't have told her. He should have waited until they'd gotten the tech and got out. He's planned on it, in fact.

But he hadn't been able to bring himself to wait. Because there was a very good chance they weren't all going to come out of this compound, if he died and she lived, she deserved to know. After what he'd done, he owed her that much.

She looked like she'd been hit on the head by a giant prefab-block, in that moment where her body was still upright only because gravity hadn't caught hold yet.

He shook his head. He owed it to her, and he'd told her. Come what may.

The wet heat from the jungle slapped him across the face like a damp towel as he stepped outside, and he blinked and almost coughed at the thick, heavy scent of flowers and green things growing. The path down from the hangar-bay to the compound was made of intricately-fitted concrete slabs, and lined with brilliant, flowering trees. It would have been impressive, if he'd been in the mood to be impressed.

As it was, he was more in the mood to throw up, or maybe turn and run back for the ship.

Still, he'd had his chance to back out when he was back in prison. And yesterday afternoon, before the hungover Jez had stumbled down to the ship, he'd seen what he needed to see. Masha had pulled up on her holoscreen a vid-feed of his family, being led out of their cells and into the open air, to show him she'd done what she'd promised.

His family was free. That was why he'd signed on in the first place. He should probably be feeling peaceful now.

Instead, he felt like someone had replaced his stomach with a pit of live centipedes.

"Any word from Tae?" he whispered over his shoulder to Masha as they walked. She gave a short shake of her head.

Her expression was, as always, perfect, the sort of calm, unemotional competence that would be expected in a highly-trained bodyguard. But he'd known her long enough to catch the tension in her posture.

Then the compound was in front of them. He closed his eyes for a moment.

Tae should have contacted them by now. Before now. But he was there. He had to be. Probably just in the middle of something, and couldn't communicate.

Overhead, another ship was coming in, a larger one this time. Lev turned, and frowned at it.

"I thought no long-hauls were allowed," he said, trying to keep his voice arrogant instead of worried. Their guide glanced up.

"Oh, don't worry. That's no long-haul. That's just the ship bringing in the guard recruits. Was supposed to be here yesterday, but they got delayed. Vitali wasn't happy to have it come down in the middle of all this, but—" he shrugged. "What can you do, right?"

Lev stared at the ship, his stomach sinking.

Tae was on that ship. Which meant no one was waiting for them at the gate.

It meant no one to tinker with the sensors.

It meant in about three minutes from now, they'd all be shot dead.

He caught Masha's face. She must have overheard, because her face had gone slightly bloodless, even if her expression hadn't changed. Ysbel still looked stunned, and he wasn't sure if she'd have understood what was going on even if she had overheard.

Maybe he really should have waited.

Then again, he'd been right—they weren't going to walk out of this. At least she'd have that before she died.

There was no way to back out now, and no way to survive this.

Unless …

He took a deep breath and closed his eyes for just a moment. He wasn't certain, even now, that he'd prefer the 'unless' to the quick death.

Still, at this point it was out of his hands.

There were two other clusters of guests waiting outside the heavy gates.

"I apologize for the delay," their guide murmured. "Vitali takes pride in the safety of his compound, and his security technology is the latest and best."

Lev nodded and tried to make his expression look interested instead of sick. Beside him, Masha stood stoically, shoulders tense, face betraying nothing.

Ahead of them, guards passed a long, wand-like scanner over the guests, then touched it to the backs of their hands.

"Non-invasive, but it does a rudimentary DNA check. You're in the system, you get the green light." The guard was still trying to carry on a conversation.

Lev watched with a sick fascination as the light on the party in front of them flashed a bright green.

"We don't do the bodyguards, of course, but the guests. These things are getting big enough he doesn't know everyone personally," the guard continued as they stepped forward in line. "There are presets in the machine, so it's not even logged to you personally. As long as there's a match in the system, light is green. As un-intrusive as possible, and still effective. Bodyguards here for their scan, and if you'd step right through there, sir ..."

Lev swallowed hard and stepped forward.

The guard with the long wand moved towards him, smiling. "Don't worry, sir," she said, "just a basic precaution. If you'll just hold out your hands palms down—"

He did as he was told.

He wondered how it would feel to be shot. Hopefully it would be quick. If he was shot with one of Ysbel's weapons it would be quick, and surely Vitali wouldn't be far behind her in innovative methods of killing.

Still, if there were people who saw killing as more of a journey than a destination, Vitali was one of them.

The wand touched the backs of his hands.

He tried to swallow again, but his throat was too dry. He wanted to look away, close his eyes, anything, but somehow his gaze was glued to the button on the bottom of the scanner wand.

It beeped.

And flashed green.

He let out his breath, feeling almost dizzy.

"Go on sir, you're clear," the woman was saying. She waved him out of the circle, and with unsteady legs he made his way to where Masha and Ysbel were waiting.

"So Tae got in after all?" Masha whispered, as they made their way through the long, domed gateway.

He gave a brief shake of his head. "No. I'll tell you later."

If there was a later. That was his only hope, really. He might still die before he'd have to explain.

Explain how his poor, impoverished family had come to Prasvishoni because of his father's stubborn morality. How he could have been rich, if he could have stomached it.

So could Lev.

If Masha had known, there was no way she'd have trusted him with a place on the team. Honestly, she would probably never trust him again, now, and nor would the others.

Because the secret he'd been trying so desperately to keep, and which was now all too exposed, was that besides being the most notorious weapons dealer in the system, Vitali also happened to be Lev's uncle.

# 20

"Go on, get out." The woman behind Tae shoved him, and he stumbled forward onto the launchpad.

He had to have gotten in before them. He had to have. He hadn't slept since he'd got the news, and he'd been holding his breath practically the whole leisurely flight here.

If his calculations were correct, there was just a chance …

His eyes landed on a familiar ship, scorch-marks scarring the sides, and bile rose in his stomach.

They'd gotten there first.

There was no way they'd get past the new system. He'd gone over it a million times. Chances were they were already dead.

He hadn't expected how hard it would hit him.

He was trapped here, of course. He'd be trapped here for the next five years, working for a man that represented everything that was wrong with this system. Slowly losing his soul. But right now, all he could think about was Ysbel's deadpan expression when she'd joked about Jez, the thoughtful tone in Lev's voice as he'd considered Tae's suggestions. As if he was an equal. As if he was actually worth listening to. And Jez, the look on her face when she'd been jumped in the alley. When she'd turned around and seen them standing there. Like she'd never had anyone stick up for her before.

He thought he might throw up.

"Pssst!"

He jerked his head up, glancing around quickly.

"Psst!"

There. Off to one side.

Jez.

His heart almost stopped, then started again, and his legs went weak with relief.

She was still alive. The others must not have gone through the scanner yet—if they had, Vitali wouldn't have left Jez alive.

It was impossible, but apparently somehow true. They weren't all dead, yet. Which meant he possibly still had time.

He quickened his walk.

Get to the guard barracks. Get to a private place and hook his com chip into whatever communicator they'd provide him. Get through to Lev and the others and figure out what the hell was going on.

Hopefully, do it before they all died.

They were led on a short walk down a paved path through the jungle before their guide stopped in front of a large, squarish building.

"You've all had time to memorize the manual," the guard said, turning to face them. "I expect you to remember it. You'll start on the outside, because that's what everyone here does. You survive that for a year, and maybe you get a post inside the compound. But surviving means two things." She ticked them off on her fingers. "First, you do your job and you do it right. That means remembering the things from the manual you should have memorized. And second, you don't be stupid, and by that I mean piss off your superiors, piss off the big boss, or wander around in the jungle. There are more things in there that can kill you than you have words in your vocabulary. Now." She turned and gestured. "Get inside, get cleaned up, and be ready to report to your posts."

He didn't have a private room. That would have been too much to ask. However, the bathroom stalls were private, and once inside he managed to pry the chip loose with his tongue. He slipped it with trembling fingers into the guards' com on his wrist.

"Masha," he hissed. "I'm not in yet. Can you delay?"

There was a long, long pause. He could hear his heartbeat, pounding in his ears.

Had he been too late? Were they already dead? Were they—

"We figured that out," came Lev's dry voice, and he was so relieved he almost collapsed.

"Where are you?"

"We're on the inside."

He stared at the com on his wrist. "How?"

Another pause.

"Long story," Lev replied at last. "Listen, you in?"

"Yes. I'm in the barracks. Still trying to work out how to get—"

There was a crackling. In the background, he could hear Lev swearing faintly.

"Tech's not going to let us—" his voice floated through faintly, and then it cut off. Tae swore and shook his wrist, tapping the button on the com.

It must be the force-field. It was interfering with their coms. He and Lev had discussed the possibility, but there hadn't been much they could do about it.

No wonder all the coms in this place were on a closed loop.

Someone pounded at the bathroom door. "You done in there? There are people waiting."

"Sorry," he said. He depressed the waste lever and stepped out, holding his hands under the blue sanitizer light for the requisite amount of time.

The mission was still on, then. He needed to steal a uniform, get through a jungle that was supposed to be an exercise in creative ways to die, talk his way into the compound, and let Jez in the back gate.

And that was just so they could get started.

They lined up outside five minutes later for their first postings.

The only bright side to all this was the core password was in the manual he'd been forced to memorize. He'd managed to get into the system, shallow, but enough for now. His name had been on daylight duty, but a quick switch meant they wouldn't be expecting him at a post until night duty.

He hoped that would give him enough time.

It would have to.

"… And Tae. Night duty."

He nodded, pretending to mutter like the others had, and moved over to the group of milling guards who had drawn the short straw.

Or hacked their way into the short straw.

Other bonus—he'd managed to hack his bunk-mates into the day shift. They were high-fiving each other, and he tried to look jealous as he made his way back to the barracks with the other disgruntled guards. His muscles were shaking with adrenalin.

Jez had seen him. That meant she'd be on her way, and he had no way to contact her. And the jungle wasn't supposed to be friendly.

He tried to take a deep breath, and only managed to give himself the hiccups.

Damn.

He waited an endless fifteen standard minutes before poking his head out of his bunk room.

The hall was empty. Good. He slipped towards the uniform closet. Jez was taller than he was, so if he got a couple sizes larger—

"Hey! You! Where do you think you're going?"

He froze. A guard was walking down the hallway towards him.

"I … um, I was … a bit sick on the ship. I wanted to grab a clean uniform."

The guard came closer, sniffing the air suspiciously. "I don't smell any sick."

"I got most of it off, I think. But I'm afraid it's going to make me sick again. I'm not much of a flier."

The guard laughed. "Well, you're in luck. You're not leaving this place for at least five years."

He tried to smile. "Yeah. That's what I've heard. Anyways, if you don't mind—"

She stepped over to the closet and, sizing him up with her eyes, pulled out a uniform and threw it at him. "There. Now get back to your bunk."

He waited for a moment for her to walk away, but she just stood there, watching him, and at last he sighed and turned back to his room.

This was ridiculous.

At least he had a uniform. Even if it was probably at least two sizes too small.

It was another ten minutes before he figured it was safe to come out again.

He'd checked the schedule and guard rotation and set them into his com, and by dint of exact timing and more than a little luck, he managed to slip outside without being caught. Once in the courtyard, he ducked low and crept around the outside wall of the building. He glanced both ways quickly, then darted past the portal and onto the main walkway.

Now all he needed was to get through the gate.

Somehow.

Then break Jez in, then break into the vault, then get through the security, then steal the tech—

He took a deep breath, and stepped out onto the path.

First, the gate. Preferably without being shot.

"… And here are your rooms. You're welcome to sleep and refresh yourself until your crew returns."

The guard leading her was clearly trying to be polite. He was clearly having a hard time of it.

Jez grinned. "What did you say your grandfather did for work?"

He turned to glare at her. "There's food in your rooms," he said through gritted teeth, "and if you need anything, you—can—call." The last words were forced out. She grinned wider.

"Oh, don't worry. I'll call you any time I think of something. Don't want Mikail's pilot needing something. He likes me. He'll be pretty ticked off if I tell him I needed things and I didn't have them. That'd be bad for all of us."

The guard looked ready to commit murder. Instead, he held open the door to a comfortable-looking set of rooms.

"I don't know if I want to rest right now," she said. "Why don't you show me around some more?"

For a moment she thought he'd actually hit her. Then his shoulders drooped visibly. She almost laughed.

"On second thought, I'll rest. Long night and all that. But if you want to come check in on me …" she raised her eyebrows invitingly.

He looked like he was holding himself back from running.

She stepped through the door and closed it, and his footsteps rapidly retreated down the corridor.

Good. No one likely to check up on her for a while. See, whatever Lev said, this was a pretty handy talent to have after all. She'd have to tell him when—

She paused, her stomach tightening.

If he was still alive. If either of them survived this.

She'd seen Tae, here, in the hangar, just a few minutes before. Which meant he hadn't been there to let them in the gates. To be honest, she hadn't paid too much attention to how that was supposed to work, because first, she wasn't involved in it, and second, that was around the time Masha had announced that the hangar was going to be turned into Prison Ship II, but she was pretty certain it had meant if Tae wasn't there, it was bad news.

Still, they couldn't have been captured. If the guards had discovered that one of the so-called weapons dealers was a scholar-type ex-con who had not only kidnapped the weapons dealer he was impersonating and stolen his identity, but also intended on breaking into Vitali's deepest vault, stealing his most valuable possession, and blowing up half his compound in the process, she probably would have heard something about it by now.

She was pretty sure.

Either way, probably best to get the hell out of here as fast as she could, because if they were still alive, they'd be expecting her to be there.

They had to be still alive. That was all. They just had to be.

Once the footsteps were gone, she peeked out of her room into the main corridor.

There were people there, but hell, it wasn't like there was a wanted sign over her head. She had just as much right to be there as anyone. She shoved her hands into her pockets and strode out into the bustle.

OK, maybe it was hard to be nonchalant when she was grinning like an absolute idiot, but honestly, everyone else here had no idea what it felt like to be locked into a damn hangar for an entire week.

Her guide had led her past three other hallways, and at the end of one she'd noticed a door. A thick metal door, the kind you'd use if the door in question opened onto, say, a jungle.

She touched the pocket of her pilot's jacket, and felt the tiny reassurance of Tae's lock scrambler.

Didn't scan the pilots, did they? Because the pilots were supposed to stay where they were, in their fancy little waiting rooms. So she had all the tech.

This was definitely a better coping strategy than getting roaring drunk.

Although the look on Masha's face had been kind of funny.

At the very least, she wouldn't have a hangover afterwards. She'd either have her freedom back, or she'd be shot, and neither of those two things would leave her with a headache.

She strolled down the corridor until she reached the hallway, then she glanced around quickly and slipped inside.

She was almost at the door when she heard footsteps. She flattened herself against the wall in the shadows, heart beating quickly, but the footsteps passed without pausing. She let out a breath, glanced around quickly, and pulled out the lock scrambler. When it touched the lock, it whirred for a moment, then gave a satisfying click.

Perfect.

After one final glance around, she pulled the door open and

stepped through it.

She was in a jungle, like Lev had warned. The air was dank and heavy, and the listless breeze smelled of something sweet and rotten.

Terraforming gone wrong, Masha had said. Well, she wasn't going to argue with that.

A path led out from the doorway, but it was narrow, and it was swallowed up by the jungle after only a few steps.

Better than nothing, right?

Her heart beat quickly, her breath coming a little too fast. It was one thing to escape from people, but this place felt … wrong. Dangerous. Sick.

She stepped gingerly out onto the path, hand tight on her heat pistol. There was a movement at her feet, and she froze.

Something long and narrow with far too many legs skittered sinuously past. She could almost feel tiny legs scuttling up her boot, down the back of her neck—she shuddered, and brushed imaginary things off her shoulders.

She couldn't let her imagination get away from her, not now.

But hell, she was meant to be in space. In space you didn't have to deal with things with too many legs.

She stepped forward again, cautiously.

Overhead, a plant that looked like a tree, but with a thick, bulbous stem instead of a trunk, towered over her head. Its leaves were broad and bifurcated.

Lev would probably look at it and know what it was. She, on the other hand, was smart enough to stay the hell out of its way. There wasn't enough nope in the system to describe her feelings about this jungle.

The path petered out a short distance later, and she fought back the unease in her stomach.

No reason to be alarmed. It's just that they didn't have any need to come out into the jungle much. Not because whoever had cut the path had died violently before they made it any farther.

She took a deep breath and closed her eyes, trying to pull up the map of the compound in her head. The hangar was about half a kilometre from the compound, if you walked up the main path. She'd come out the back, so the compound was to her left, but the path she'd followed had been weaving around to the right, towards the guards' quarters. Which meant—she opened her eyes. Which meant the compound was that way. And also meant that wasn't going to be a path.

She paused for a long moment. Then she stepped out into the virgin jungle.

Things squished under her feet. Something brushed against her cheek, rough edges scratching her skin, but when she turned, there was nothing there except a hanging vine.

She shuddered, and started forward again.

The air was so humid she felt like she was trying to breath under water, and the heat of it pressed down on her like a weighted blanket. In the background, insects ticked and buzzed, the droning a thick undercurrent in the muggy air.

A few steps later, something brushed the back of her leg. She whirled around, gun at the ready.

Nothing. Just the never-ending greenery, thick and foreboding

A few more steps, and something touched her shoulder.

She almost didn't catch it. She almost turned around and studied the jungle behind her and didn't see it.

Then she did. The hanging vine that had scraped her cheek.

That had somehow bunched up behind her, and over her, and around her.

She whipped out her heat pistol and fired it into the thick, encroaching green. The vine reared back, its leaves reaching out like writhing fingers, and she ran.

Tendrils twisted around her ankles, but she yanked herself free. If she went down, she'd die. The compound was ahead of her, she was sure of it, but it was impossible to tell exactly where.

Behind her, the vines—if that's what they were—slithered through the trees, rough edges of leaves dropping down around her.

She wasn't going to make it. It was impossible. Whatever this was was going to catch her, and she'd be nothing but a lump of decaying matter on this jungle floor …

To hell with that. She turned around and snapped off three shots with the heat gun, then pulled out the other gun strapped to her calf. She took careful aim, and pulled the trigger.

A wave of fire shot out, enveloping the creeping vine. Clutching leaves burst into flame, and something that sounded like a scream echoed through the thick trees.

That scream could have been hers.

She turned again and ran.

She was lost. She'd missed the compound, and she was lost in the jungle, and she'd never find her way out—

And then she burst through the wall of trees and into the cleared perimeter of the compound.

She almost dropped to the clipped grass and kissed it, but there was no time. She had to get around to the back door, and she had to do it before Tae was noticed or she was eaten.

She gritted her teeth and slipped back into the jungle.

She had to skirt the edges of the jungle half-way around the massive compound before she got to the small entranceway in the back. She kept checking over her shoulder, but everything behind her was the same dark, foreboding green. If there were vine tendrils there, creeping after her, there was no chance she'd see them.

The entrance had obviously been cut clean recently, but already the jungle was pushing in towards it, taking it back. Vines dropped down from the overhanging trees, obscuring the entrance, and the shadows of the jungle let barely any light through, even down the cleared perimeter around the wall.

She shivered. The jungle was thicker and darker on this side.

That was a good thing. Meant she could get close without being seen.

She ignored the creeping feeling on the back of her neck, the memory of the brush of leaves against her cheek, and stepped out onto the grass.

Almost there …

Her foot sank into ground that should have been solid. She jerked it back out in a panic, and for half a moment thought she'd dodged a bullet. And then a writhing mass of whip-like, many-legged creatures swarmed out of the hole.

She ran for the wall.

"Tae!" she shout-whispered into her com. "For heaven's sake open the gate!"

Behind her, the wriggling mass of creatures flailed for a few moments, whipping their thin bodies through the grass. Then one seemed to pick up her scent. As one, they turned and flowed towards her.

"Open the gate!" she hissed.

The only reply was static.

She swore and pulled out Ysbel's fire-blaster gun. She lowered it towards sinuous mass of creatures flailing across the thick grass towards her. A shot of fire here would almost certainly attract the guards. But on the other hand—

They were only a meter away from her. She jammed the button on her com. "Tae! Open the damn gate!"

Nothing.

Half a meter.

She aimed.

She'd die either way, but at least the guards would take a few moments to get to her.

She'd die either way, but if she shot, and they found her, Lev and Masha and Ysbel and Tae would die too.

She took a deep breath and shoved the gun back into its holster.

The vines. There were vines across the door to the gate.

OK, they were carnivorous vines, but at this point ... she jumped and grabbed for the hanging tendrils as the creatures arrived at where her feet had been moments before.

They could probably climb, but they didn't seem to have eyes. So maybe if she was far enough up, and her scent wasn't on the wall ...

One of them reared up, tiny pin-like head weaving back and forth, as if trying to catch a scent.

The leaf on the vine she was holding snapped shut around her hand, and she bit back a scream.

The creature started up the wall, sinuous and snake-like, movements leisurely.

The hairs on the leaf scraped against the skin of her hand, surprisingly sharp.

She raised her free hand to her mouth, pushing the com button with her chin. "Damn you, Tae—"

The gate swung open, and Tae stood gaping at her. Then he jerked a short knife from his belt and shoved it at her. She grabbed it and slashed at the vine.

The vine drew back, its tendrils curling around her. The many-legged snake-creatures bumped its narrow head against the opening to the door. And with one final, desperate shove, she fell forward, through the door and into the compound. Tae slammed the door behind her, cutting the snake-creature in half.

She collapsed against the wall, gasping, her heart trying to pound its way completely out of her chest cavity.

"What—the hell—" Tae began. She glared at him.

"Don't you even start with me, smart-ass. I almost died back there. Where the hell were you?"

He was staring at her. "I—I was—"

She shoved herself to her feet, scowling. Her hand was bleeding where the cut-off leaf still clung to it, and she pulled soggy bits of vegetation off herself.

The tiny hairs inside looked uncannily like teeth.

"What kind of a hell-scape was that?" she whispered. "And why didn't you open the gate when I called?"

"I couldn't hear you," he snapped. "The coms aren't working. Force-held interference. Anyways, I was trying to get into the compound myself without getting everyone found out and locked up. You're just lucky my com picked up that you were calling at all." He picked up the knife she'd dropped and shoved it back into the holster sewn into his pants-leg.

She stared at him. "Lucky? You think—" she threw up her hands. "You know what, never mind. Give me the plaguing uniform."

He scowled and dropped the uniform in her hands. "Keep your voice down. No one can see in here unless they come looking, but if they hear you shouting, they'll probably come looking."

She scowled back, stripped down, and pulled on the uniform. He turned his face away, clearly embarrassed, and she rolled her eyes.

He was such an innocent.

The shirt pinched her shoulders as she pulled it on, and she glared at it in disgust. "How small do you think I am? I can't even get into this."

He turned back, exasperation clear on his face. "Sorry I couldn't get your exact measurements."

"Look at this!" She held up one hand, where the uniform shirt sleeve pulled part-way up to her elbow. "How the hell am I supposed to pretend to be a guard in this? Oh, don't mind me, my uniform just shrunk in the wash?"

"Do you think it was easy for me to get that and get out in time? You're lucky I have one at all. I was supposed to have a day and a half to get a uniform and get over here to let you in. I had less than a standard hour. You should be counting every lucky star you have that I made it here at all, and that I got the gate open before you got eaten out there. I almost died, more than once. But no, you're complaining your uniform doesn't fit."

She didn't bother to answer, just glared as she buttoned up the too-tight shirt and clipped the too-short pants. She didn't even attempt to shove her feet into the boots. The ones she was wearing were basically the same colour, and it was the best she was going to do. Then she threw her old stuff into the standard-issue backpack, clipped it shut, and took a deep breath.

Much as she hated to admit it, Tae was right. They were both lucky to be alive.

"How long do we have before Ysbel sets off the diversion?" she whispered. Tae, still glaring, raised his com.

"About twenty standard minutes. If all goes according to plan."

"So we wait here?"

"At this point, I don't see that we have much of an option."

She raked her fingers though her hair and pulled out a large leaf.

It bit her.

She swore and dropped it, crushing it under her boot with a shudder.

"As long as I don't ever have to go back out into that again, I frankly couldn't care less," she said.

# 21

For perhaps the first time in her life, Ysbel had no thoughts to spare for her explosives.

Lev walked casually ahead of her through the compound, occasionally responding to one of their guide's comments, but none of his words penetrated her brain.

Tanya was alive. Olya and Misko were alive.

"Ysbel," Masha hissed in her ear.

She blinked and shook her head, taking in her surroundings for the first time.

Everything around them spoke of decadent opulence, combined with military-level paranoia. The walls sparkled with the glittery sheen of delicate ravanite, which would have cost thousands of credits per square metre, and on top of them were mounted sleek black heat-rifles and projectile cannons, the smoothness of their design doing nothing to hide their deadly function. Like wearing combat boots with an air-dancer's dress.

A look, certainly. You wouldn't do something like that unintentionally.

The ground-cannons and the shielding. That's all she should be thinking about right now.

Tanya. Alive.

"And when will we be invited to see the new technology?" Lev had a knack of sounding both imperious and slightly condescending at the same time. Which wasn't actually all that far off from his normal voice.

"Shortly, sir. In the mean time, may I interest you in a brief tour of the compound?"

She glanced around quickly, orienting herself. They'd only be taken places that Vitali thought were appropriate for his guests to see, but she'd planned for that.

Her plans seemed a million years ago, and a thousand light-years away.

"Thank you." Lev glanced backwards with studied nonchalance, and she found herself almost smiling.

Poor boy. He was trying so hard to be a weapons buyer.

She flicked her eyes meaningfully in the direction of the back wall. He turned back to the guard.

"I'd love to see the, uh, walls over there. The finish is beautiful."

Again, she almost smiled. Almost.

The guard led them towards the back wall, and Ysbel grunted and moved to adjust her jacket. The heat inside the compound was dimmed somewhat by the second force-field surrounding it, but it was still warm enough that the movement was natural.

Discretely, she loosened one of the gel packs and dropped it into her hand. She palmed it, slipping it partway up her jacket sleeve, and then with a quick tug, ripped back the opening.

"… And this is put up to keep back the jungle," the guard was saying.

There. In the ground. A hairline crack, so small you wouldn't see it if you didn't know what you were looking for. Carefully, she pulled back her sleeve and let a thin trickle of the substance drip down onto the tiny crack.

She smiled to herself as it pooled, then disappeared.

They could put their force-shield reactors under the cobblestones. That didn't make them safe.

"Not bad. Not bad. And now, why don't you show me that, uh," Lev was looking at her for help. She flicked her eyes to the spot where, if the diagrams Tae had shown her were correct, she'd find another hairline crack in the stones.

"The lovely, uh, architecture there in the corner."

The guard gave him a strange look, but led them over.

Another crack. Perfect.

More of the viscous substance dripped and pooled and disappeared.

One more.

She gestured with her eyes towards the back of the courtyard. Lev cleared his throat.

"And over there?"

The guard looked blank. "The—wall, sir?"

"Yes. I'm impressed with the—reflectivity of it. I'd like to take a look."

"Very well, sir," said the guard, and led them over.

Again she fed the goop down through the tiny crack, and again she watched it as it soaked through. She squeezed the last of the packet onto the rapidly-disappearing puddle on the ground, and then let the packet itself fall behind one of the massive trees in the courtyard.

Tanya. Tanya. Her name beat in Ysbel's chest like a second heart, and she was almost dizzy with the sound of it.

The cannons. There were three of them, all wall-mounted, but, if Tae was right …

If Tae was right, one more packet of gel, dropped into the base of the largest gun, over to their right, should take down the power to all of them.

When Lev had maneuvered them into position under the first of the guns, she surreptitiously removed one of the neat packages and tossed it upwards. The explosive packet teetered on the edge of the gun base for a moment, then rolled slowly off.

She'd missed.

Still, she'd planned for something like this. She palmed a second packet then glanced up quickly to make sure she wasn't being observed. Masha had moved to stand close to Lev. Ysbel frowned and moved slightly closer as well, looking around.

There. At the gate. A young-looking guard, with dark, wavy hair almost obscuring his face.

Ysbel looked away quickly.

Tae would make it. And if he didn't, she realized suddenly that she wouldn't be able to watch him be shot.

Yes, she had planned to bring down an entire building on top of him and all the others, but she was suddenly unsure she'd have been able to.

And then Lev had disrupted her entire world. The future, which had seemed so certain only a couple standard hours before, had disappeared.

Beside her, she heard the faint sigh of relief from Masha, and turned back to see Tae, through the gate now, hurrying across the courtyard.

She tossed the packet, and this time it went in.

Thank goodness. She glanced at her com. Only a few more

minutes now. Had she got everything?

Yes. She was certain she had. She had to have.

But her family's faces, flooding her brain, were the only thing she could think of, and all she could remember.

She swore internally.

"And now, sir, if you'll come with me, I believe it's time for us to take our seats."

Lev glanced back at her with something like panic.

"Sir?"

"Of course. We're on our way."

She looked around quickly, and took a deep breath as they walked towards the building in the centre of the compound courtyard.

It was too late now. She'd done her job or she hadn't, and they'd all find out soon enough.

She glanced over her shoulder one last time as the door closed behind her, fingering the controller sewn into the lining of her jacket.

She couldn't see Tae or Jez.

Ten minutes. They'd better be ready.

They'd all better be ready.


Tae glanced at his com for the fiftieth time.

On the other side of the narrow doorway, Jez was—well, doing whatever Jez did when normal people would be sitting still. Pacing back and forth, swearing to herself quietly, putting her hands on the expensive-looking walls as if contemplating climbing them.

Two minutes. They should head over to the vault entrance.

He looked at Jez, wrists and ankles sticking out of her too-tight uniform, battered pilots boots on her feet, dirt and scattered vegetation strewn through her hair, even after she'd tried to brush it out.

He blew out a long breath and shook his head.

Not really guard-material.

Not like they had a lot of choice at this point.

"Come on, Jez. Time to move."

"About time." Her tone made it clear that she considered the risk of being caught and killed in all sorts of messy ways preferable to one more moment's waiting.

Well, she'd likely get her wish.

"Follow my lead. Keep your head down, and try not to do anything that attracts attention. And try not to annoy anyone."

"Oh come on. I do this kind of stuff all the time."

He turned and glared at her. "Yes. And every single time, it ends up with people shooting at us."

"Not every—"

"Have you ever, even once, in your entire life, pulled off a job without getting shot at?"

She paused, and seemed to be considering. He shook his head in disgust.

"We don't have time for this. Listen, I got guard's training and you didn't, so follow me. OK?"

She rolled her eyes, but nodded. He took a deep breath and stepped out into the courtyard.

It was busy, but not as busy as he'd hoped it would be. They must have already started taking people down into the conference room.

Blast. This was going to be a problem. He and Jez would stick out like a smuggler in a government vault.

He walked as quickly as he could, ignoring the glances, and tried to look like he had something important to do. Tried not to glance around at the heads turned in their direction.

His palms were sweating, his legs shaky. He couldn't do this. Why hadn't he learned his lesson in prison? He was a no-one. He was a tiny cog, in a cog-crushing machine.

Except now there were four other cogs that depended on him. And they would all die if he failed.

When they reached the door to the vault he blew out a breath and glanced at his com. Jez, against all odds, had followed his instructions and kept her head down, but she was far from inconspicuous. The sooner the distraction came, the better for all of them.

If his com was right, something should happen in three... two ... one.

Nothing.

He held his breath for a moment. He couldn't call them on the coms, couldn't know what had gone wrong.

More heads were turning in their direction.

And then an explosion cracked the air, and guards ran for the wall. He blew out a sigh of relief and held out his hand, and Jez, who had already pulled open her backpack, handed him his lock scrambler and wires.

He pressed the lock scrambler to the door, and as it whirred and clicked, he flipped the holoscreen on his com open and clipped the wire into it. He fed it gently into the system, and gave it a delicate tug to make sure it had gone in.

Perfect.

He began typing feverishly, connecting the system he'd built back in the hangar bay into the security.

It beeped softly.

Damn. The system had been updated since Lev had given him the specs. Should still be able to get it to work, but it would take a few moments—

Beside him, Jez was tapping her foot against the cobblestones impatiently.

She probably wasn't trying to get on his nerves, but she had a knack of doing it anyways.

Abruptly, she stopped.

He turned at the unexpected silence. She was looking behind them, her whole body tense.

He realized, belatedly, that after that first explosion, he'd heard nothing more.

He turned back, fumbling with his equipment. But he'd only managed to pull his com-chip free and shove it back into his mouth before he heard the running footsteps.

"You run," Jez whispered. "I'll hold them off."

"No!" He grabbed her arm. "Leave it. We'll both be killed if you try that."

She turned on him, jerking her arm free, but before she could do anything else, rough hands grabbed them.

Jez flailed and twisted and once actually bit one of the hands holding her.

Tae didn't fight. There was no point. Unlike Jez, he could tell when he'd been beaten.

Someone hit Jez across the head, and she went down. Before she could scramble back to her feet, they'd locked her arms behind her.

Another guard was behind them, smirking at the lock scrambler and the bundle of wires on the ground, where Tae had yanked them free in his panic.

"Well, guard 57223," she said, turning back to him. "Would you like to explain exactly what you planned to do in Mr. Vitali's vault?"

The cold hit Lev like a wall as they passed through the doorway. It was probably meant to be refreshing, but after the stifling heat of outside, instant goosebumps rose on his arms.

"Right this way," said the guard, and led them into a large, circular room, with dim, opulent lighting. There were generous half-circle rows of seating, and a low podium in the centre with a presentation table beside it, but what caught Lev's eyes and held them were the display cases around the edges of the room.

He stepped towards them unconsciously, almost forgetting the reason he was there.

They were genius. They were works of sick, twisted genius.

No wonder his father had wanted nothing to do with his erstwhile brother.

He was no Ysbel, but the craft that went into these killing machines was nothing short of breathtaking. He stopped in front of the first display. Inside the case lay a small item, about the size of a drinking bottle, but sleek and gleaming. One end was smooth and rounded, the other circled by a row of raised bumps.

The holo-plaque beneath showed a masked and padded person tossing the device into an empty field. It landed on its rounded end and emitted a low-lying hiss of something that looked like gas.

The padded person disappeared from the screen, and in their place a group of marsh-gritha, lowing in deep, sonorous tones, wandered into the cloud, as if they'd been herded. They sniffed at the gas, but it didn't seem to bother them, and after all, it was only as high as their hooves.

In the centre of the screen, the tiny contraption blinked red, red, red, then yellow, then green.

The raised bumps on the upper end shot—something—into the gas.

There wasn't even a scream. The cattle, dozens of them, dropped to the ground like puppets with cut strings.

The smoke dissipated, leaving nothing but the bodies.

Lev hid his shudder as he moved away, trying to paste an impressed expression over his horror. Ysbel was studying the displays with interest, but he found he'd lost the desire to see more. He took his seat near the edge of the room as other buyers filed in, and glanced down at his com.

Two more minutes.

Ysbel had been distracted—his fault. But these were explosives. Surely she wouldn't have made a mistake.

One minute.

Ysbel was fiddling with her sleeve, where the controller was concealed.

Thirty seconds to go.

Ten.

Five.

"Excuse me, sir, could you come with me?"

He looked up. An unfamiliar guard stood beside him. And behind that guard three others.

His stomach twisted.

Ysbel's hand twitched, and a second later an explosion rumbled through the courtyard above. The other weapons buyers looked around nervously, but the guard standing over him didn't even blink.

Slowly, he stood.

"Your bodyguards too," said the guard. His words were polite, but his tone made it clear that this wasn't a request.

The next explosion should have gone off by now. But there was nothing. He glanced at Ysbel, and saw confusion turning to disbelief on her face.

"What is the meaning of—"

"You'll see in a moment." The guard studied him dispassionately.

"Follow me, please."

He drew in a long breath, then gestured Masha and Ysbel to follow, and walked in silence after the guard.

They were led down a long, narrow corridor that wound towards the centre of the compound. Lev's stomach was clenched, his muscles shaky.

Then again, he supposed he'd always known it would end like this.

Finally, the guard stopped in front of a blast-shield door.

"Arms against the wall," one of the other guards instructed, and he, Ysbel, and Masha put their hands and foreheads against the wall and spread their legs as they were patted down and their weapons removed.

At least his stint in prison had taught him how to do that.

Once the guards were satisfied, the leader spoke into his com. The blast doors slid silently open, and, at the guards' prodding, they stepped through.

A man waited for them.

He wasn't tall, but he was thick and heavily muscled. Like the courtyard outside, he was a mix of brutality and sophistication, his silver hair cut and styled elegantly, his shirt half-way unbuttoned around his thick neck and hairy chest.

He nodded at them.

"You know," he said, with a predatory smile, "I've had a bit of a puzzle here this morning." His voice was rough, but the accent genteel. "You see, everyone here today passed through our new DNA scanners. But there was a problem—there was one set of DNA that never got scanned. An alert popped up in the system. At first my guards thought someone hadn't arrived yet, but on checking the guest list, no one was missing. And so they brought it to me."

His eyes narrowed. He was clearly enjoying this. "It was a puzzle.

If the full complement of guests had arrived, and one of the DNA presets was missing, that meant someone uninvited had come in. But who could it be, and how could they have passed through the scanners?"

Lev closed his eyes, clenching his hands inside the sleeves of his coat.

Just a few more words, and the secret he'd worked so hard to keep would be out in the open.

The man in front of them leaned forward. "The DNA scans aren't exact, of course. We're still working on that. Close family members, for example, could pass through without triggering the alarm. That didn't help me, though—Even if one of the buyers had brought a son or daughter, why had our last guest not arrived, and how did we not catch it? But they don't call me a genius for nothing. It only took me a few minutes before I figured it out." He laughed.

"Brilliant, really. Whoever it was passed the DNA scans, but not because they were a match for one of the presets. No. They were a match for someone who had been entered into the system for a long time." He leaned back in his chair expansively, and and put his hands behind his head. Then he turned to look directly at Lev.

"Welcome home, nephew. How's my brother?"

# 22

As the guards dragged her away, Jez cast a last, desperate glance over her shoulder. Tae was being led away in the opposite direction, but he was staring back at her as well, his face panicked.

A guard cuffed her across the face. "Keep moving," he snapped.

She couldn't completely blame him. She'd fought until she was physically incapable of fighting anymore. She now was restrained with handcuffs on her wrists and another set on her elbows, and a magnetic gag had been slapped across her mouth. Her head throbbed where they'd hit her, and her shoulders ached and burned from the cuffs.

"Come on," said one of the guards, shoving her roughly forward. She tried to take a step, lost her balance, and went down hard, her face slamming into the rough cobblestones. A guard grabbed her cuffed arms and pulled her to her feet, and she bit back a yelp of pain, then they shoved her forward again.

She was going to be locked up again. They were going to throw her in a tiny cell, and she'd stay there forever. Tae had grabbed her arm to stop her fighting, and he probably thought he was doing her a favour. He'd wanted to stop her being killed.

He had no idea how much she'd prefer that to being locked up again.

They manhandled her into a small lift, and when it finally whispered to a halt, the guards shoved her off and into a short, dimly-lit corridor. The walls were lined with six cells, but they were all empty, and for half a moment she felt a sliver a hope. Maybe some of the others had got away. Maybe they'd rescue her. Maybe—

The guard shoved her forward into the first cell, and again she lost her balance and landed hard. They kicked her legs into the cell and slammed the door behind her, and the magnetic lock clicked shut.

"How many of them were there?" one of the guards asked.

"Five," the other grunted. "Got them split up, though. Vitali doesn't want them talking."

"All of them still alive?" the first guard asked, and Jez could hear her grinning.

"Yes. Because you'd never believe who was the ringleader," said the second guard. "Vitali's nephew."

Jez felt suddenly cold.

Nephew. Not Masha, then. And it wasn't Tae, they'd have said something. Which meant—

Lev.

She rolled on her side, feeling tears welling up in her eyes.

She'd trusted him. She'd liked him. Hell, she'd almost let herself— She bit back the thought.

It had been a trap. She'd known he was hiding things, just like all the rest of them were. But after everything that had happened over the last couple weeks—she'd thought, somehow, that no matter what he'd wanted, betrayal was a step too far.

Stupid. She knew better. There was a reason she always worked alone. It was because people were stupid.

No, it was because she was stupid. Because society was built on a long list of rules, top of which seemed to be sit still and shut up. They were unwritten, and unspoken, and you were just supposed to know what they were and follow them, but she couldn't. Rules for how you act around other people, and what you say and don't say, and how you should dress and how loud your voice should be and when it's an appropriate time to laugh, and some secret code of what a look means, or how you interpret this word said in that tone. And she didn't know them, and even if she had, she couldn't have followed them, no matter how hard she'd tried. Her whole life she'd never been able to.

Her parents had thrown her out when she was fourteen, but she'd been a disappointment since the day she was born. It wasn't because she hadn't tried. Oh, she'd tried. She's tried to sit still, and shut up, and only say things that were appropriate, whatever that meant, but she'd always been too loud, too careless, too flighty, too rebellious, too impulsive. Too stupid. She'd spent most of her childhood locked in her room for some infraction or another, and when she couldn't handle it and snuck out, the punishments had only gotten worse. Flying was the only freedom she'd ever found, and she'd been good. Even as a kid she'd been good.

Trouble was, her parents never wanted a good pilot. All they wanted was a good, quiet, obedient daughter.

And when she finally got free, and finally started flying, she learned something else—the people who hired her needed good pilots. But they wanted the same thing as her parents did. They wanted someone quiet and obedient, or even someone with the right amount of calculated, roguish disobedience. They didn't want her. So they'd keep her as long as they could stand it, or hire her to fly for them, as long as she never stayed too long or worked too closely with them.

She'd known, by then, they wouldn't want her. She'd always known they wouldn't, and so she'd never looked for anything except hatred, distain, cold shoulders and badly-hidden loathing. And she worked alone.

Until now.

Why had she thought this would be any different?

But she had. Somehow, when they'd pulled off that job with Mikail, when the others had come back and stood up for her when she'd been jumped in the alley, when Ysbel had cracked a joke and not locked her door despite Masha's instructions when she woke up with that pounding hangover—she'd thought maybe, for once in her life, they'd not just needed her. They'd liked her. They'd wanted her.

And now they were locked up. She was locked up. And Lev had been the one who betrayed them.

Her shoulder was cramping from her weight and the hard cold of the floor. She rolled over, and by dint of shoving her bruised face into the rough cement, she was able to get her legs under her and push herself to her feet.

They'd come remove her cuffs, eventually.

Probably.

Maybe.

She sank down onto the small cot and leaned up uncomfortably against the cell wall.

This cell was even smaller than the one on the prison ship.

She wasn't going to cry. She wasn't. She wasn't some kid, she was a pilot, and she wasn't going to—

A tear trickled down her cheek, then another and another, and with her hands cuffed behind her back, she couldn't even wipe away the snot.

* * *

She didn't know how long she sat there, shoulders aching, then burning, then screaming, muscles in her chest knotted and cramped, hands going numb. She cried for a while, but eventually she ran out of tears.

It hardly mattered, really, at this point.

Sometimes, you just had to give up.

She fell asleep eventually, head leaned against the wall, until the pain in her shoulders woke her.

The dim lights of the cell block hadn't changed, and she suspected they wouldn't. She could have been in there hours or years, and there was no way to tell. But judging from the dull, hungry ache in her stomach, she'd probably been there for about a standard day.

Maybe they wouldn't be coming to remove the cuffs after all. Maybe they'd just leave her here until the pain in her shoulders was so great that she simply died of it, if she didn't die of hunger first.

When she heard the gentle clicking, she thought at first it was footsteps, and she looked up with a sort of dull relief.

Even if they were coming to kill her, they might take the cuffs off first.

It took her a moment to realize that the sound was coming from behind her.

She turned, frowning. There was nothing there.

*Click. Click. Click.*

It was her com.

The clicks made a pattern that seemed vaguely familiar.

*Click. Click. Click. Clickclickclick. Click. Clickclick.*

She frowned. It was the pilot's alphabet.

*J-e-z-d-o-y-o-u-c-o-p-y-J-e-z-d-o-y-o-u-*

Gingerly, she wriggled so that her bound arms were up against the wall. It took some doing, but she was finally able to mash the com button against the bare pre-fab blocks.

*W-h-a-t-t-h-e-h-e-l-l*

A pause.

*Jez. Can you get into your pockets?*

*No.*

Pause.

*Are you still handcuffed?*

*Yes.*

*There's a piece of tech in your inside pocket. Can you get to it?*

She glanced down.

*Nope.*

Another pause.

*Jez. I thought you said you could do anything.*

She almost mashed out a rude word. But instead she gritted her teeth.

Damn Tae. At least, she assumed it was Tae.

She leaned over, wincing at the pain, and grabbed the edge of her guard's jacket in her teeth. She pulled it back, then leaned over.

The tearing pain in her shoulders almost made her black out, but as darkness danced on the edges of her vision, she heard the tiny *clink* of something falling.

She pushed herself back upright carefully.

*Got it,* she tapped.

*OK. I'm going to set it to pop the lock on your cuffs. You need to get your com in contact with the connector end.*

She looked down to where it had fallen on the floor.

Even imagining what it would take to get her com touching it was making her feel lightheaded.

*Give me a sec,* she tapped. Then she closed her eyes, took a deep breath, and gingerly rolled herself onto the floor.

She almost screamed. She almost blacked out. But instead, she rolled over on her burning shoulders and maneuvered herself into position.

She was gasping in pain. But at last she heard a soft *click* and a *whirr.*

*Done. Put the connector in contact with the handcuff lock.*

With one final effort, she rolled herself up so her elbow cuffs touched the tech.

They clicked open, and she moved again so it touched her wrist cuffs.

They fell to the ground beside her.

She tried to move her arms, then sucked in a sharp breath as feeling rushed back into them, bringing pain that left her lightheaded for a moment.

She leaned her head against the floor, whimpering. Her com clicked again, but she couldn't decipher the message through the fog of pain.

*Jez. Are you alright? Jez. Jez, can you hear me?*

Finally she managed to move her dead arm around to where she could tap out a painful message.

*I'm fine. Cuffs are off.*

*OK. I need you to get a wire out of your outside pocket and open the back of the com.*

Painfully, her fingers so numb they were almost non-responsive, she did as he instructed.

*You see the switch connected to the green wire?*

*Yes.*

*Flip the switch, then remove the green wire and plug it into the third hole on the other side of the switch. I won't be able to talk to you after you do that, so ...*

His taps cut off as she flipped the switch.

Which hole had he said to put it in? She glared at the inside of the com, and finally shoved it into one of the holes.

Nothing.

She tried again.

This time the holoscreen on her com popped up, and Tae's worried face appeared. He looked more exhausted than she'd ever seen him, his face drawn, his eyes hollow.

She'd never seen anything so beautiful in her life.

"Tae! What's going on? Can you get me out of here?"

He shook his head slightly. "I'm working on it." He looked at her more closely, and winced. "You had the cuffs on all night?"

She nodded.

"You must have really ticked them off," he said, voice sympathetic.

"I have a knack for that."

Wisely, he didn't comment.

"What's going on? How did you get out?"

He sighed. "I didn't. I'm still locked up."

"Are we breaking out?"

He paused. "It's a bit of a long story. I ... Lev managed to contact me."

"Lev? I thought he—"

Tae held up a hand. "Yes. He's Vitali's nephew, apparently. I wish he'd thought to mention that. But anyways, Vitali has him somewhere that's much more comfortable than this, although he's still a prisoner. I managed to hide my com chip, and once I was in my cell I pulled it out and found he'd been trying to get a hold of me."

"I thought the coms didn't work in here."

"They don't. Or at least, they didn't. That's why they didn't bother to remove ours. But they click when someone tries to call in.

He figured that out, and was clicking out a message in pilot's code until I answered. He'd been trying to figure out how their closed system worked even with the shielding, and he was able to give me some ideas. Took me all night, but I re-conned the com system and made us a private closed loop. I managed to contact the others earlier and get them hooked in. You're the last one."

She winced and gingerly rubbed her arms, trying to bring her circulation back.

Of course she was the last.

The heaviness from earlier settled back into the pit of her stomach.

"So. Everyone else is on?"

Tae nodded and pressed a button. Ysbel's and Masha's faces popped up on the screen.

"Jez," said Masha. Her face was graver than Jez had ever seen it. "We've been talking this through. Tae has a proposition for you."

Jez frowned. "What?"

For a moment, Tae didn't speak. Finally, he said. "We're pretty far down in the cell-block. Hard to escape from here. Masha thinks that with Lev's help, she may be able to persuade Vitali to keep us alive. But—you're in a different block than the rest of us." He took a deep breath.

"If you can get out of your cell, we'll use the coms to make it look like you're still locked up, and Lev says he'll keep Vitali distracted for a minute or two. That should give you long enough to get out the back way. Then, if you can get to the ship, you can get off the planet. You won't have the cloaking tech, but Lev thinks he can convince Vitali you're just a pilot and not worth hunting down."

She stared at the com for a moment. What Tae was saying didn't make sense.

"And then what?" she asked finally.

Ysbel spoke, finally. "You're the only one who has a chance, you stupid pilot. The rest of us figured you might as well take it."

"And the tech?" she asked dumbly.

"It stays here."

"The rest of you?"

Tae shrugged. "I'm sorry. That's the best I can do."

There were a few moments of silence. Jez's heart pounded painfully, tears pricking at her eyes.

She'd be out of prison. She'd be back on a ship. Yes, Lena would be after her, probably Vitali too, and yes, she'd still have to find a gig to work. But she'd be alive, and she'd have a ship. That's all she'd ever wanted, right?

"Jez?" asked Tae.

They'd offered. They'd practically insisted. Anyways, she wasn't a team player. She'd told Masha that from the beginning. This was everything she wanted.

Except—except she couldn't stop seeing Tac's face, back on the pleasure planet, when he'd pulled off his own mask and shoved it over her face to keep her from passing out, Lev's small smile when he'd climbed into the cockpit with her the day before, Ysbel, shoving the painkillers under her door when she was half-dying from a hangover.

"Not happening," she said finally, her voice low. "I'm not leaving you."

"Jez!" Tae exploded. "Do you know how hard I worked to come up with—"

"Shut up, Tae. I'm not leaving. We all get out, or none of us do."

Tae took a deep breath. For a moment, Jez swore she could see tears in his eyes, but maybe it was just the exhaustion.

"Alright then," said Masha at last. "Since the only way to get all of us out is with Sasa's cloaking and hyperdrive tech, I suppose we'd best figure out a new way to pull off this heist."

# 23

"Lev? Lev, do you copy? If you can't talk, tap twice."

There were two quick taps.

Jez sighed. "So we can't get a hold of the one person who might have a plan to get us out of here."

Tae nodded grimly.

"Well, let's take stock of what we have," said Masha, her voice brisk and businesslike. "Jez."

"They didn't search me," said Jez. "I guess they figured they'd just leave me in cuffs until my arms fell off, and then it wouldn't matter what I had in my pockets. I assume they planned to pat me down whenever they came to take off the cuffs."

"OK. What do you have for now?"

She checked her pockets. They'd taken the knapsack, but there were still a few pieces of Tae's tech crap in her pocket. She emptied them onto the cot and pointed her com at them so Tae could see.

He frowned. "Not bad. A lock scrambler and a couple of my tools. I have nothing. They patted me down before they threw me in my cell. Masha?"

Masha reached down offscreen, and came back with a slim, sharp blade. She reached offscreen again, and pulled out a flabby-looking pouch.

"What's that?" Jez asked.

"Sleeping gas," said Masha, with more than a hint of satisfaction.

"Where were you hiding—" began Tae.

"Don't ask."

There was a moment of awkward silence.

"Ysbel?" asked Tae at last, clearly embarrassed.

"I have these." Ysbel reached inside her shirt and pulled out two packets of clear gel from under her breasts.

"Ysbel!" said Tae, looking away quickly.

"He did the same thing when I was changing into the guards uniform," said Jez in a stage whisper, grinning broadly. "I think he's a bit innocent."

"Who's innocent?"

They looked at each other.

"Lev?" asked Jez tentatively, after a moment.

"Yes. Is everyone alive? Is Jez on her way out?" They couldn't see him on the com, but his voice was strained.

"We are all alive," said Ysbel. "But our stupid drunken pilot refused to leave. So now we have to finish this stupid heist."

"What?"

"She says she won't go unless we all get out, and we don't get out without the tech. And I don't think any of us can handle Jez locked in a cell. Not even you, mister Nephew of Vitali."

"I'm sorry." He sounded faintly irritated. "Trust me, it wasn't my choice." He paused. "Jez, don't be an idiot."

She grinned, swallowing back a lump in her throat. "Tall order, genius-boy. I'm not leaving you knuckleheads, so you'd better come up with something."

He paused a moment. "What are we working with, Tae?" he said at last through his teeth.

Tae gave him a brief rundown. She could picture Lev frowning in concentration.

"Here's the thing," he said at last. "Vitali was hurt that my father disowned him. He thinks he can get back at my father through me. So for right this moment, I'm not in prison. Thanks to Tae's com link, I know your cell coordinates, and I managed to get my hands on a map of the compound."

"How did you—"

"Never mind. The point is, if Jez can get out, I should be able to tell her how to get to the rest of you. I'll try to keep Vitali occupied in the meantime. It'll be next to impossible to break out into the compound from where you are in the cell blocks, but if Tae can use the tech to get you out of your cells, I may be able to direct you through to an underground entrance to the vault."

"Tae's the one who's innocent, by the way," Jez broke in. Tae glared at her through the holoscreen.

"I'm not—"

"OK. OK. Tae may or may not be innocent, I get it. Now, how are we going to get Jez out so she can find you? The tech is in her cell, right? Tae, can you just explain to Jez how to—"

"No," said Tae and Jez simultaneously.

"Fine. Then we need—" There was a pause, then Lev said, his voice obviously trying to be calm. "Listen, I'm going to have to shut this down in a minute. Jez, Tae is on level five, hallway fourteen, and I'll pass the info on the others through to his com. You'll have to— Oh, thank you." His voice was slightly distant, as if he was talking away from them. "Yes, I'm ready. I'll come right—"

His voice cut out abruptly.

There were footsteps on the narrow corridor outside of Jez's cell.

"Hold on," she hissed.

The footsteps came to a halt outside her door. She slapped her hand over the com, kicked the cuffs under the cot, and dropped onto the cot with her hands jammed behind her back and her butt covering the contents of her emptied-out pockets as the door swung open.

Two guards stood there, faces grim, weapons in hand, the same two from yesterday.

She looked up at them pitifully, and one of them laughed. "Guess that will teach the little leech-eater a lesson." He rubbed at his shoulder absently. "She has teeth on her like a jungle-frog."

The other guard sighed. "Let's get this over with. Get up, you. We're going to take your cuffs off, and you're going to stand up against the wall nice and easy while we pat you down. OK? Or, you try to be smart, and we leave you in your cuffs. Got it?"

She nodded, biting the inside of her cheek to keep back a grin.

Bastards had no idea what was coming.

"Come on, up!" the guard said. When she didn't move, he prodded her with the nose of his gun. She whimpered.

"I can't—" she whispered, making her voice as weak and pathetic as she could.

The guard rolled his eyes. "Cover her," he said. "I'm going to get her up."

He holstered his heat pistol and reached down. She finally allowed the grin to spread over her face, and for half a second, he stared at her in confusion. Then she grabbed him by the front of the shirt with one hand and yanked the heat pistol out of its holster with the other, then brought her forehead hard into the bridge of his nose. He screamed. She threw him back into the other guard's gun hand, and heat seared the air above her head. She jumped up and bowled into the two guards, knocking both of them back onto the floor. The woman pawed at her com, but Jez brought her boot down hard on her wrist with a satisfying 'crunch'. The woman screamed in pain. Jez spun, smashing the hilt of the heat pistol into the other guard's temple. He dropped, and Jez turned, kicking the last pistol out of the woman guard's hand. Then she pointed the heat gun at them and stepped back.

"One move, and I barbecue both of you," she said.

They froze.

She bent and reached carefully behind her, still holding the pistol steady, and pulled the cuffs out from under the cot.

"Now, stand up and turn around," she said to the male guard. "No sudden moves, and keep your hands where I can see them."

He did as she asked.

She clipped the first pair of magnetic cuffs around his wrists, and pulled off his com. Then she did the same to the female guard.

"See how you like the handcuffs now," she said, with some satisfaction. She rummaged through their pockets until she found the magnetic key, then she slapped her own com.

The holoscreen sprang open.

She turned slowly, so the others could take in the full effect.

"I think I solved the problem of getting us out," she said, and scooped up the miscellaneous tech she'd emptied from her pockets earlier.

"Wait," called Tae. "All the guards have a standard-issue code break wand. It'll come in handy. They'll be in their inside pockets, or else on the belt loop."

Jez nodded. "Sorry," she said to the guards, making it very clear that she wasn't sorry in the least. "Just going to pat you down."

She rummaged in their pockets again, and finally held up two small cylindrical items. "These them?"

Tae nodded.

"OK. Hold on a sec."

She stripped down, and by dint of holding the heat gun in one hand and maneuvering the handcuffs with the other, she managed to get the female guard out of her uniform.

"Jez, you could just turn off the holoscreen for this," said Tae, in a long-suffering tone. She grinned.

"No one cares except for you Tae. Get over it."

She pulled on the uniform, raked her fingers through her hair, and grinned. "How do I look? See Tae, works better when you're not trying to put on a uniform that's three sizes too small."

"I told you," he muttered, "I was doing the best—"

"Level five, hallway fourteen. Be there in a jiff," she said, grinning. Then she slapped her com, straightened her jacket, and stepped from the cell, locking it carefully behind her.

It took her some time to find the right floor, and even longer to figure out which of the maze of hallways was number fourteen. But when she found it, and shoved the tech that Tae requested through the cracks between the bars, it was only moments before his cell popped open.

"Jez," he said in obvious relief once he was out, his voice thick with fatigue. He was still dressed in his guard uniform, although it was decidedly more rumpled than it had been last time she'd seen him. "I have the coordinates for the others. Let's go."

Tae had, it turned out, memorized a map of the cell block as part of his training, and it was surprisingly useful. With hardly any wrong turns, and only one near-miss discovery, they managed to break out Ysbel. When the door to Masha's cell popped open, Jez couldn't hold back her grin.

They'd done it.

Well, they still had to find the tech, break out, and rescue Lev, with Vitali's entire guard on full alert.

But that was the fun part.

# 24

"Lev. Nephew. It's so good to have you here." Vitali was grinning widely, but his smile had a vicious twist to it. "Your father never approved of my business, I understand. Willing to let his family starve rather than come to me. But you. You're a smart boy, Lev. I heard all about you. I was proud of you, of course. On track to become a professor. But then you had to drop out, didn't you? Pity your father was still too proud to ask me for help. He was willing to sacrifice you rather than his principles. But now, here you are." He opened his arms, gesturing to the room around him. "More than you deserve, really. I should have you thrown into prison with the rest of them, but I couldn't bear to do that to family."

Lev just stared at his uncle—the vicious killer. The reason the rest of his team was locked up.

He tried to hide the nausea twisting his stomach.

Jez would be going mad. He could picture her locked up, and it wasn't a pleasant picture.

Why hadn't she got out when she had a chance? He'd been sure she would.

He'd hoped she would.

Because even after everything, despite everything, he couldn't stand the thought of her with that trapped, desperate look on her face.

"So, nephew, instead, I'm going to ask you to come dine with me."

She'd die here. In a tiny cell. The others thought they could still pull off the heist, but there was no way. Why in the hell had Jez picked this moment to be a hero?

"Lev! We're out!" The voice hissed into Lev's earpiece. He started in shock, then quickly tried to fix the expression on his face that he'd been wearing the moment before.

"Uh. Dine with you?"

He tapped nervously on his wrist, where the com was concealed.

*How? All of you?*

"Yep. And I'm a genius, that's how."

He closed his eyes, body sagging in relief.

"Yes." His uncle looked slightly irritated. "Dine with me. I have a few people I'd like to introduce you to."

Damn.

*Give me a second,* he tapped. *Not a great time right now.*

"OK, but there are guards coming." Pause. "Don't worry. We'll be fine. I think Masha has—" The com cut out.

He swallowed hard, heart pounding. "Uh. Yes, uncle. I ... thank you."

What were they doing?

"You did it for the money, I realize that. That Masha woman was only too willing to confess, when I threatened to have the rest of you shot. You were working for the government, and you were here to steal tech from me. But really, you hurt my feelings. You know you could have asked, and I would have given you what you needed. For a price."

Lev tried to look concerned. It wasn't actually difficult. "What price?"

"You, of course! Your father broke my heart when he disowned me." He leaned forward, showing his teeth. "And you coming here to work for me would break his."

The com crackled in his ear. "We're good. It's all good. We took care of it."

*How?* He tapped out. *Never mind. Doesn't matter.*

"Great. So what now?"

*OK.* He closed his eyes and tried to concentrate. *You'll have to get up ... let's see, about three floors. Then you're going to find a large barracks room. Can you get there?*

"I said, this may be the only chance you have to keep your friends alive. Are you listening?"

Vitali was sounding definitely irritated now.

Lev opened his eyes and shook his head. "I'm sorry. I didn't mean to—I'm sorry. I'm a bit distracted is all." He tried to smile. "I'm—just worried about them."

"Then maybe you'd do well to listen to me when I speak to you," Vitali growled. Lev dropped his head, and after a moment, Vitali's voice grew slightly softer.

"I can go send my guards to check on them. Will that make you feel better?"

"No! I mean, no, there's no need for that. I'm sure they're fine. I —"

Vitali waved a hand. "It's no trouble. Besides, if I'm going to break all protocol and give you a chance here, I would appreciate your undivided attention."

"Yes. Uh. Of course. Thank you."

*Heads up. Guards on their way,* he tapped frantically. In his earpiece,

Jez swore.

"Follow me, then." Vitali glanced at him. "I'm glad you deigned to dress for dinner, at least."

Lev followed Vitali out of the room and down a hallway into a large conference room. There was a long table, with comfortable antique seats, which probably each cost as much as Jez's whole ship, around the edges. Vitali took a seat and beckoned Lev to a seat next to him.

"I'm not going to introduce you as my nephew just yet," he whispered, as the other men and woman at the table who must be the other weapons buyers stood. "For now, you're just another buyer. We'll see how you comport yourself. And I'll make a decision from there."

"Yes, sir," said Lev.

Jez was still swearing.

"Masha. You have the—yes, yes, I see it. OK, get—no! Damn."

"Welcome, my friends," Vitali was saying. "I'm thrilled you could be here with me on this memorable occasion. Now, please, let's serve the food." He clapped his hands, and a series of automatons rolled forward into the room, one for each guest. "Simply order what you will. If you are unsure, place your fingers over the buttons and you'll be able to taste each dish."

An impressed murmur rippled around the table.

"Really, Vitali," said a man from across the table. He had sharp eyes, and the imperious voice of someone who was used to being listened to. "I am beginning to wonder if your genius for weapons is matched by your genius for comforts."

Vitali smiled, an expression of equal parts pleasure and menace. "Well. You only say that because you haven't tested my latest batch of weapons."

The man smiled. "I look forward to it."

"We're at the guard room!" Jez hissed into his earpiece. "Just going in now." There was a pause, then muffled shouting.

"It's not empty. But we're going in anyways."

Lev could almost hear her grinning.

He started to roll his eyes, but caught himself. His automaton sat patiently in front of him, beeping softly. With a guilty look over his shoulder at his uncle, he placed a finger over one of the buttons.

Something rich and creamy and sweet exploded onto his tastebuds, and he jerked his hand back in surprise.

The taste was gone.

Behind him, his uncle chuckled. "Not bad, is it?"

"It's amazing," he said, trying to smile.

With his hand under the table, he tapped his com against his thigh. *Are you alright?*

No answer.

*Jez. Answer me. Is everyone alright?*

"Go ahead, try another one."

He shoved his finger on another button at random. Salty and meaty, with just a hint of a citrus tang.

*Jez!*

"Define 'everyone.'" He could hear the smirk in her voice, and gave a quick sigh of relief. "Guards are all sleeping soundly in the corners. You should ask Masha about that sleeping gas stuff. I'm impressed, and seriously, that's saying something. Because, not to put too fine a point on it, I'm the one who—"

*Jez. Shut up.*

"Sorry."

He touched his finger to a third button, and gasped at the bite of spice on his tongue.

"Where to next?"

"You're going to have to chose one of them, you know." His uncle sounded amused.

That was good. That meant he wasn't angry, and right now Lev didn't have the mental space to deal with pacifying him. He was trying desperately to remember which of the passageways led to the vault, and which security they'd have to get there to get through it.

He depressed a button at random, and the automaton beeped in affirmation and rolled off. Vitali raised his eyebrows.

"Bold choice, Lev. I'm impressed."

He groaned inwardly. He could safely say he was many things, but a person who intentionally made 'bold choices' when it came to dining was not one of them.

The woman beside him gave him a piercing glance. "I don't recognize you," she said. "I pride myself on knowing most of the people in the business. I'm Nonna. I understood that Mikail would be here as well, but I haven't seen him."

"Yes," said Lev, trying to make his voice bland. "I ran into him a few days back on a pleasure planet. I understand he got—distracted."

She raised an eyebrow. "I hadn't thought Mikail the type to get distracted. Still—" she shrugged. "I have heard that on some of the pleasure planets it's hard not to be."

"So I'm told," Lev murmured.

"Lev!"

*Sorry. OK. Go out the back door. It will be locked, but Tae should be able to deal with that. It should open onto a narrow maintenance shaft. You'll want to go through there and ...* he paused, trying to count in his head. *Five doors down on your left.*

"Got it, cap'n. Hey, Tae. Get over here. Lev says you're supposed to do something useful."

He glanced around the table. Some of the others had already received their dishes. They looked and smelled mouth-wateringly good.

"So," said Nonna, leaning over. "You're here buying as well, I presume?"

"I, uh, did feel it important to come for a look," he said, trying to keep his tone neutral.

"And?"

He sighed, trying to keep the irritation from his tone, and searched his memory for everything he'd recently read on the latest weapons tech. Really, it was Ysbel who should be having this conversation. She'd probably actually enjoy it.

"Well, the truth is, I'm not quite certain whether the reactor-core on the cylinder-bomb will be affected by the energy-signature of my weapons launcher, since my launcher runs off-centre bursts and the cylinder-bomb core runs in-line."

Vitali turned to stare at him, a slightly-impressed look on his face. "You know," he said slowly, "I will have to look into that. I hadn't thought of that particular interaction."

Lev bit back an exasperated sigh.

Perfect. Now he was helping the most murderous individual in the system make his weapons even more effective.

In his earpiece, Jez swore again, loudly, and he jumped.

"Hey genius-boy, did you mean for us to end up in a robotics closet?"

He swore under his breath, although with less creativity than Jez exhibited.

"What?" Nonna gave him a sharp glance.

"Nothing," he said hastily. "I stubbed my toe on the chair leg."

She gave him a strange look, and he realized belatedly that the chairs were suspended by one leg, far in the back.

He shot her a guileless smile.

*Sorry. Four doors to your left. Go back one.*

"And here's your food, boy," said Vitali, leaning over to get Lev's attention. Lev glanced over and almost gagged.

The platter the automaton was bearing was more of a horrific *tableau vivant* than a meal. It appeared to depict a giant centipede that had wandered into a blast from a heat gun, then dragged its charred, smoking body through a sludge-hole before crawling onto the plate to die.

Nonna raised her eyebrows. "Bold choice."

He tried to give her a carefree look as he lifted the plate onto the table.

He would not throw up. No matter what happened, he would certainly and definitely not throw up.

"I didn't see you in the exhibition," she continued. Lev bit back a groan of irritation. He'd had no idea that weapons buyers were such a chatty group.

"I was there. I, ah, suffer from occasional bouts of *amicus insanus*, and it can prevent me from staying seated for long periods. I stood in the back to watch."

"*Amicus insanus?*" she asked, still looking slightly suspicious. Vitali caught his eye and shot him an amused glance.

Of course. Of course his uncle would know latin.

Lev picked up his knife and gingerly poked at the thing on his plate.

Vitali seemed to be biting back a smile.

"We're in. It's a sort of hallway thing."

*OK. Now listen closely, because this is important. Does Ysbel have any explosives?*

"Are you even asking me that question?"

*She needs to put just a dab of explosive on the left side of the door. Right under the bottom hinge. That's where the security port is plugged in, and if she can take that out, you'll be able to open the door.*

"OK. On the right under the bottom hinge."

*No! Left! Left under the bottom hinge.*

"Ysbel! Wait! He's changing his mind. Now he says left side."

*There's not even a hinge on the right side.*

"Yeah, that's exactly what we were wondering about. So why did you say—"

*I didn't ...*

He blew out a breath through clenched teeth. There was no point in getting in an argument with Jez right now.

He cut his eyes quickly to his left, and lifted a large fork-full of centipede into his mouth.

It was rubbery, and he had to chew it far too many times before he could force himself to swallow.

In his earpiece, there was a muffled 'boom'.

"Got it. Now what?"

*Now get Tae to open the door. The blast should have cut out the alarm. You want to get down to the end of the corridor, and there'll be a lift. Ride it to the top, and it will put you inside the structure that leads down to the vault. I'll meet you there as soon as I can.*

"Sweet! We should have thought of this getting locked up thing in the first place. Hey! Tae! You don't have to break us into that stupid door again!"

*He's still going to have to get through all the same security! It's just the outer door he's skipping. And he's going to have to open that anyways, to let me through.*

"... And which new technology was your favourite?" the woman was asking.

"Um. Probably the ... third one, I think it was, that they demon-strated?"

She frowned. "The ship cannon? I preferred the gas canister."

"Well, I could certainly see the attraction of it. However, in my experience, the admittedly-large amounts of overheated air that would escape from the reaction of the mixed gasses would be highly-pressurizing in a system like this one that is already running at a surfeit of overheated gas."

She looked confused.

This was stupid. Every person at this table could probably kill him without a second thought, although to be fair, he was fairly certain she'd never actually figure out the insult.

He forced himself to take another bite, and almost gagged.

"You alright there?" asked Vitali. He was grinning broadly.

"Um. I'm sorry, it may have been too bold of a choice," he said. He didn't have to fake the look on his face. "I ... may have to run outside quickly."

"Go on, then," said Vitali indulgently. He beckoned to a guard, who came over to stand beside them.

"Please. Take him out for a moment. I believe he needs some fresh air." Vitali waved a hand, and the guard nodded. Lev stood and made his way out the door, the guard close on his heels. They walked down the long corridor, and then up the lift to the outside.

"Hey! Lev, you OK? We're here. Tae is working on the door."

His stomach was clenched tight, not just from the centipede, and his hands felt shaky.

He was no Jez. He really, really wasn't a fighter.

The guard pressed the button to open the outside door, and beckoned him forward. He walked out, and the guard followed.

But he knew a lot. A lot about the human body.

The door slid silently closed behind them.

Enough to know that if he were to do this ...

He spun around and brought the edge of his hand down at a point between the guard's ear and his collar bone, once, then twice.

The guard slumped to the ground. Lev gasped in a breath, then bent over and threw up centipede all over the cobblestones.

He was vaguely grateful that Jez hadn't been watching this.

He pulled off the guard's jacket, removed the standard-issue knife, and cut strips of it to bind his hands and mouth. Then he pulled off the still-unconscious guard's com, dragged him behind a decorative planter, and sprinted for the door to the vault.

"Jez, I'm on my way. Does Tae have the outside door open yet?"

"Working on it," said Tae into the earpiece. "Just give me—"

Just as he reached the tall plinth in the centre of the courtyard, the door set into it cracked open. Lev slipped inside, and closed it behind him.

# 25

Tae was dizzy with exhaustion.

He had no idea how long it had been since he'd last slept. He had no idea how long it had been since they'd been captured, or since Lev had contacted him over the com. Everything had turned into a sort of frantic blur in his memory.

And now, however many standard hours later, he was again standing in front of the vault, trying desperately to break into a security system that was basically unbreakable.

Lev stood beside him, scrolling through something on his holoscreen.

He should probably be relieved to see Lev, but he was so tired it had hardly registered. To be honest, when Lev had first arrived, he and Jez had gotten into an argument that, Tae was pretty certain, had involved Lev snapping something about how he'd eaten a giant centipede and it was her fault. So he wasn't entirely sure he was running at a hundred percent at this point.

"Tae. Here. This is the latest update."

Tae glanced over quickly. He'd patched Lev through into the system, and trusted that Lev would be able to figure it out.

"Thanks," he said, glancing through the information quickly.

He probably had about three chances before the system caught him and kicked him out. And he'd used one already.

Behind him, Lev said quietly, "Alright, Masha. I'm guessing we have about ten minutes from when I showed up. Later than that, and my uncle will come looking for me, and someone will have noticed the guards that went down to look for you never came back."

"Damn right they didn't," said Jez, with a self-satisfied smirk.

"So we need to get in, get the tech, and get out. What are we working with right now?"

Masha's voice was grave. "Not a lot. Tae rigged our ship so they can't lock us out, so if we can get to it, we can fly it. But the explosives didn't work, so we'll be up against both the shields and the ground cannons, as well as Vitali's entire fleet. The cloaking device and the hyperdrive tech won't be any use to us until we're out of atmosphere. Also, we don't have a good way out of here except out through the back entrance Jez came in, and that's only if he hasn't already locked it down. There's a good chance he has. I don't know how much more we can expect out of Tae. He's been working non-stop since he got here, over twenty-eight standard hours ago."

Even hearing her say those words made him feel woozy.

No. He had to be able to do this, because he was the only one who could.

He leaned up against the wall, as inconspicuously as possible. He couldn't fall over, not right now, and his knees were feeling distinctly unreliable.

Damn. He hadn't been this tired in a long time.

It took him a moment before he noticed the flash of green on his holoscreen, and he was almost too tired to feel relieved.

He was through the main system. Now he had to hook into the

overlay, which would be ten times more difficult. He closed his eyes, just for a moment, and bit back a groan, then started typing again.

"You through, Tae?" Lev asked.

"Yeah. Through the basic system. Now I need to take down the overlay."

"Let me see if I can find any more specs on that system you hooked me into," said Lev, and swiped his own screen in front of him again.

"OK. So once Tae gets us in, then I get through the physical system and grab the tech, yes?" Jez was asking. "Do we even know what this looks like?"

Masha shook her head. "I have no idea. But I can give you some likely dimensions and a possible shape."

He could almost hear Jez rolling her eyes. "Fine. But don't blame me if I come back with the anti-grav system or something."

"Jez. You know your ships. You'll know what the standard components are, and what's out of place. And you can have your holo-screen on. Lev and Tae will be able to help."

"Oh, so I'm so smart now? Not just a disrespectful drunken useless no good solo-player?"

"No." Masha was speaking through her teeth, and once again Tae felt a sort of awestruck wonder at Jez's ability to get under peoples' skin. "You are definitely all of those things. You're just also a decent mechanic."

'Well, now I definitely feel good about myself. Lots of confidence. Thanks for that, Masha."

"Shut up, Jez," said Ysbel in a tired voice.

His eyes were blurring, and he blinked hard, squeezing them shut.

He could do this. He could keep his eyes open, and he could keep his focus, and he could get this stupid system down, because right now he didn't have any other options.

Right now, the rest of the tiny, bedraggled team was waiting on him, and he was their only chance at getting out of here alive.

And then, finally—he stared at his screen stupidly for a moment before his brain registered.

Green.

"We're in," he whispered, and for some reason the floor seemed to sway. A pair of arms caught him before he could fall.

"Tae! Tae, you alright? What's the matter?"

He blinked up into Jez's slightly-blurry face. She looked—worried. He'd never seen Jez look worried.

"Masha! What's wrong with him?"

"He's fine." It was Ysbel's voice. "He hasn't slept for over a standard day, and I doubt he got much sleep before that either. He's just tired."

"Yeah, well, maybe I don't like it when my teammates are passing out in front of me, OK?" Jez grumbled, and he felt himself being lowered to the floor, back propped up against the wall. He took a deep breath and shook his head, and the world fuzzed back into focus.

"I'm fine," he said. "Just a little—"

"Oh for goodness' sake, just sit down for a minute," Jez snapped. "Take a catnap. This next part is mine anyways."

He groaned, and struggled to his feet. The word 'nap' almost made him want to pass out again.

"Jez. Lev ran you through the specs, right?"

She grinned at him. "Specs are for people like you."

"Jez! You need to at least—"

"Relax! Yes, he ran me through the specs." She stretched her shoulders, and winced. "It would have been easier if I hadn't just spent twenty-odd standard hours with my arms cuffed behind my back. But what the hell?" She grinned again. Tae handed Lev the scrambler, and Lev clipped it to the door, under the handle.

In theory, now that the security was down, the scrambler should just pop the door open.

In theory.

There were a few moments, while the lock scrambler whirred quietly to itself, where it sounded like all five of them had stopped breathing completely.

And then there was a *click*, and a communal release of breath, and the doors slid silently open.

"OK, Jez. Remember, this is a physical system. Tae can't shut it down from here, so you'll have to get through it on your own. Once you're through, there should be a shut-off switch on the inside."

"How does Vitali get through it?" she grumbled. Her arms still felt half-way dead from the cuffs, and she kept rubbing her fingers together, trying to make them act the way they were supposed to act.

She'd better not need any manual dexterity for this, that was all.

"He has a sensor. He keeps it on him, and it de-activates the system with a magnetic code as he walks past. They reactivate as soon as he's out of range. And no, I didn't get a chance to steal it."

"Some good being his nephew is," she said. "Centipede-eater."

He gave her a flat look.

If she was being honest, she was only harassing him because she was nervous. She shouldn't be nervous. But she was. These people had been willing to give up their own chance at freedom to let her escape.

She couldn't let them down.

She took a deep breath, pasted on a jaunty grin, and stepped through the doorway into the wide, high-ceilinged corridor.

Her first step was almost a disaster. She saw the hair-thin trip-thread on the floor a millisecond before the toe of her boot would have hit it, and barely jerked her foot back in time. She squinted in the dim light and carefully stepped over. She held her breath as her foot came down on the other side, but nothing happened.

Either she hadn't triggered the alarm, or else it was an alarm none of them would hear until it was much too late.

Either way, she didn't have much of a choice except to go forward.

The massive space was lit with a dim glow, reminiscent of the emergency lighting in a ship. She'd wanted to hit the light on her com, but Lev said there were light-reactive sensors. So she was doing this in the murky twilight.

She bent and yanked off her boots, placing them gently on the ground, then her filthy socks. She wriggled her toes against the smooth ground, took a deep breath, and started forward again.

She avoided two more tripwires and managed at the last second to duck out of the way of a trailing thread hanging from the ceiling.

She was a quarter of the way across.

"Jez!" Lev hissed into her com. "In front of you!"

She glanced up, and came to an abrupt halt. Swaying in front of her was—

Damn.

It was one of the giant, cannibalistic vines from the jungle, almost invisible in the dim light. It spread across the entire width of the corridor, tendrils swaying gently even without a breeze.

"What kind of lunatic is he?" she hissed back. "His magnet crap isn't going to work on this thing. Trust me, I know."

"Maybe he just stays out of its way. Can it—smell you or

anything?"

"I have no idea!"

Right beneath the vine, three strands of trip-wire, the height of her thigh, her knee, and her ankle, stretched thin and gleaming across the passageway.

If you had a magnetic sensor, you could simply duck under the vine and step through the loosened trip wires.

If you didn't …

She looked up again at the thing.

Maybe Lev was right. Its leaves seemed to be turning gently in her direction, like ears pricking at a faint sound.

They couldn't smell her. There was no way.

More leaves turned, and the rustling growing louder.

"You need to hurry, Jez." Lev's voice was strained ever so slightly. "I'm getting some feedback on my com. I think someone has seen something."

"Do you know what's after this?" she hissed back. "More tripwires? Traps? What?"

"No idea. But we're running out of time."

She stared at the vine for a moment. It was trembling now, leaves fluttering open, showing the teethlike hairs inside them.

She swallowed hard, took two steps back, and whispered, "if this damn thing eats me, promise you'll set it on fire, OK?"

Then she gulped in a breath and took a running jump over the trip wire, and right through the centre of the plant.

Leaves caught at her hair and face, closing around her body and grabbing at her clothes, and then she'd wrenched herself free and rolled to a stop on the floor, panting and gasping. Blood trickled down cuts on her face, and her hands looked like she'd shoved them against a grinder and accidentally turned it on.

"Jez! Are you alright?"

"I'm fine," she said, hoping she didn't sound as shaky as she felt. "All good."

Slowly, she got to her feet.

"They've figured out what's happened. Tae patched into their coms system. They're looking for us, and they already have a pretty good idea of where we'll be." His voice was the kind of calm that meant something really bad was happening.

She looked at the passage ahead of her.

One way to do this.

She took a deep breath and blurred out her brain, like she did when she was flying. When she wasn't thinking at all, just reacting. Then she rose up on her toes, bounced a couple times, leaned forward, and broke into a sprint.

She hurdled one trip wire, slid under another, rolled beneath a cluster of hanging threads. Her eyes didn't have time to register the threats, but her body moved to avoid them without her conscious thought.

Just like flying.

Three tripwires in a row, which she hop-scotched over, then twisted between two hanging sheets of something, then a two metre stretch of metal bars set into the ground that must be pressure sensors. She leapt the gap, landing on her shoulder and rolling, and jumped another wire, and then …

It took her brain a second to realize what the thick obstacle in front of her was.

A wall. The back wall. And in it, a massive open doorframe.

"I made it!" she panted into the com. "Tell me where the off-switch is!"

"Door frame, top third, right hand side. It will be a manual switch."

She groped around frantically until her hand caught on something.

She flipped it.

"Done! It's off! Get in here, and for heaven's sake, stay out of the way of the vine!"

Over the com, she heard Lev's muffled commands to the others, and then running footsteps. A few moments later, they were all there. Ysbel pulled a scrap of leaf off her shoulder with a disgusted look on her face, and dropped Jez's boots and socks at her feet.

Jez could have kissed her.

"We're good for the moment," said Lev. "The door's closed, and without hacking in, they won't be able to see that the security's been overridden. So that's bought us maybe five minutes. Let's get the tech and get out." His voice was thick with worry, and even Masha's usually-mild expression was cut with concern. Ysbel looked tired, and Tae looked like 'tired' was a word he'd outgrown about twenty hours ago. He swayed slightly on his feet, and for a moment she thought he was about to pass out again.

"Where do we go," she hissed at Lev. He turned on his holoscreen and pulled up the map.

"Follow me."

She grabbed one of Tae's arms as he swayed again, and Ysbel grabbed the other, and the five of them sprinted down the hallway.

On either side were display cases, illuminated with a low light, of chip cylinders containing unimaginable amounts of credits, holo-screen plans, weapons prototypes, and probably a million other things that could kill you or make you rich beyond your wildest dreams, or, more likely, both.

She didn't care.

Get in, get the tech, and then, somehow, get out.

Lev screeched to a halt and turned through a doorway, and the rest of them followed.

Then Jez stopped short.

There, in front of her, was the *Ungovernable*. The Ship.

It wasn't a short-hauler like the one she'd so reluctantly left in the hangar bay. This was a long-haul ship, built for deep space, and it took up the entirety of the large, open room where they were standing.

The ship was clearly old. It had clearly been old when whatever-their-name-was had crashed it here. It glowed with the sensuous gleam of old metal polished into something beautiful. The hull was joined with old-fashioned rivets. She'd never seen rivets like that, except in history texts. They invited your hands to run over the hull, to feel their raised lines against the perfect smoothness of the gleaming plates. Despite its bulk, there was something sleek and weightless about it, like it was straining against gravity, like it's natural place was in the sky.

She wanted it. She wanted it like she'd never wanted anything in her life.

"Jez!"

She blinked.

"I said, let's get this done and get out." Lev stood on the ramp into the ship, Masha beside him, waiting for her.

"Oh. Yeah."

He paused. "Jez. We're ten metres underground, half a kilometre of corridors away from the exit. We can't take the ship. I'm sorry."

She swallowed hard. "Yeah."

She glanced over at Tae, who was looking around in a bemused way and clearly struggling to keep his eyes open. "I'd better go in.

Ysbel, don't let him fall down again or anything."

She sprinted up the lowered ramp, and into the body of the ship. The Ship. She'd never be able to think of it in anything other than capital letters.

It was exquisite. The inside was as breathtaking as the outside, with that same old-fashioned ambiance, a restored ship that somehow was even more perfect restored than it could possibly have been new. The walls were set with actual wood, dark and gleaming and exuding the faint, sweet aroma of evergreens and crystallized sap. The ceilings were low, the corridors narrow, but somehow it felt comfortable rather than cramped.

She should be walking. She should be running her hands along the smooth, smooth, old-fashioned walls. She should be breathing in the smell of it, the atmosphere. No wonder Vitali had kept it in his secret vault.

She'd be almost tempted to be a weapons dealer herself if it meant she could have a ship like this.

And then they stepped into the cockpit, and Jez thought she might actually faint.

She steadied herself against the wall and breathed in deeply.

This was heaven. If she died, she wanted to end up right here. In this cockpit. If that was the reward for being good, she'd spend the rest of her life trying.

"Jez," Lev said, concern in his tone. "You alright?"

She turned dreamy eyes towards him and nodded through the lump in her throat.

She was more than alright. She was floating.

And when she left here, she'd never be alright again, for the rest of her life.

"You might want to hurry," Ysbel's voice came in over the com, cutting through her reverie. "I'm going to go flip the physical securi-ty system back on so we're not leaving them a trail, but I don't think it will hold them off for long."

There was a pause.

"Tae's staying here. I'm leaning him against the walkway. Don't step on him, please."

Her com cut out. Jez, Lev, and Masha looked at each other, then Jez pulled a wrench out of her uniform pocket and gently, reverently, began removing the panel under the controls.

It took her only a moment, but Ysbel's voice came back online as she carefully pulled it free.

"I'm guessing you've got two more minutes. Grab the tech and come. I'd prefer not to fight them off by myself."

"We can still get out," Lev murmured to Masha, as if trying to reassure himself as much as her. "If we have the tech, and Tae is conscious, we can still make it."

Masha nodded, but she didn't look convinced.

Jez laid the panel to one side, and the three of them leaned over and stuck their heads inside.

For a long moment, none of them spoke.

The tech was there, alright. Even Jez's untrained eyes could see it, spidering through the *Ungovernable's* controls. If she hadn't known what it was, it would have looked like some quirk in the wiring.

"It's completely integrated," said Lev softly, his voice holding the smooth bite of despair.

Jez shook her head silently.

They'd have to take this beautiful ship apart piece by piece.

Masha's face was pale and stricken.

"You have it?" asked Ysbel over the com.

Lev touched his own com button, looking like he was

sleepwalking. "No," he said, his voice hollow and quiet. "We don't. The tech is staying here. Maybe you and Tae should move inside. Take them a few minutes longer to find us that way."

He put a hand gently over the com, cutting it off.

# 26

Lev watched with a sort of abstract calm as Ysbel appeared in the cockpit doorway, half-dragging an almost comatose Tae.

Vitali wouldn't show them any mercy this time. And he had a pretty decent guess what 'no mercy' meant to someone like his uncle.

Ysbel glanced around the cockpit quickly. It only took her a brief look to take in what he, Jez, and Masha had already seen.

"We could defend this, if my explosives were reliable. But I don't know what's wrong with them." She gave a small shrug, looking more defeated than Lev had ever seen her. "I suppose I must have made a miscalculation somewhere. I've never had my explosives not work." She paused. "I'm sorry."

Lev shook his head wordlessly. It hadn't been her fault. He'd been the one to distract her.

Not that it really mattered. They were all going to die horribly. Allocating fault seemed a pointless exercise at this stage.

"We can't get the tech out?" Tae asked, blinking awake enough to look around. "What—oh."

He'd seen the same thing they'd all seen. Lev had had, for one brief moment, the wild hope that perhaps Tae would see a solution where he hadn't. But it had been a dream. Tae was good, but he wasn't a miracle worker.

"We'll split up the weapons," Ysbel was saying matter-of-factly. "We aren't going to win, but we can make a few of them wish they hadn't come after us. If you're going to die, you should have company on the way down."

"Wait," said Jez slowly. He turned to look at her. She still had the slightly-dazed look on her face that she'd worn since she'd first seen the ship.

"What?" Ysbel snapped impatiently. "Shall we just wait until they show up?"

"No." She still had that far-away expression. "I know how we can get the tech out after all."

He stared at her for a moment, hope battling with concern. It had been a long—well, whatever it had been. Day. Week. Month. And he knew how much she hated being locked up. Maybe it had finally pushed her over.

"Jez," he said gently.

"I can fly us out."

Now they were all staring at her.

A slow, slightly-goofy grin had spread across her face. "This angel is in perfect running order. I looked through the controls. I think there's a break on it, but I should be able to pop it off."

"Jez," Lev said through his teeth, "that's impossible. You saw the corridors we came through. I don't even know how they dragged it in here."

"They're plenty big enough. We'd have to smash out of the door," for a moment her face betrayed a pang, "but other than that—"

"Plenty big enough? You'd have maybe a finger's width on each side of this thing."

"Like I said."

Masha was shaking her head slowly. "It is impossible. Or should be. But—this is Jez. It's just possible that she could pull it off. Even if she did, though, we'd still need a distraction, or the other ships would be on us before we got out of the vault. And we'd need the shields down. This thing doesn't have the mods our ship does."

Lev stopped abruptly.

The shields down, a distraction. The explosives hadn't worked last time, but why? Ysbel would never have made a mistake, not with her explosives. So it had to be something else, something …

He spun around. "Ysbel! I know what happened with your explosives. It had nothing to do with how you made them. It's the closed loop! Just like the coms—they only worked sporadically because of the force-field interference. The same thing was shorting out your controller. It only worked on the one at close quarters to you."

Ysbel frowned, but he could see the dawning relief on her face. "Perhaps you are right," she said slowly. "Can we fix it?"

He glanced over at Tae, who was still on his feet, but barely. Tae forced his head up with an effort. "I can—" he began, words slurring with exhaustion.

Lev gave a decisive shake of his head. "I'll do it. I should be able to patch your control into our closed loop pretty quickly."

"We'll need to be closer. My control won't work from here—we're too far underground. And I'll need to be with you. I know my explosives."

"Alright," he said. "It's settled. I'll go with Ysbel to set off the explosives. That will take down the ground cannons and the force-field for a minute or two before they get it switched over to alternate power. And, it should cause enough of a distraction to get people looking away from you. As soon as you hear the first explosion, get going."

"And you?" asked Jez.

He shrugged. "If we can, we'll get out to the other ship. That's our best chance."

His heart was pounding strangely.

Neither he nor Ysbel was going to get out of this alive. A glance at Ysbel told him she'd realized the same thing. But then, this whole thing had been just a wish and a prayer to begin with. At least this way, the others stood a chance of escaping.

Jez looked slightly panicked. "Wait, you don't know what that jungle is like. You're not—"

He drew in a breath, then took her gently by the shoulders. "Trust me, Jez. It will be fine. Just worry about getting the ship out."

She looked into his eyes for a long moment, her face, for once, deadly serious. Almost afraid.

He'd never seen Jez afraid.

"We're about to have company," warned Ysbel. "Come on. If we don't go now, we're not getting out."

He took one last look at the three of them, Masha, still with her impassive expression, Tae, trying desperately to stay on his feet, Jez, who he somehow couldn't look away from …

Nope. Not the time for it.

He turned resolutely, and followed Ysbel out of the ship at a run.

Tae took a deep breath and pressed his fingers to his temples.

This was going to end, one way or another, in a few minutes. The least he could do was stay awake for it.

His head felt like it had been stuffed with cotton, and then repeatedly smashed with a hammer.

"Tae. Can you help Jez with the lock?"

Masha was standing in front of him. He blinked, and her face seemed to waiver.

"Can you slap me?" he said, his words indistinct.

"What?" She frowned.

"Slap me. Maybe it'll wake me up."

She raised her eyebrows, drew back her hand, and slapped him hard across the face. He staggered, tears coming to his eyes, then shook his head.

It seemed to have helped, anyways. Even though he'd probably have a bruise.

"Oh, can I play?" Jez had looked up from where she was kneeling under the control console. She was grinning, but it was obviously forced.

Was she actually worried? About him? Jez?

He shook his head again. The day couldn't possibly get any weirder.

"Here. Let me in." He came over and knelt beside her.

"I thought I had it," she said. "I got the cylinder off, but it's not sparking."

He glanced quickly at the wiring. "There," he said. "That black wire. Clip it, and twist the live end into the red wire connector."

She looked closer, frowned, then grinned. "Got it. You're not too bad at this, you know?"

"Thanks. We're waiting for explosions?"

That was what he'd thought they'd said. But then, there were a lot of things he thought people had said today that they probably hadn't.

"Yep. Lev figured out what was wrong with the explosives." She jerked at another wire, and he winced.

"There's a secondary choke. I can't fire this little beauty up until we get it off, and I can't figure out where he put it."

"Move over."

She shifted, and he peered into the compartment, frowning.

"Jez. Tae." Masha's voice was grim. "Vitali's here. How much longer do you need?"

"I—" he tried to focus his bleary eyes. "A few minutes?"

She turned to them, face set. "Fine. I'll hold him off as long as I can."

He stared at her blankly for a moment. "You're going to get into a firefight with Vitali and his guards? Don't you think—"

She shook her head with a faint smile. "No. I'm just going to talk. Get the ship ready and fire it up. I doubt even Vitali has any idea what Jez can do."

She flashed them a quick grin, then disappeared back through the ship. A moment later, he saw through the cockpit window her slip out through the doorway.

"Vitali!" Her voice drifted in over the com. She must have turned it on so they'd know if things were going sideways.

Whatever the slap had done, it was wearing off quickly.

"What the—" Over the com, Vitali let loose a long string of expletives that would have made even Jez proud. "How did you get out, and where are the others? Where is my nephew?"

"I honestly don't know where Lev is right now. He's not with me. Did he run?"

"Don't act the fool, Masha Volkova," Vitali said, his voice low and dangerous. "I looked you up. You told me you worked for the government. And it's true, you do. But you didn't mention the mafia."

"I—don't know—" she sounded suddenly uncertain. Tae looked up from the tangle of wires and frowned at Jez. She shrugged, and gestured with her chin at the controls. He sighed and went back to work, his pulse throbbing dully behind his forehead.

"Don't play games with me, Masha!" Vitali growled. "What are you trying to steal, and what you have done with my nephew?"

"So many things to steal here, aren't there," she said musingly. "What do you think I was going for?"

"I could shoot you now."

"You could, but then you'd never find out what happened to Lev, or the others. And you'd never know what I did while I was down here."

There was a long pause.

"I know how to get people to talk," Vitali said, his voice a menacing purr.

"You said you'd done your research on me," said Masha lightly. "I would have thought you'd know better. Do you want to take the chance? How many mafia operatives have you found who don't carry a suicide pill?"

"I could stop you."

"Could you? Are you a gambling man?"

There was a long sigh.

"What do you want? Do you think you can stand there and negotiate with me, when your only bargaining chip is that you can kill yourself before I can kill you?"

"No." Masha's voice was her typical calm politeness. "My bargaining chip is that I know what the mafia sent me here for, and I know what the government sent me here for. I know what they want from you, and why they're after you. I could tell you what happened to Lev. I know how the others escaped. So I don't think you're correct that I don't have bargaining chips. It just depends on what you're willing to bargain for."

"And what are you willing to bargain for?" Vitali asked at last, in a low voice.

"Tae! I said, are you finished?"

He glanced down at the mass of wires in his hands, and forced his eyes to follow the colours. Red to red, green to green, yellow to yellow.

"Yes. I think so. It should start up now."

He sounded drunk. Or maybe high. Or both. It was hard to care.

"Oh, I have some ideas," said Masha lightly. "For instance—"

Her words were drowned out by a *boom* that shook the entire building.

Jez shot Tae a quick glance and hit the ignition.

He held his breath.

It purred to life, and he let out his breath in a rush. He honestly hadn't been sure he could keep the wires straight.

And then, through the com, there was the staticky fizz of a heat-gun blast, and a strangled grunt of pain. Three more blasts, and Masha came stumbling into the hangar, clutching her side.

He slapped his com. "Get in!"

"No." Her voice was choking with pain. "Get out of here."

There was another explosion from outside.

Jez scowled and slapped her own com. "Get in, Masha, you idiot. This isn't the time to play games."

"No. Trust me—on this one. I'll be—fine. Just go."

"We're not—"

"You're running out of time!" Masha snapped, life coming back into her voice for just a moment. "For heaven's sake, trust me! Get out!"

Jez looked at Tae.

"Go, damn it!" Masha called.

Tae glanced from Jez's stubbornly-set face to Masha's determined one.

Why did he have to make these decisions when his brain had been removed and replaced with cheap cotton stuffing?

But there was something about the way Masha was looking at him …

"Go," he said quietly. "Just go."

"I can't—"

"Trust her. Go."

Jez took a deep breath. Another explosion shook the ground overhead. Already, Vitali's guards were appearing in the doorway.

She glanced one last time at Masha, and he followed her gaze. Then she dropped into her seat, and he grabbed for his harness as she jammed the throttle forward.

The figures in the doorway dove for cover as the ship skimmed past them, and for half an instant he caught sight of Vitali and his guards staring after them, mouths gaping open.

And then there was nothing but the flight.

Tae had seen Jez fly before. He'd seen her fly the skybikes, skimming the surface of the force field, he'd seen her pilot their stolen short-haul ship between the buildings and down the alleys of Prasvishoni.

But this was something orders of magnitude beyond that. This was the precise moment he realized what Jez meant when she said she was born to fly.

She seemed formed to the controls, part of the ship itself, or maybe it was that the ship was part of her. Her eyes were half-closed, every muscle in her body relaxed, her mouth curved in a wistful smile of pure pleasure. The huge ship careened down the corridors like a bubble on a stream, dipping between walls, spinning around corners, threading through passageways as if borne on an invisible current. Jez's fingers played the controls like an instrument, and the music was the speed and the thrill and the glorious, death-defying flight. The acceleration pressed him back into his seat, and his harness was the only thing holding him as they spun and dipped, but he didn't care.

Maybe it was just the exhaustion, but he swore he felt tears coming to his eyes.

And then they were through the passageway, in what must have been only a few seconds, and then the massive stone door loomed in front of them. Jez winced, and Tae ducked instinctively, and they crashed through the entryway and into the open air, debris scattering around them.

# 27

Ysbel sprinted down the corridors after Lev. He paused when they reached the doorway for long enough to shut off the physical security system, then they raced across the tripwires and around Jez's cannibalistic vine, past the massive hallway, and through the heavy door. She shoved it shut behind her, and Lev tossed her the lock scrambler. She clipped it on, waited for the click, then snatched it back, and the two of them dove for cover behind a low decorative wall as what looked like a full squadron of guards pounded towards the door to the vault.

The leader grabbed the handle and pulled. "Still locked," she muttered into her com.

"Doesn't mean they're not still down there," said another. He typed in a passcode and waited.

Nothing.

"Hand me your controller," Lev whispered. She lifted her sleeve to her mouth and delicately ripped through the stitches one by one with her teeth. A tiny device dropped out from her cuff, and she caught it deftly, then handed it to Lev. He looked at it, frowning, and she found herself wishing Tae was here. She didn't trust anyone else with her explosives.

Still, a half-comatose Tae probably wouldn't be any better than Lev, if push came to shove.

She glanced back out at the guards.

"Lock's scrambled," one of them grunted. "They got through."

"Is the security down, do you think?"

"Don't know how they'd get past it, but—" the speaker shrugged. She typed in what must be the override, and slowly, the door swung open. "Come on." They jogged inside.

"Come. They'll see the security is down within a couple seconds," she whispered, and, crouched low, she and Lev sprinted for the courtyard.

The benefit of everyone going after the three in the vault was that the courtyard was practically deserted.

The disadvantage was, of course, that everyone was going after the three in the vault, who currently had no way of defending themselves. If she'd been there she could have brought the whole place down on them, but that would have been ultimately unproductive if the goal was to live through this.

"Do you have it yet?" she hissed at Lev.

"Give me a minute." He was frowning in concentration, typing slowly on his holoscreen, the device touching his com. Then he sucked in a quick breath and grinned.

"Got it."

"Then let's blow some things up. Stand back."

He tossed her the device, and they ducked down behind a massive potted tree.

Ysbel had never worried about her work. She couldn't remember a time when she had, since she was five years old, sitting on a too-tall bench in her mother's shop as she showed her daughter how to pour granules into the casings, or watching her father design a new and improved explosive formula. The explosives she had built, the weapons she had created, had always worked.

Until the time a few standard hours ago, when they hadn't, and everything had ended in disaster.

She took a deep breath and depressed the trigger.

"For you, Tanya," she whispered.

And then, with a thick low-pitched roar, like thunder except a thousand times louder, an entire section of cobblestones, and whatever controller had been underneath it, vaporized.

She let out her breath in relief, a grin she couldn't contain spreading across her face. Lev was grinning as well.

Since the moment her explosives had failed to ignite, she'd felt crippled, broken somehow.

Now she was whole again.

From all over the courtyard, guards were converging on the site of the explosion, coughing and choking on the fine dust of what had once been one of the power sources for the force field.

"Four. Three. Two. One," she counted quietly.

*BOOM!*

Another section of the courtyard exploded.

Lev watched the expanding cloud of dust as guards raced about like insects whose nest had been kicked, then turned to her with admiration on his face.

"Ysbel, I'm impressed. This was your gel?"

"It's a new one," she said. "The others were too viscous to drip down and coat the insides."

He raised his eyebrows. "No wonder you're famous."

"Yes, well I'm also a mass murderer."

*BOOM!*

Now the guards were frantic, calling in on their coms, darting back and forth between the explosions. She almost expected them to start bumping into each other, like the clown shows she and Tanya had shown to little Misko.

She turned back to Lev. "Were you telling me the truth? About my family?"

His face was deadly serious. "Yes. I was. They're all alive, all three of them."

"You know, my baby would be six now. Almost seven."

"He is, you mean."

She nodded. For some reason, tears wanted to come to her eyes again, but this wasn't the time for them. She glanced out. "How long do you think until they find us?"

Lev looked at her, a small, wry smile on his face. "You know?"

"I always knew. We're going to die." She shrugged. "At least I know about Tanya and my babies. That was the best gift anyone has given to me."

He nodded, but didn't meet her eye. "You think the others will get out?"

"Jez will get them out," she said. "She may be crazy, and the most irritating person I have ever met, but that girl can fly."

He nodded, and tried to smile.

"You're sweet on her."

He reddened suddenly. "I—don't know what—"

Ysbel smiled slightly. "If it makes you feel better, she's sweet on you too. I've seen her watching you. Even if she won't admit it."

*BOOM!*

He chuckled softly, looking down at the cobblestones. "Well, I suppose I can only be so embarrassed if I'm going to die in five minutes." He glanced over at her. "Do you have extra explosives?"

She nodded, and handed him a pouch. "When they come, you'll want to drip some on yourself, and then toss the rest at them. I have one too. I'll hit the switch right before they reach us."

He nodded. His face, under the blush, was pale. He was afraid to die.

Well, perhaps she was too, if she was being honest with herself. For the first time in a very long time, there was something she could have lived for.

And that, of itself, was something she'd always be grateful for.

Across the courtyard, one of the guards had caught sight of them. She was shouting and pointing.

It would be a matter of moments now.

There was the splinter of shattering rocks and masonry, and, from the centre of the courtyard, a ship exploded from an opening that looked far too small to have ever contained it. Lev gave it a wistful smile, then turned back to her.

"Ysbel—since we're about to die, I suppose there's something I should tell you."

She only half-heard him. She was frowning at the ship. It should have burst through the shield, but instead it had whipped around into a tight turn.

What was wrong? Had she mis-calculated? Still, even if the shield was up, she couldn't see Jez not at least trying to …

The ship came to a shuddering halt directly over the top of them. A hatch opened, and a worn rope-ladder came slithering out of it.

At the top, Tae's face peered over the edge.

"Get on, you two idiots," Jez's voice crackled over their ear-pieces. "You think it's easy to hold this thing steady?"

Ysbel felt her face crack into a smile. "For you, you crazy drunken lunatic, I think it's as simple as breathing."

Lev was staring like his brain hadn't quite registered what his eyes were telling him. The guards were sprinting for them now, and already heat pistol blasts seared the air around them.

She grabbed him around the waist and flung him bodily upward. He caught at the rope, and she jumped after him as the ship slowly began to rise. The air rippled around them as heat blasts scored the air.

"Up!" she hissed at Lev. He was staring downward, his face pale, and clinging to the ladder with both arms, but at her words he swallowed hard and began to climb. She followed.

Another heat blast scorched through one side of the rope just below her hands, and she barely managed to catch on to the length above her before she lost her balance. Tae was leaning down from the hatch on his stomach, and he caught Lev's hand and hauled him inside, then reached down again for Ysbel. He dragged her onto the ship's floor and slammed the hatch behind them as another heat blast burned through the last of the connecting rope, and the ladder fell away below them.

The three of them scrambled to their feet and stood looking at each other for a long moment. Tae, the circles under his eyes so dark he looked like he'd been punched in the face, managed a weak smile.

"You didn't think we'd leave you, did you? Jez said you'd never make it to the ship, and even if you did, and I quote, 'that idiot Lev probably flies like your grandfather's three-legged cat.'"

Lev took a deep breath and managed his own weak smile. "Hate to say it, but she's probably right." He paused. "Thank you."

"You're ..." Tae swayed for a moment on his feet, looked vaguely confused, then fell face-first onto the floor. Ysbel and Lev looked at each other in alarm.

"Hope you got those force-fields down," Jez called over the ship's com.

"Who do you think you are working with?" Ysbel grumbled into her com, dropping down beside the comatose Tae.

"Was he shot?" Lev mouthed, forehead creased with worry.

The ship accelerated alarmingly, and Jez whooped. "We're through! You're beautiful, Ysbel!"

"Piss off," she growled into the com. She rolled her eyes at Lev, then felt Tae's pulse and gingerly patted him down. "No. He's fine. I think his long day finally caught up with him."

At her words, her own exhaustion came crashing in. She closed her eyes and tipped her head back, just for a moment.

She'd almost died several times already in the last standard day or two, not to mention finding out that the people she'd been mourning for the last five years were, in fact, still alive. It was enough to wear someone out.

She could use a bit of a rest sometime soon, if that was in the cards.

"Strap down, kids." Jez's voice crackled out of the coms in the ship walls. "Things are about to get interesting."

Lev appeared in the doorway, and, face pale but set, strapped himself down into the copilot's seat. Jez raised an eyebrow.

"I thought you hated flying with me."

"I do." He already sounded slightly sick. "But on reflection, I prefer it to getting shot down with you. I thought you might want updates on the defences."

"Yeah, well I'm pretty sure we're about to get updates in full size and full colour, any second now." She glanced behind her. A flight of ships had already taken off, small and lean and dangerous, and were swooping low over the compound.

"Do we have any weapons on this thing?" he asked.

She glanced down at the controls. "Technically, yes. Also, technically, a cloaking device and a hyperdrive. But Tae and I barely managed to get the flight controls online before we had to blast out of there, so nothing we can use." She paused, her euphoria slowly fading. "I—we left Masha behind."

He turned to her, frowning, and she bit back her irritation.

"She was trying to distract Vitali while Tae and I got the ship going, and she wouldn't get into the ship. Kept saying to leave her, she had something she needed to do."

She waited for the condemnation in his eyes.

Not that she needed it. She'd been feeling sick about this since she'd nodded her head, started the ship, and flown off without the calm woman in the pilot's coat.

But he didn't look accusing. He just nodded, face a little sad. "I'm sorry, Jez."

"Don't be sorry for me," she snapped. "I'm the one who left her."

"You left her to save Tae, and me, and Ysbel," he said. "It was Masha's decision. You did what you had to do."

"Yeah." She couldn't meet his gaze.

She glanced at the ship's holoscreen, and her stomach dropped, from fear, or excitement, or dread, or some mixture of all of them.

They were going to die. No matter how well she flew, no matter how the ship responded to her, like it could read her thoughts, there was no way they could get past that many ships. And they didn't even have guns online to fight back.

"Can Tae—" she began, but a glance at Lev's face confirmed her fears.

"He passed out when Ysbel and I got up. Honestly, I'm surprised he lasted that long."

She gave a tight nod, and tried to grin. "Well, it's been good knowing you."

They were passing through the atmosphere now, the ship trembling ever-so-slightly at the air resistance. Her fingers shook just a little, cold tingling in the pit of her stomach.

It had been a good run, for what it was worth. At least she'd die in the air. Flying. Like she'd wanted.

The short-haul fighting ships below them spread into formation as they pulled free of the confines of the planet. Any second now they'd begin to fire. The *Ungovernable's* shielding was impressive, but against that level of concentrated weaponry, even that wasn't going to save them.

The ships swung, and her screen lit with the flash of fire. She winced, glancing down for a damage report.

There was nothing.

She frowned at the holoscreen. Maybe Tae hadn't fixed it as well as he'd assured her he had. In fairness, he'd sounded half-way drunk at the time, so—

No. The ships were firing at something behind her.

She looked up in confusion and met Lev's equally-confused stare.

Then the ship's com crackled.

"Jez?"

The voice was faint, but unmistakable.

Jez sat flabbergasted for a moment, then hit the com.

"Masha? Is that you?"

She caught a glimpse, on the screen, of the tiny blip the ships were firing on. Frantically, she expanded the screen.

She felt suddenly sick.

A short-haul SRS 17, with understated grace and scorch-marks on the body panels.

"Masha! What are you doing with my ship?" she shouted into the com.

"Jez, listen to me. I can draw them off. They don't know how many of us are in here. Can you fly like you're on autopilot?"

She stared at the com dumbly. "Yes," she managed, finally. "But they saw me stop and pick up Lev and Ysbel. They know we're in here."

"You remember the mod that Tae put on this ship? The tracker? As far as anyone else is concerned, about twenty seconds ago an escape pod jettisoned from that ship you're on. Just trust me, and fly like I told you."

"Yeah." She was too stunned even to think of a smart remark.

In a daze, she set the controls to auto and moved over to the cockpit window.

Her ship was flying, not brilliantly, but competently. The shields Tae had installed glowed as blasts ricocheted off them, and the weapons Ysbel had installed vaporized ship after ship into clouds of glittering space-dust.

It was beautiful. Yes, she was in the *Ungovernable*, but that little short-haul beauty had been her first love, and she could almost feel the shape of the controls against her palms.

But even with that, even with the weapons and the shields and everything else, Masha wasn't going to be able to out-fly all Vitali's ships.

Jez wasn't certain that even she would have been able to.

Ysbel joined them in the cockpit, and the three of them watched silently.

The shield was beginning to flicker now, even as the ship's weapons fired harder.

Jez clenched her fists.

She felt numb, like she was watching the whole scene from outside her body.

Two ships swooped in close, firing heavily. For half a moment, she thought maybe her little short-haul would survive one more assault, just one more …

And then it exploded, disintegrating into chunks of rubble that drifted outward in an ever-expanding cloud.

# 28

She stared at the place where her ship had been. Where Masha had been.

Both gone now.

Beside her, Lev wiped a hand across his forehead in a sort of exhausted admiration.

"Well," he said into the silence. "I will say one thing about Masha. She knows how to go out in style."

"They're still following us," said Ysbel, glancing at the ships.

They were, but at a distance, and they weren't firing.

That was the genius of Masha's plan—Vitali wouldn't want to fire on this ship. No one in their right mind would want to fire on this gorgeous, perfect ship. And as long as they'd given him some excuse to think that it was empty, he'd have his people follow it until he could figure out how to retrieve it without damage.

Of course, that meant they'd still be caught eventually. But they had Lev, and Tae, sort of, and Ysbel, and her. Maybe the most naturally-talented team that anyone had ever put together. Between now and when they were caught, Masha had given them a chance.

"She was a good woman," Jez said, surprising even herself with the words. "I mean, she was a lunatic, and I never trusted her, and she had stupid notions about keeping people inside of hangar bays. But she was a decent person after all, I guess."

"I suppose you're right," said Ysbel, her accent thicker than ever. "I mean, it is her fault we were here in the first place to get shot at. But—" she shrugged.

"What—what happened?" Tae staggered into the cockpit, supporting himself against the walls. He looked a little like he'd died, been buried for a few days, and then dug himself out of his grave with a teaspoon.

"What the hell are you doing up?" Jez snapped.

"Good to see you too," he groaned. "What happened?"

"Masha blew up my ship," she said in a hollow voice.

She still couldn't believe it. To be honest, she wasn't sure how much of the ache in her chest was for the woman in the pilot's jacket, and how much was for her lovely little short-haul ship.

"Wait." He shook his head as if trying to get his bearings. "Masha blew up your ship? Why?"

Lev shot her a long-suffering look, then turned to Tae. "Masha took off in our old ship. She sent out a tracer that made it look like we'd bailed from this ship, and told Jez to run it on autopilot—"

"I was wondering why I hadn't thrown up yet," Tae murmured.

"And then she drew their attention with our old ship. And—" Lev trailed off, shrugging helplessly.

Tae stared out the window. "You know," he said after a moment, "I was actually starting to like her?"

They stared out at the blackness of space outside their cockpit for a while. Vitali's ships were trailing them at a respectful distance.

"We'll need to think of a plan," said Lev at last.

"I believe I have one." The voice was faint, but distinct.

They looked at each other.

"Who said that?" asked Jez finally.

"I did. Jez, please open the airlock. We have about two minutes and thirty-seven seconds before we all explode."

She stared at the ship's com, for the first time in her life completely speechless.

"Masha?" said Lev at last.

"Yes. We're down to two minutes and twenty-six seconds."

There was something in her tone that snapped Jez out of her paralysis, and she jumped for the controls.

"I can set the airlock," said Tae, pushing himself upright. "Ysbel and Lev, go down there and get on the manuals. Masha, what are you coming in on?"

"Escape pod," she said.

Jez frowned and stared at the holoscreen.

There was a tiny blip, clinging to their starboard side.

"Got it!" Lev called over the com.

Tae was fiddling with something from the co-pilot seat, and he glanced up. "Got the airlock working. Jez, open it up."

She flipped the switch. Her body was moving on something like autopilot itself. She assumed that at some point her brain would catch up and this would all make sense, but until then, she was running on instinct and adrenalin.

"She's in," said Ysbel, and then there were running footsteps up the narrow corridor to the cockpit. Masha burst through, breathing heavily.

"Tae. Listen. Bottom panel, where the tech is. Do exactly what I tell you. Jez, stay where you are. I'm going to need you in a moment. The rest of you, tether down."

Tae didn't even stop to ask questions, just bent down and got to work. A moment later he had the panel open.

"Alright. Here are the specs." She pulled something up on her holoscreen and crouched down beside Tae. "We need to get the hyperdrive functional, right now. Can you see what's wrong?"

Tae squinted at the diagram, then at the mess of wires. Then his face cleared, and he started pulling delicately on the coloured wires. "They have it mis-connected here," he said, almost to himself. "If I just switch these two—"

An entire section of the control panel lit up under Jez's fingers, and suddenly she didn't care that she had no idea what was going on.

This was something she had to try.

"On my mark, Jez," said Masha, looking down at her com. "I assume you can make this go?"

"Oh, I can make this go," Jez murmured. A feeling like electricity was running through her fingers, up her arms, and straight into her brain.

Hyperdrive.

This would make ordinary flying look like a stroll down the avenue.

Wormholes were one thing. This ship was about to make its own wormhole.

"Two. One. Now!"

Jez pulled back on the newly-lit-up lever with one hand while pushing the throttle forward with the other.

For half a second, time seemed to stretch. Space warped around them like a rubber band stretched too far, and behind them she caught an oddly-distorted view of the escape pod exploding into dust. And then time snapped back, and she was shoved into her seat, and Tae and Masha went flying into the cockpit window behind them, and then they were drifting through an odd, strangely coloured and patterned expanse that she'd never seen, but something inside of her recognized and wanted like she'd never wanted anything else.

Behind her, she could hear Tae and Masha getting to their feet, but she just stared out the front window at the achingly-beautiful expanse.

She felt a hand on her shoulder, then Masha's voice said quietly, "I think we've tested the hyperdrive long enough. Let's get back to regular speed. I believe we have some things to discuss."

Slowly, hardly knowing what she was doing, Jez reached out for the controls. Reluctantly, almost painfully, she flipped them back into position while easing back on the throttle. Time stretched around them again, and when it snapped back, they were in the place that was more hers than any home had ever been. Deep space.

But something inside of her longed for that feeling, that place, that moment of nothing and everything at once, and she found there were tears in the corners of her eyes as she took her hand off the throttle.

# 29

Masha looked around at her motley crew as they gathered into the common area of the ship.

Tae was almost dead on his feet, and Lev was wearing a sort of stunned expression. Only Ysbel was as stoic as ever. Jez was still in the cockpit. She'd looked so distraught to pull out of hyperdrive that Masha had taken pity and asked her to run the ship through a couple maneuvers while the rest of the crew gathered, to test that everything was working.

"Masha," said Lev, voice strained, "I'll be the first to admit that that was wildly impressive. But if you'll excuse me for asking, what the actual hell happened back there?"

She smiled slightly. The heat-blast she'd taken in her side throbbed with an almost luminescent pain, and now that the adrenalin of the chase was fading, the edges of her vision were starting to fuzz. But she felt, somehow, that this conversation deserved to happen while she was still standing.

"I'm sorry I didn't have time to explain it more thoroughly," she said. "But thank you for trusting me. Once I realized we wouldn't get the weapons online in this ship in time, I decided our best chance was for someone to get the other ship in the air and draw their fire."

"But how did you get out?"

Her smile widened. "Half the courtyard blew itself up piece by piece, and Vitali's prize ship blasted out through the vault. It distracted a lot of attention. I slipped out the front way, and thanks to Tae's delightful modifications, was able to get it into the sky relatively quickly. The rest, I think, you saw."

Lev was shaking his head slightly. "Jez is going to want to hear this, and I don't want to have to be the one to explain how her ship got blown up." He tapped his com. "Jez! Get in here."

A few moments later, Jez wandered through the doorway. Her face had the kind of rapturous glow that only happens to most people once in their lifetime, if they're lucky.

"You know when you're having sex?" she began. "And there's that one moment?"

"Jez!" Tae yelped.

"That one, perfect moment?"

"Jez, no one needs this information," said Lev, resignation in his voice.

"Well, that's what flying this ship is like," she said, ignoring them both. Her voice had a dreamy quality to it. "It's like—"

"Jez. Shut up," said Ysbel, but she was grinning.

Jez dropped into one of the chairs and stretched her long legs out in front of her. "I'm just saying."

"Nobody wants you to just say that, Jez," said Lev. "Anyways, Masha's about to tell you why she blew up your ship."

Despite the pain, despite the fact that Jez definitively did not know how to shut up, despite the fact that she would probably feel slightly dirty every time she touched the controls on this ship from now on, Masha smiled to herself.

It had worked. She hadn't been certain, at first, that it would. But she'd done it.

They were the ones that had pulled off the heist, of course. With her assistance, but still—the point was, she'd done something much more important.

She'd made these four into a team.

Jez turned to glare at her. "Yeah, Masha. Why'd you blow up my ship? And how did you get away?"

Masha gave her a pleasant look. "I watched a pilot, once, play a little trick with a transport pod. She did it with handcuffs on. I'm not quite that caliber, but with both hands free and a bit of luck, I managed to pull it off, even if it wasn't quite as graceful."

"You got out behind their line of sight and went dark," said Jez, a hint of admiration in her tone.

"And," Lev continued, "you set the pod to self-destruct, and got Jez to make the jump at the same time as the explosion. And despite the huge disparity in the two masses, you gambled that since none of our pursuers knew about the hyperdrive tech, they would assume the explosion must have been from this ship."

"Yes." Masha spread her hands and gave him a fond smile. He was a smart kid. "But you missed the best part. Yokov wiped every trace of us from every database, and Vitali and his pilots saw us die. Now, as far as anyone in the system knows, we no longer exist. So, Jez, to answer your question, that's why I blew up your ship. But," she smiled apologetically and gestured around her at the gleaming dark-wooden walls, and beyond them, the endless expanse of deep space, "I like to think the exchange was worth it."

There was a long moment where no-one spoke.

Masha leaned up against the low table behind her, inconspicuously. The encroaching blackness on the edges of her vision was growing more solid, and her legs weren't as steady as she could have wished.

"This wasn't really about the tech, was it, Masha?" Lev said at last.

"Oh, it was certainly about the tech," she replied, trying to keep her voice light. "It was just about other things as well."

"But if we've disappeared," said Tae slowly, "the government won't get it."

She was mildly impressed that Tae could form complete sentences. He looked like death by exhaustion had come by, seen him, and given it up as a bad job.

"No," she said, and for a moment she couldn't keep the hardness from her tone. "The government will not get this tech, nor will the mafia. But we will." She paused a moment.

"Tae. I know why you were in prison. You wanted something of your own back. You wanted to get back at everything that kept you and the other street children starving and freezing, unable to get a job or schooling or any way of bettering your lives."

"It did nothing. It got me thrown in jail." His voice was flat, bitter.

"Yes. But that was when it was just you. Now you have a team. I know you have friends in Prasvishoni you want to help. But I'm asking you to consider how much more you could do than just get them out of the city, to live out their lives struggling to survive on some outpost fringe planet. You were powerless before. But now?"

He was staring at her, his expression, under the overlay of exhaustion, a mix of residual anger, irritation, and what she'd been watching for. The tiniest spark of hope.

"And Lev. What do you have to go back to? Your family is free. I know that's what you wanted. But your professorship was gone a long time ago. Will you go back to working for a government that has proven it will never trust you? You're too smart for them. You know too much. You'd be back in jail in three month's time. But here —" she broke off and gestured around her. "Sasa Illiovich built this ship. There will be information here that no one else in the system has access to."

She turned to the lanky pilot. "Jez. I know I blew up your ship. But this—"

Jez held up her hand. "Look Masha. I can see what you're doing. But right now, where I'm sitting, I have a ship, I'm out in deep space, and no one knows where I am. You really don't have to convince me."

"It will mean being part of a team," Masha said, trying and failing to hide a small grin.

Jez looked around her. "Well, I suppose if being around these idiots means I can fly this ..." her expression turned dreamy again. "It's like—"

"Shut up, Jez," said Ysbel.

Masha turned to the stocky woman, with her cropped hair and her foreboding expression, and felt a pang of sympathy. "Ysbel," she said softly. "I can't give you back what you want. I wish I could. But —"

"No." Ysbel cut her off. "You can't. But here's the thing—Lev already did. My family's alive, somewhere, and Lev knows where. I don't know what you're angling for, and to be honest, I don't care. I will fly with you. But the first thing we're going to do, with our new ship and our new tech, is we're going to find my family, and we're going to rescue them. Those are my conditions."

For once, Masha was taken by surprise. She wasn't sure she enjoyed the feeling. She looked at Ysbel, then at Lev, who nodded slightly.

"It's true, Masha. If you recall, I have access to some rather classified information."

Masha glanced around at the others.

"I'm in," said Jez, shrugging. "As long as it means I can fly this little beauty, I don't actually care where we go. Although," she raised her eyebrows suggestively, "I'm just going to say, Ysbel's wife might be a little jealous of my dashing—"

"Piss off, Jez," said Ysbel, but she was smiling. Actually smiling.

"Right now, I'm going to sleep for a full twenty-four standard hours," said Tae emphatically. "But if and when I wake up, I'm going with Ysbel."

Lev turned to Masha and shrugged. "I'm sorry, Masha. It sounds like we're doing this with or without your permission."

"Well then," said Masha after a moment. "I suppose it's settled." The room was starting to spin around her.

"One thing that I still don't understand," said Lev softly. "I checked up on you. Before I agreed to come, I looked through all the information I have, and believe me, it's a lot. You're exactly who you told me you were. You started out in a low-level bureaucratic job out of college, and worked your way up. You've worked for the government for seventeen years. You have a spotless record, and not because something was wiped—I would have been able to tell. And yet, here we are. We've deprived the government, and the mafia, who you were also under contract to, of tech that would be invaluable to either of them, and we've disappeared with it. Not only that, but you were much too quick with your confession that you were working for the government when Vitali caught us. And I checked—even though everything in your record was wiped, your contract with the mafia was mysteriously still searchable. If my uncle didn't find that before we left, he's found it by now. It will be a long time before Vitali will deal with either the government or the mafia again, and it won't take long for the government and the mafia to realize that each used you to go behind the other's back to extract the tech. We didn't just steal some tech. We've done the equivalent of dropping a plasma bomb on the entire Svodrani System government and organized crime infrastructure. That wasn't just chance. So tell me, Masha. What are you really doing here?"

She shook her head fondly, even through the jagged lighting-streaks of pain. He was really very clever. She'd chosen well.

"I suppose," she said, "that I'm rescuing Ysbel's family. At least, that's what I've been informed."

"We have no supplies, no funds, nothing," said Tae. "It's all well and good to talk about ideals, but—"

She reached into her pilot's coat and pulled out a small canister, which she placed carefully on the table. "I forgot to mention. What with all the confusion in the vault, I grabbed this on my way out. Thought it might come in handy." Her head felt like it was floating, the pain shooting through her side alternating fire and ice.

"That's—" Lev began, staring at the canister.

"Credits. Lots of credits," she said faintly.

Her last conscious thought was that maybe she should have sat down after all.

Lev jumped forward as Masha collapsed, but he wasn't as fast as Jez. She caught the woman before she hit the floor, her face creased with concern.

"What—" he began.

"I forgot," she said, lowering Masha gently to the ground. "She was hit with a heat gun before we took off."

Lev swore. "Get a first aid kit. If Vitali restored this thing so well, he'll have stocked it with the basics."

Jez stood. "If he did, there should be one right about ... here."

He pulled off Masha's pilot coat as Jez handed him the kit, and winced at the scorched hole in her shirt. "Ysbel," he said, "get me a heat-blast kit and a razor, please."

Ysbel handed him the kit and a small medical knife, and he gingerly sliced charred cloth away from the wound, feeling slightly sick. Where the heat-blast had struck, Masha's flesh looked like meat that had been left on the barbecue too long.

"You haven't done this before, have you?" asked Ysbel, crouching beside him. "Let me help."

She sprayed sterilizer on the injury as Lev finished peeling away the shreds of fabric, then opened the heat-bandage. "Roll her over just a little," she instructed, and Lev complied. She gently pressed the edges of the compress around both sides of the wound, and there was a faint hiss as it sealed. The cooling gel would stop any further damage, and the enzymes inside would eat away the dead flesh before it could become infected, while stimulating cell repair on the healthy tissue.

Technically, as long as it took properly, she should be fine in a week or so.

Reluctantly, he stood.

Masha was stone cold dangerous. She was far too good at keeping secrets, and she was playing a long game that neither he nor any of the rest of them understood.

But she had saved their lives back there, and she'd almost died doing it.

Ysbel lifted the woman gently. "Jez. Where are the cabins in this thing?"

"I'll find them." Jez jumped to her feet, starry-eyed once again at the prospect of exploring her beloved ship.

"Tae, follow them," said Lev. "You need a bed as badly as Masha does at this point."

Tae didn't even bother to argue, just gave him an exhausted look and stumbled after Ysbel.

Lev sat down in the chair, the weariness of the past few days finally washing over him.

It had been a long run. But somehow … he glanced out the window.

He couldn't remember the last time he'd felt like this. Satisfied.

Happy.

Jez came back a few minutes later and flopped down into a chair next to him. "The others are all in their cabins. Tae almost started crying when he saw the beds, and Ysbel said she'd had enough excitement to last her for a few lifetimes and now she was going to get some sleep because if she had to listen to me for three more seconds she'd blow this whole ship up and all of us with it. So—" she shrugged, grinning. "You don't know how to blow things up, so I figured this should be safe."

He smiled back at her, despite himself. "Aren't you tired, Jez?"

"Nah. I have my ship. I think I could stay awake for the rest of my life if it meant flying this beautiful angel."

They were quiet for a few minutes. Finally, Lev said, "Why didn't you leave? Back there, I mean. In prison. You could have gotten away, gone off and flown for yourself. I thought that's what you wanted."

She turned to look at him, and he was surprised at the seriousness in her expression. "Here's the thing, though," she said after a moment. "You didn't leave me. I thought you would. I was certain you would." She paused. "Back there in Prasvishoni, when I got jumped in the alley, and then again when we got thrown in prison. I was sure you'd all take off, and I'd get left behind. But you didn't."

He was shocked to see tears in her eyes.

"I—no one's ever done that for me before. Not left me, I mean."

It was still there, that magnetism in her gaze. That thing in her face that made it almost impossible for him to look away.

Somehow he'd turned in his own chair to face her, and they were much closer than he'd realized. His heart pounded strangely. Her eyes held his, and for once there was no sarcasm or mockery in her expression, just something vulnerable and almost questioning. Like she wasn't entirely sure what was happening either. For half a second he thought she was going to lean forward, and that he was, and that

—

And then she turned away quickly, and gave a slightly-shaky laugh.

"Maybe you're right. Maybe I should get some sleep. I'm going to the cockpit and put back the chair, set the autopilot alarm so that if anything happens it'll wake me." She paused, not meeting his eyes.

"Um. You should get some sleep too. But when you're done, I—I mean, Tae's not going to be up for a while, and I could use a copilot. If you want. For a bit."

He smiled. "I'd like that."

She stood, then paused again, looking at the ground.

"Um. I—know you said you got thrown in prison because you knew stuff you weren't supposed to know. I ... OK, so while I was waiting by the ship, after you all went into the compound, I did some research. Ship's database wasn't hooked in until we reached Vitali's planet, and I managed to pull our information onto my com before it was erased. You—wanted to be a professor, didn't you?"

He nodded, even though she probably couldn't see.

"And you couldn't. Because …" she swallowed hard. "Because your family lost everything. I—I guess you're probably pretty mad about that still."

"Jez." He stood, and after a moment's hesitation, put a hand gently on her shoulder. "I was. I used to be. But—I'm not. Anymore. Life is crap, and crap happens. People do stupid things because they don't think they have a choice. I certainly have."

Finally, she met his eyes, and there was something in her gaze, regret, and weariness, and underneath it, a sharp, painful glimmer of hope.

"I got over it," he said quietly. "It's OK. I'm OK."

She blinked hard, as if pushing back tears. "Really?" she whispered at last.

"Really."

And as he said the words, he knew they were true.

"I—that's good," she said at last, voice choking only a little. "I'm glad. That you're OK, I mean. Because I need a copilot, and I sure as hell don't want to have to learn all the crap you know by myself."

"Yeah," he said, smiling despite himself. "That'd be rough. Go get some sleep."

She turned and started for the cockpit with her jaunty gait, and he smiled after her.

Whatever Masha's long game was, maybe it wouldn't be so bad to play after all.

In a cabin down a hallway, Tae lay on the small ship's cot, which felt a little bit like paradise, with the angels singing and everything.

His friends back in Prasvishoni would hear what had happened soon enough. They'd think he was dead. They'd think he'd abandoned them. But they'd be wrong. Because Masha was right. He couldn't really save them by himself. He could take them somewhere where things would be marginally better, for a little. But by himself, that was the best he could do.

But this team. They'd already pulled off the impossible once. Maybe, just maybe, they could do it again.

He drifted off to sleep, visions of Caz and Peti floating through his brain and leaving a smile across his face.

In the cabin next door, Ysbel slowly pulled off her boots and ran her hand over her shaved head.

It had been so long that she hardly remembered what this felt like. This thing inside of her, that bubbled up from her stomach through her chest, burning and bright and searingly intense.

Happiness.

Hope.

Did it used to make her cry? It had been so long she couldn't remember.

She lay back on her bed and closed her eyes. A slender, brown-haired woman waited behind her eyelids, like she always did, and a small, tenacious little girl and a chubby, solemn baby boy.

They'd be older now. Olya would be eight, and Misko six and a half. Was Olya still as determined and headstrong as she'd been as a three-year-old? Had Misko grown out of his baby fat?

She'd never let herself think that far. She'd never let herself wonder what might have been, because the pain was too much even for her. But now it wasn't what might have been. It was what was.

"Tanya," she whispered. "Soon, my love. I'll see you soon, if I have to move planets to get to you."

In the cockpit, Jez leaned back in the pilot's seat, eyes half-closed, and stared out at the blackness surrounding her.

She was in her ship. She was back in the sky.

And behind her, sleeping, were her team.

Her friends.

Who'd have thought this was what perfect felt like?

She closed her eyes. For the first time in her life, there was nothing she was running from.

Masha stirred on her cot, her thoughts coming back to her groggily.

She was alive. That was good.

The cooling gel from whatever they'd put over her wound was soothing, and there must be a pain inhibitor as well, because her mind was clearer than it had been in a while.

She allowed herself a small smile as she lay back on her cot.

They'd agreed.

Everything was going exactly as she'd planned.

They had no idea what it was they'd agreed to, of course. And she had no intention of telling them just yet. She'd wait until they were hers, body and soul. This crew was the sharpest set of tools she'd ever had to work with, and she had no intention of wasting that.

At least, not until she had to.

Because once they were hers to do with as she wished … what was coming would shake the foundations of the entire Svodrani system.

This was only the first move, and they'd pulled it off beautiful. But even a crew like this one was unlikely to survive an explosion like the one that was coming.

The End

## ENJOYED THE BOOK?

I HOPE YOU'VE ENJOYED Zero Day Threat, the first book in The Ungovernable series. Thank you for reading!

If you did, I have a small favour to ask you: would you please leave a review on Amazon? It may seem like a silly thing, but reviews are very important to authors like me, as they help other people find my book, which in turn helps me to keep writing. Even a line or two would be unbelievably helpful.

The series continues with *Jailbreak*, which is available on Amazon.

In the mean time, if you'd like to connect with me on my website, www.rmolson.com, you can subscribe to my mailing list and I'll send you an exclusive short story prequel featuring Jez Solokov, *Devil's Odds*. I'll also let you know about future launch dates, give-aways, and pre-release specials. And I always love to hear from my readers, so feel free to drop me a note!

Also, feel free to connect with me on Facebook (RMOlsonauthor) or Instagram (rolson_author).

**Read on for an excerpt from book 2 ...**

# JAILBREAK

## Chapter 1

Jez grinned at the man sitting across the table from her. He smelled of sour sweat and too much sump, and his pilot coat was thick with grease and dirt.

He didn't grin back. "Well, you scrawny plaguer? You going to call, or fold?"

She leaned back on the rickety metal stool, still grinning. "Neither. I'm raising."

The small kabak was noisy, crowded with hard-drinking, grim-faced men and women in tattered pilot's coats or grubby peasant smocks, but a handful of the man's crewmates had gathered around the gambling table. At least, she assumed they were his crewmates. Couldn't imagine anyone else would stand that close to him on purpose.

"Raise with what?" he grunted, clearly skeptical.

She grinned wider. She didn't look like much right now, sure. But she plaguing well smelled better than he did. That should count for something, right?

Casually, she reached into her coat and pulled out a small chip. She kept her fist closed around it for effect as she touched it to the betting chip in the centre.

The six pairs of eyes widened as the numbers clicked higher, and the man's heavy eyebrows dropped into a scowl.

"What?" she asked innocently. "Can't meet it?" She shrugged. "You could always fold."

"You damn—" he half stood, leaning forward.

Her heart was pounding, every muscle in her body tingling with anticipation.

This was what she lived for.

"Or," she said casually, "I suppose you could put in that information chip my friend was asking you about earlier. I'd take that as a call."

He would probably just kill her. Or try, of course. But what the hell. If you weren't about to be killed at least a couple times a week, were you even really alive?

"Why do you want it so badly?" he grumbled. She shrugged.

"That's fine, you can fold. I don't care. Got plenty of credits in there, I could buy myself enough sump to last me five standard years. Or maybe one really, really good night."

"How did some scum-sucking lowlife pilot like you come up with that kind of credits?"

She raised her eyebrows. "You calling, or folding? Don't got all day."

He looked down at the symbols on the smooth tokens in his hand and scowled.

He had a good hand.

She'd checked.

Slowly, he pulled a small chip out of his inner pocket. "I lose this, my job's not worth spit."

She shrugged and made as if to scoop the betting chip towards herself. He slapped his meaty hand down on her wrist.

"Damn you." He dropped the small chip into the centre of the table. "Now, I say we're dropping tokens."

With a dramatic flourish he spread his tokens out on the table and broke into a slow, mean smile, the expression ugly on his stubbly face.

It really was a good hand.

She would have let her grin drop if she could. But she couldn't help it. Never been that good at modesty, really.

So she was grinning so wide her face felt stretched as she tossed her tokens casually onto the table.

There was that one delightful moment, as he saw the symbols and made the calculations in his head. Then his eyes bugged out, his face darkening with rage.

She scooped up the betting chip and the information chip and shoved them in the inside pocket of her jacket. Time to leave.

His fist caught her in the ribs as she stood, and she grunted and stumbled sideways. He shoved the table out of the way and grabbed her by the shoulder, hoisting her bodily into the air.

"You cheated! You plaguing scum-sucker."

She turned her head and bit down as hard as she could into the fleshy part of his hand. He howled in pain, and she dropped to the ground. She grabbed the stool she'd been sitting on and swung it into position just as he lunged down at her. The stool legs caught him under the ribcage, and for a split second he stood, face frozen in agony, gasping for breath. She rolled out from under the stool, spun around, and flung it into the face of the man next to her, who, in fairness, looked like he had been about to recover his wits and grab for her. He grunted and stumbled back, cursing, and she turned and brought her forehead down on the bridge of her erstwhile gambling partner's nose. He fell against the broken table, clutching his bloody face, just as another one of his friends grabbed her from behind. She threw her head back, connecting squarely with his jaw, and then took advantage of the momentary slackening of his grasp to drive her elbow hard into his sternum. She dropped to the floor as another man and a woman grabbed for her and rolled between their legs. Then she jumped to her feet, checked her coat pocket, and sprinted for the exit, still grinning, the man and all of his friends hot on her tail.

She burst out of the kabak, glanced quickly in both directions, then took off down the dirt street towards the edge of the shabby town. She slapped the com on her wrist as she ran.

"Hey kids, time to go!" she called. A moment later, Lev's long-suffering sigh came through her earpiece.

"Where are you, Jez?"

"Be there in a jiff."

"And someone's after you."

A heat blast scorched the dirt beside her, sending up a thick scent of ozone and burnt earth. She yelped and dodged as another blast sizzled past her and left a charred mark across the colourful shutters on the dingy prefab house across from her.

"Yep. Don't call you genius boy for nothing!"

She ducked down an alley, dodged into another street, and took a sharp right.

There, ahead of her, was the wall marking the end of town, the intricate carvings and once-brilliant colours now faded and shabby. And after that …

The crew behind her were gaining. She half turned, and squeezed off a shot from the modded heat pistol she'd borrowed from Ysbel.

The street in front of her pursuers disappeared in a ball of smoke and flame, and from behind it she heard strangled cursing.

"Ysbel! You're beautiful," she called over the com.

"Piss off."

"Pees oaf yourself," she called back, imitating the woman's heavy outer-rim accent.

She sprinted through the gates of the town—no city force field on this dump of a planet—and slowed, grinning.

Three figures stood in front of the loading ramp to the most stunning ship she'd ever seen in her life—a sleek long-haul, with beautiful old-fashioned rivets and smooth metal panels, its body the dull, glossy sheen of something old that had been restored and polished to perfection.

Yes, she'd been flying this little beauty for the last two weeks, but honestly, every time she saw it again her heart skipped a beat.

Tae was glowering at her—nothing new there—Ysbel was giving her the usual flat stare, and Lev was shaking his head slightly, his expression resigned.

All three of them had drawn heat-guns, and they were holding them in a no-nonsense way.

"What did you do, Jez?" Lev asked as she jogged up to them.

"Nothing," she said. "Just making new friends. Hey! You figured out how to hold a gun!"

Lev gave her a look that was almost as flat as Ysbel's. Granted, he didn't look nearly as intimidating as the stocky, muscular woman, with her shaved head and obvious familiarity with weapons, but Jez had to admit that being on the run had been good for him. He still looked more like a scholar than anything else, with his messy cropped hair and the thoughtful, calculating expression on his face, but at least he'd figured out which end of the gun to point at the bad guys. Or the good guys. Whoever was chasing them at the moment.

Two weeks of Ysbel's tutelage would do that to a person, even a soft boy like genius over there.

She reached them and turned around, drawing her own pistol. "Ysbel, don't take this the wrong way, but I think I might love you mostly for your weapons."

"That's good. I might kill you with them one of these days."

Tae shoved his dark hair out of his eyes and glared at her. "Can we spend one day getting supplies without you getting into a fight Jez? One day?"

"Nope." She grinned at him.

The gambler's crew had come through the gates and slowed on seeing their company. They'd all drawn weapons, and now they were approaching cautiously.

"Your pilot stole something from me," the man in the dirty pilot's coat called out. Jez was gratified to see that his nose was swollen to twice its previous size.

"Hey now, can't handle the pressure, stay out of the game," Jez called back. "Not my fault you can't pay what you play."

"You cheated!" he growled.

She shrugged, still grinning. "How do you cheat at fool's tokens?"

Lev sighed and slapped his com.

"Masha, you were right. Jez found someone who wants to kill her. We've got to go." He glanced at the scowling young man beside him. "Tae, can you throw the last few boxes in? Ysbel and I will hold them off."

"And me," said Jez. Lev glared at her.

"Hand the pilot over and we'll call it even," the man called. "There's more of us. You don't want a fight, and neither do we."

Ysbel turned her flat stare on the approaching group, and they slowed further.

"It's tempting," she said. "But I have dibs on killing this idiot, so I'm afraid I can't."

The man shifted his grip on his pistol.

Ysbel raised one eyebrow. "I don't think you want to do that."

"Tell your pilot to give me back what's mine."

"Was yours. Until I won it," Jez shot back. She glanced quickly over her shoulder. Tae was carrying the last of the boxes up the ramp, and she could feel in her bones the slight vibration that told her that the ship was running.

Damn.

She slapped her com. "Masha, stay out of my cockpit!"

The man in the dirty pilot's coat whipped his pistol up and cracked off a blast. Jez dove for the ground, knocking Lev out of the way as Ysbel fired.

The force of the blast from Ysbel's modded gun threw Jez against the ramp, practically on top of Lev. He shoved her off him, and she rolled to her feet, yanked him up, and pushed him up the ramp.

"Get in, genius."

Ysbel had holstered her weapon and was running in after them. Jez took one last look around, grinning, paused long enough to make a rude gesture at the stunned gamblers, and swung herself up the ramp.

Tae was already closing it behind them.

She shoved her way past him into the cockpit, where a pleasant, competent-looking woman in a long pilot's coat sat in the pilot's seat, her black hair pulled back into a simple rat tail and her expression one of bland helpfulness. You'd hardly see the calculation beneath it unless you were looking.

"You've already blown up one of my ships, Masha," Jez growled. "Move over."

Masha stood, giving Jez a cold look. "If you had fewer people trying to kill you, I suspect it would be easier to keep your ships from getting blown up," she said, words tinged with ice.

"Shut up," Jez grumbled, sliding into the pilot's seat. She rested her hands on the controls for half a moment, letting the perfect, perfect feeling of the ship wash over her. Then she touched the stick, ever so slightly, and the ship lifted delicately off the ground.

"Strap in, kids," she called over the ship's com.

On the holoscreen in front of her, the right shield glowed as a heat-blast bounced off it.

She gave a beatific smile, settled herself into her seat, and pulled back smoothly on the control stick.

The ship pointed its nose to the sky and streaked towards the blue line of atmosphere, leaving Jez's stomach far behind. The speed of it shoved her back into her seat, and she half-closed her eyes in pure bliss.

This was life.

This was what she was born for.

The shields glowed a dull orange as they shot through the atmosphere, and the controls trembled against her hands, and then they were through.

She let out a long breath as the rich black of shallow space enveloped them, tension draining from her body.

Finally.

They'd been planet-side for less than a day, but she already hurt from missing this.

She leaned back in her seat, staring out at the vast expanse, the tiny pricks of fire that were the stars, the brown-blue glow of the planet through the rear window.

Every time. It almost made her cry, every single time. She'd spent three plaguing weeks on a prison ship back when she'd been picked up for smuggling, and every moment of every day in that tiny, miserable cell she'd longed for this. She'd needed it like she needed the blood in her veins and the air in her lungs, and every day she couldn't have it she'd died just a little bit more.

And now that she was back in the sky, it took her breath away every single time.

Freedom.

Home.

The only thing she'd ever wanted.

She let her hand rest on the control stick and closed her eyes, feeling the ship in her bones, the rightness of it.

She was jolted from her reverie by the sound, from somewhere behind her, of someone swearing loudly.

That would be Tae. Probably hadn't strapped down in time.

She opened her eyes and turned back to the cockpit window, staring at the endless expanse surrounding them. Then, reluctantly, she glanced at the com screen, set a few calculations into the controls, and stood.

Even after two weeks, leaving this perfect, beautiful cockpit was almost a physical pain.

She patted her coat pocket and grinned.

This time, though—

She couldn't wait to see the expression on Ysbel's face.

Made in the USA
Middletown, DE
05 December 2022

17072900R00187